8/12/14

ALWAYS CHARLIE

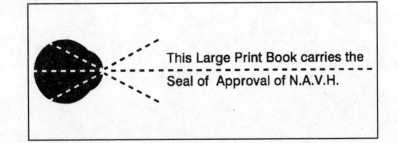

This Large Print Book carries the
Seal of Approval of N.A.V.H.

ALWAYS CHARLIE

MARGARET P. CUNNINGHAM

THORNDIKE PRESS
A part of Gale, Cengage Learning

Detroit • New York • San Francisco • New Haven, Conn • Waterville, Maine • London

GALE
CENGAGE Learning®

LIBRARY OF CONGRESS CATALOGING-IN-PUBLICATION DATA

Cunningham, Margaret P.
    Always Charlie / by Margaret P. Cunningham. — Large Print edition.
        pages cm. — (Thorndike Press Large Print Clean Reads)
    ISBN 978-1-4104-5735-6 (hardcover) — ISBN 1-4104-5735-4 (hardcover)
    1. Large type books. I. Title.
PS3603.U668A49 2013
813'.6—dc23   2012050576

Published in 2013 by arrangement with Black Lyon Publishing, LLC.

Printed in the United States of America
1 2 3 4 5 6 7 17 16 15 14 13

For Julia, whose story is just beginning.

MACONDO

The guitar player who'd come on at 9:30 strummed a half-hearted *Happy Birthday*. Friends, staff and a few over-served patrons of Casa Crab, home of the world-famous Pink Meanie, got into the spirit, singing the usual off-key rendition of the B-day song. Liza Jane Bradford and Charlotte Turner raised their drinks in a mutual toast. Though a decade apart in age, the cousins had both been born April twentieth.

When the smattering of applause and well-wishes subsided, Janine Jett set fresh Meanies in front of the cousins.

"They're on the house," she said. "Just don't mention it to the Crabman." Her large brown eyes rolled in the direction of Casa Crab's proprietor who occupied a stool behind the cash register. "And drink 'em slow," she added with a wink.

"Thanks," said Liza Jane. "But, hey . . . we don't want to get you in trouble with the boss man."

"Ahh, don't worry about it." She smiled at the women. "Today's my boyfriend's birthday, too. And I hope somebody's doing something nice for him."

"No kidding?" said Charlotte. "How old?"

"Bobby's twenty-five today. Works the oil rig out of Louisiana or we'd be celebrating. Shame to be working on his birthday."

Charlotte followed Janine's gaze over the railing of the Crab's deck, out past an expanse of sand that could pass for powdered sugar. Except for phosphorous-tinged waves and a freighter headed to who knew where, the gulf was an infinity of black. *What would it be like to spend night after night surrounded by all that darkness?* Charlotte wondered.

"But we got one heck of a party planned for him when he gets back," Janine was saying.

"Well, here's to Bobby," said Liza Jane, raising her glass to the inky water.

"To Bobby," Janine said and looked at her watch. "Now I got to get back to it. Enjoy your evening."

An hour later Charlotte was at home receiving birthday calls from her sons. Liza Jane was still at the Crab easing the pain of another year's passing with mediocre coun-

8

try music, almost-cold beer and a dwindling supply of male attention. Charlotte yawned and turned off the light. Another year and it seemed that nothing much had changed.

1.
ART LOVERS

Harrison McMillan watched and waited as a collecting dusk washed the acacias in blues and grays. Behind the acacias, a blue-black fringe of plane trees stretched against a sky just purpling with night. As his eyes adjusted to the shadows, he began to notice them — figures, barely discernible in their translucent state, floating toward one another from out of the mist.

The aura radiating from the ghosts was conveyed through an intricate layering of glorious color that lightened to a pure white as it rose heavenward. Harry realized that he was witnessing the spirits' triumph over the darkness. He was reminded of Marie and Simone, and it made him smile.

The painting was titled *The Gathering*. It hung alone and unframed on a side wall of the gallery where it could be seen and enjoyed through the front bay window.

Charlotte Turner sat behind a desk tucked

into a corner of the room and watched the man watching her creation. The painting drew viewers into it like the gallery's air-conditioned interior sucks the tourists in from East Oyster's sidewalks on summer afternoons. So his reaction was not unusual. She saw him smile and knew that he was remembering.

Finally, he looked at the discreet price card below the frame, let out a low whistle and walked over to the desk. As recognition dawned, his face broke into the grin that had melted Charlotte's heart — what was it, twenty-five years ago?

"Charlie? Is that you? I can't believe it!"

When was the last time anyone had called her Charlie?

He leaned across the desk and kissed her cheek, his familiar smell a caress from another lifetime. And when his lips brushed her cheek, that summer in France came rushing back — the vendors and their wares, awash in the morning's first light; the market with its smells bursting from pungent cheeses and spices and just-picked fruits and vegetables piled on every avail-able surface; the aromas, salted by sea air, mingling with the laughter and conversation and delighted groans of tourists sampling the local delicacies. It was just the thing for

12

a twenty-nine year old artist who'd lost her husband to their accountant and her will to paint to a nasty case of the blues.

"Sugar, a change of venue is what you need," her Aunt Maisy had said, handing Charlotte an envelope.

Inside were an airline ticket, registration for art classes and directions to a house in Saint-Yves-Sur-Mer. The mer of St. Yves just happened to be the Mediterranean.

"If it was good enough for Henry Matisse, it ought to do the trick for you."

As usual, Maisy knew exactly what she was talking about.

On this particular Friday afternoon — her first in Provence — Charlotte and two fellow art students sat shaded by a café awning in Cassis, the seaside town tucked into limestone hills where Matisse had indeed summered. Provencal's celebrated sunlight danced on the bay, setting boats and cobblestones, shade trees and buildings a dazzle until Charlotte was itching for her palette and brushes.

Tourists milled around them, a blur of color and language moving at leisure speed when suddenly the rhythm of the crowd was upset. Charlotte turned in time to see a muscular, young man sprinting through the crowd. He clutched a white handbag, looking comical and at odds with the mask of defiant fear on his face. Several other young men and a purse-less woman cursing in French raced ten or fifteen yards behind.

Deciding that the fellow bearing down on her was not simply in a hurry and making an unusual fashion statement, Charlotte stuck a foot into his path as he passed. The thief sprawled onto the cobblestones, losing his grip on the bag which sailed across the street. It was picked up by a woman in bulging spandex who wrapped her arms protectively around the pocketbook and glared at the perpetrator, her chin raised in triumph. He glared back at the woman, scrambled to his feet and into the hands of two gendarmes who knew a purse snatcher when they saw one.

The pursuers and the owner of the purse skidded to a stop beside Charlotte's table.

"Merci, merci beaucoup," said the woman before moving on, wooden clogs clattering on the uneven stones, to retrieve her handbag and berate the man who seemed much more afraid of her than the policemen gripping his arms.

"That was quick thinking."

The voice was masculine and southern, and for a second Charlotte was overwhelmed with homesickness. The man was leaning over, his hands on his knees, trying to catch his breath. He looked at Charlotte and grinned. One very deep dimple appeared. His eyes were brown. Full of flirt is how Maisy would describe them. It was a face made for smiling. And with that smile all Charlotte's thoughts of home evaporated into the Provencal air.

"What are you, some kind of undercover cop or something?"

Charlotte grinned back. "Art student."

"Well, I sure would like to buy you a drink. I don't think I could have run much farther."

He looked questioningly from Charlotte to several vacant chairs around the table.

"You don't have to do that," Charlotte said, "But you and your friends are welcome to sit with us," she added.

"Thanks. I'm Harrison McMillan," he said, folding his tall frame into a chair next to Charlotte.

Two hours and several bottles of Doucillon Blanc later, Charlotte and Harrison were calling one another Charlie and Harry. Despite varying ages and backgrounds, the little group became fast friends, connected in the way of fun-loving expatriates determined to wring the most out of a foreign holiday.

"New Orleans? Really?" said Harry, "Now that is good news. I've got another semester at Vanderbilt, but after graduate school I'm moving to New Orleans. I've been offered a job there." He stared at Charlotte for a few seconds. "I can't believe you're from New Orleans. Chasing that guy and everything . . . it's like we were meant to meet, you know?"

Charlotte was convinced this was true when Harry explained that, as he had for most of his life, he was spending the summer with his aunts in the seaside village of Saint-Yves-Sur-Mer, not far from where she was staying.

He spoke fluent French and offered his services as a tour guide to them all, but he was looking at Charlotte when he said, "Why don't y'all meet us here tomorrow?" He finished his wine, and gesturing toward his buddies with his empty glass, he said, "I'm showing these guys around, and I've got my aunt's van. There's plenty of room."

The women looked at one another, remembering warnings to beware of cute strangers enticing naïve American females into their cars.

"I'll show you some places that aren't on the tourist maps," he prodded.

And as he walked away he turned back,

flashing that amazing smile at Charlotte.

"Don't forget, Charlie!" he called. "Tomorrow, okay?"

2.
SPIRITED ENCOUNTERS

In the weeks that followed, the artists and grad students spent their free time swimming and picnicking along the Cote d'Azur and soaking up local color they would never have discovered on their own. Evenings usually found them at a peculiar outdoor disco owned by two women who called themselves and the disco, Deux Rienes, which means two queens. The bar served up cheap wine, a funky, strobe-lit atmosphere and live entertainment consisting of the Deux Rienes who sang French versions of ABBA songs. Of course, Dancing Queen was their big number.

Harry claimed to hate disco but could always be counted on to cut an impressive rug to Dancing Queen. This was due to the fact that the singers saved this favorite until later in the evening when the crowd, including Harry, had consumed enough wine to loosen their inhibitions.

Harry and Charlotte soon had a series of exaggerated spins and twirls saved especially for this final number. It ended with Harry dipping Charlotte dramatically (and precariously), finished off by what Harry referred to as a Hollywood kiss. Before long, Harry was requesting La Riene de Danse whenever they visited Deux Rienes.

The friends came and went that summer, depending on the length of individual vacations, but the pretty, blue-eyed blonde artist Charlie (as she was now known to everyone) and Harry, the tall, dark and very cute architect major, were a constant. When Charlotte revealed her age and marital status, Harry insisted he'd been looking for an older woman — preferably a divorced one — since puberty.

"Seriously, Charlie," he added. "I've just gotten out of a very immature relationship. I didn't realize how immature until I met you."

After that, the subject was never mentioned again.

Harry's aunts, Marie and Simone, treated Charlotte like one of the family, showing great interest in her art, her family, her home state of Louisiana and all things American. They were soon calling her "Harry's girl Charlie," and inviting her to join them for meals in the stone farmhouse they'd occupied since their birth.

On Charlotte's first visit to the house, Harry explained that the ladies were actually his great aunts and quite elderly. Though they had always lived in the little town of St. Yves, they had an interesting past and were local celebrities of a sort. They — and the house — had an unusual story.

At an early age, Simone and Marie discovered they possessed a talent for water divining. Their first discovery was an underground spring on their father's property. Before the year was up, two more springs were discovered by the petite filles.

Their father, on the verge of losing his parched land, sunk wells. He then constructed one of the largest water basins in Provence. Two hundred thirsty olive trees began to bear fruit in abundance. The whole town prospered as the girls divined water running beneath the land of their neighbors.

In a flood of gratitude, the townsfolk planted roses all around papa's house and constructed a large fountain several meters from the front door. In its center, they placed a sculpture of the two little sisters, smiling sweetly as water poured from cradled buckets. The ever-flowing fountain and the now-thick stems of climbing pink roses were the first things visitors saw when they arrived at the house. The fragrance of blooms and sound of the splashing water divined by Marie and Simone served as a reminder to all that the girls had saved the town of Saint-Yves-Sur-Mer.

"And you've never lived anywhere else?" Charlotte asked one day. They were having lunch in the shade of the olive trees made possible by Simone and Marie.

"Non, Charlie. We love this house, the oliviers, the roses," said Simone.

"And the ghosts," added Marie.

"Ghosts? You have ghosts here?"

Simone waved her hand in dismissal. "We have some spirits without rest, you understand? They are troubled, but they do not trouble us, so it is . . ." She threw up her hands. "No trouble."

"Most of these old places are haunted in one way or another," said Harry. "You know, a spirit that's stuck can't evolve, is how Marie puts it . . . yet a spirit that's not supposed to be here." He grinned at her and shrugged. "But like Simone says, they don't bother anyone."

"It is very sad, just the same," said Simone, shaking her old head. Then she smiled. "But there is no room for sadness at

21

my years, yes?"

"Marie and Simone have a rule" explained Harry. "To have a happy house. They think they've earned it," he said, winking at Simone, "Just because they're in their nineties."

"And beside it," said Marie, "I once am seeing one of our ghosts leave this place." She stared ahead remembering. "It is in the final moments of twilight. The spirit rises and blends into the light . . . such peace, such hope. It is a gift for me to witness such a thing."

The old lady smiled and for an instant Charlotte could see the young girl who still resided there. Marie was bathed in the reflected light of the memory. Charlotte looked at Harry and Simone to see their reaction, but there was none. Maybe they had seen it before. Maybe only Charlotte was privy to it. Maybe she had imagined it. Whatever the explanation, it was something she would never forget.

Simone and Marie were dependent upon a nephew — Harry's uncle — who ran the farm and lived nearby. He took care of their finances and repairs to the old house. A woman came in the mornings to clean, take the laundry and cook the noonday meal. The old sisters retired early and napped after lunch, floating through their days half hearing and half seeing, using all of their energies, it seemed, in remembering things and staying awake. If they had any inkling what Harry and Charlotte were up to as they slipped away to Harry's room late at night or on sleepy afternoons, they did not let on.

On Charlotte's last day in Provence before heading on to Paris, she enjoyed a farewell lunch with Harry, his uncle and his aunts. They ate lavender crème brûlée and sipped coffee beneath an arbor burdened with grape vines, and Charlotte realized that this was very likely the last time she would ever see Marie and Simone. She dabbed at her eyes with a linen napkin, and they seemed to know what she was thinking.

"Oh, non, non," said Simone. "C'est la vie."

Charlotte had learned to follow their odd conversations — a mixture of French, then English as Harry reminded them Charlotte wasn't quite fluent in their native language. They would laugh and apologize and speak their heavily accented English for awhile before lapsing into French again. Harry would smile and shake his head and translate for Charlotte.

"Anglais, Simone," Marie reminded her

sister. She turned to Charlotte. "Oui. It is true," she said. "It is life." Her bony shoulders went up in a weak approximation of a Gallic shrug. She smiled. "We are so old. We learn to make every minute happy. No sadness. No upset. It keeps us going, you understand? It is all we know to do."

Harry took Charlotte to the train station with promises to call as soon as he got back to the states. He would come to New Orleans first chance. She would come for football weekends at Vanderbilt. They would get to know one another's lives in the real world of the states. And one day, they would build a home together.

But you know what they say about best laid plans.

lifted her mouth to his. And before reality overtook her, for a fleeting moment or two, she tasted his kiss.

Simone survived for a month without Marie. As everyone expected, the farm was left to Harry's uncle. Harry was surprised, however, to find that he had inherited his aunts' house and its garden. On the advice of his parents, he placed the house with a rental agent.

As he and his mother gathered up the remnants of the aunts' lives, his thoughts returned to his future. The job in New Orleans was no longer an option. His prospective father-in-law had arranged an interview with a commercial real estate company. It was one of the largest in Nashville and a great opportunity — though it had little to do with architecture.

The job was interesting. Harry was good at it. So good, in fact, that he was soon a partner in the business. His wife, Annie was attractive and energetic. And they were happy for a while. But before long, he began to feel like one of his wife's chores — a bill to be paid, a tub to be cleaned, a husband to be serviced.

Like Charlotte, he often awoke with memories of that summer, memories so vivid he would be surprised to find Annie in his arms instead of Charlotte. He felt guilty about the dreams, about how real they were, and he vowed to take Annie back to the farm house as soon as the present tenant moved out. Maybe then he would see Annie's face beneath the arbor, curled up on the old chaise and next to him in his bed.

But by the time the lease in Provence was up, Annie was too busy with their baby. He understood, but as time went on, her excuses for not going became increasingly transparent. Finally she admitted that she was not interested in traveling beyond her parents' home in the next neighborhood. Harry might as well have asked her to go to the moon as travel across the ocean to France.

After six years and a daughter together, Annie filed for divorce and promptly married her divorce lawyer. Harry was hurt, humiliated, and angry. But not surprised. Not really.

In spite of doubts that she would even speak to him, he inquired about Charlotte. He found she had married, so he immersed himself in work and the role of single dad. Each summer he took his daughter to the house in Provence, and the place grew rich with new memories. He expected his recollections of Charlie to become as faded as the fabrics and furnishings of the farm house. Instead, they remained as vivid as ever.

4.
DÉJÀ VU

"So tell me about your life," said Harry.

Charlotte told him she had married, but was long since widowed with two grown sons.

"You're still painting, I hope." He grinned at her. "Unless you've gone into police work, that is."

"I hate to disappoint you, but the French purse-snatcher was my last collar."

They laughed like old friends, remembering how they'd met.

Finally Charlotte said, "But I am still painting. What do you think of my little gallery?"

"Your gallery?" He looked around the space, taking in the white-washed brick walls and high ceilings, the shining wood floors, the paintings and frames, ceramics and small statues.

"It's very impressive. You've certainly made the most of this space."

"Thanks."

"It's a great building. And how you have everything displayed is . . . it's really beautiful, Charlie."

Charlotte was touched by his sincere admiration. But that's how he'd always been. Sincere and funny and charming — until the end, anyway. The I-apologize-for-dumping-you letter wasn't all that charming and definitely not amusing. But she wasn't one to hold twenty-five-year-old grudges. Besides, Harrison McMillan was still extremely cute.

Finally, he motioned behind him. "I'm interested in that large piece called *The Gathering.* It's magical. And I was wondering if you had any information on the artist. He must be an interesting old guy."

"I'm glad you like it," said Charlotte, "because I'm the old guy who painted it."

He laughed and his face reddened, making Charlotte laugh, too.

"I'm sorry," he said. "But it's really a compliment. The painting is amazing. I figured it would take someone with the wisdom of the ages to produce something like that."

Charlotte waved his apology away. "It's okay. I use my first initial and my married name in the signature. There was no way for you to know it was mine."

"Well, I apologize for assuming it belonged to a male."

"I accept your apology," said Charlotte. "Like I said, I'm just glad you like it."

Harry looked back at the painting. "I'm no expert, but I've never seen a painting, especially an abstract piece that could evoke such peacefulness. It makes me feel nostalgic." He shook his head. "I'm not expressing myself very well."

"Actually, those are the feelings I had when I painted it." She smiled at him. "Thank you for putting it into words for me."

"Well, Ms. Turner, it looks like you've made a sale. Although I must admit, I've never paid this much for a painting."

"You're in luck. I'm giving a twenty percent discount to all old friends I haven't seen in over twenty years."

"You don't have to do that."

"I know. But between you and me, it's a bit overpriced."

Charlotte walked over to the painting and placed a sold sticker on the price tag. She could feel Harry's eyes on her as she returned to her desk.

"What about a frame?" she asked.

"I think I like it just as it is."

"Me, too," she agreed.

"Charlie," he said, "I want you to know that . . . well . . . that owning this painting means a lot to me."

To seal the transaction, he smiled and put out his hand, and Charlotte placed her own hand in his. The warmth of it was so comforting, so right that she didn't move. She could tell by the pleased, perplexed look on his face that he was feeling the same. So they stood like that for several seconds, each searching the other's face, and each falling deeper under the sweet spell of the moment.

Finally, he smiled and let go of her hand. Charlotte felt herself blush, embarrassed that she had not made the first move to end the prolonged handshake. Seconds passed as she once again lost herself in the warm eyes and handsome face. She couldn't believe it. Harry McMillan, standing here in her gallery. And that magic they'd had in Provence? It was still there! She realized she was staring at him.

"So what brings you to East Oys—" she began but was interrupted by the bell on the gallery door.

"Hello?" called Abigail Pitt, the mood-buster of all mood-busters, prancing toward Charlotte with that model-walk affectation of hers.

Does anybody — even a real model — naturally put one foot exactly in front of the other? mused Charlotte. *And that pretentious speech with its unnatural intonations! Being around this woman is like standing in an ant bed.*

Abbie's hellos ended high, like a question, sounding irritable, accusatory even. Her questions, on the other hand, were flat, making her sound bored, as if any information the questionee might impart would surely be inadequate. Everything in between rolled out of her mouth on a sigh.

Local gossip had it that Abbie, a gorgeous, thirty-five year-old associate director of sales at a big-time New York ad agency, was in town refurbishing her family's bay cottage. The house had the distinction of being the setting for *Moonlight Charade,* a movie that was a huge hit back in the seventies. The screwball romantic comedy/mystery was still a popular rental. Because of the movie, the lovely but somewhat derelict Victorian bay house at the end of Pitt Ferry Road became an instant tourist magnet. And for a hefty sum, it could even be rented. Until recently, that was.

The area had suffered back-to-back hurricanes followed by an economic downturn the likes of which most of the citizenry could only imagine. Now a busted well was belching oil nonstop into the Gulf of Mexico. As oil was the lifeblood of the nation, tourism and seafood were the lifeblood of East Oyster.

The Pitts had long since left their southern roots for the more socially rarefied environs "up east," but the East Oyster house with its sprawling porches, lofty ceilings, oak-shaded grounds and cinematic history was a favorite of Abbie's grandfather, the last of the soft-hearted Pitts, and he'd never been able to part with it. According to Craig Bloom, co-owner of the antique and garden shop three doors down from Charlotte, Pitt Cottage was one of the Pitt family's last real estate holdings. Apparently the Pitts, like so many others, had "suffered a reversal of fortune." This and the dwindling market for pricey vacation rentals had forced Abbie to reconsider the last southern vestige of the Pitt dynasty.

In other words, times were tough all over, and Pitt Cottage with its quirky charms would be a nice trade-off with her friends from up east who weren't yet as financially challenged as she, but who were nonetheless watching their pennies like hawks. It was Abbie's plan to issue invites for long winter weekends at the cottage on Palmetto

Bay. The favor would need to be returned in the form of invitations to summer weekends in all manner of less humid environs.

Craig had shaken his head and added, "Of course, with an out-of-control oil well belching a thousand barrels of crude per day into the gulf, Abbie's plans are probably doomed."

Movie buffs might equate Pitt Cottage's sloping floors, antiquated plumbing and lack of air-conditioning with a sort of vintage ambience, but Abbie's friends would expect more in the way of creature comforts. According to Craig and Leon, his "partner-in-all-things," Abbie just happened to have her own in-house architectural consultant — an older man who knew a thing or two about restoration — who also happened to be her fiancé.

"Oh, here you are, Harrison." Abbie smiled languidly at Harry as if he were a naughty four-year-old.

As she approached the desk, Harry said, "Abbie, this is Charlie." He grinned at Charlotte. "Sorry, I meant to say, this is Charlotte."

"We've met," said Abbie. "I've actually found a few things in her gallery."

She was looking back and forth from Charlotte to Harry as if she were watching a tennis match between an aardvark and an iguana.

"So how on earth do you two know each other?" she asked, sounding as if she really didn't want to know.

"We met in France, the summer after college," said Harry.

Abbie's mouth dropped open as her eyes closed in concentration. "You're the same age?" Translation: Charlotte, there is no way you are as young as Harrison.

Charlotte sighed. Abbie could really take the starch out of a girl's bloomers.

"No, I'm older. By five years. It was just after Harry graduated. We were neighbors in Saint-Yves-Sur-Mer."

Abbie made a fake, I'm-so-shocked face and said, "Ooh la la. Sounds very romantic."

If you only knew, thought Charlotte.

Harry just smiled. At Charlotte.

"Well, we have to get to Palm World before it closes," said Abbie. She pushed a strand of dark hair behind her ear and a sizable diamond sparkled on her left hand. Realization hit Charlotte like a bucket of ice water.

Oh my God! It's happening again! Harry is her fiancé! Sweet, funny Harry McMillan is going to marry Abigail Pitt!

Now it was Charlotte's turn to gawk at the twosome as if they were an alien species

37

who'd invaded her gallery. But she managed to compose herself and say, "Oh, you go ahead. I'll hold the painting for you."

"What painting?" asked Abbie.

Harry guided her over to the best work Charlotte had ever done.

"Oh, sweetie, no. You didn't. It's so . . . so spooky. And my God, look at the price. And who is the artist? I've never heard of C. Turn . . . oh."

Charlotte pretended to busy herself with papers on her desk as Abbie attempted to get her foot out of her mouth.

"Oh, it's a fine painting, I'm sure," Abby said. "It's just that my color schemes . . ."

"It's for me," Harry said, steering Abbie toward the door. "And it suits my color scheme just fine." He turned to Charlotte. "I'll be in soon to pick it up."

"Oh, uh . . . goodbye then. And thanks."

And so the man who had been Charlotte's lover once upon an enchanted Provencal summer, headed out of her gallery with his sleek, young fiancée. To Palm World.

5.
LIZA JANE, COUGAR IN TRANSITION

Liza Jane Bradford, owner of Pelican's Nest Interiors was not only Charlotte Turner's first cousin, but her best friend. On the momentous day that Harry McMillan materialized in Turner gallery, Liza Jane dropped by Charlotte's apartment for some conversation and a late-afternoon toddy. Her first bit of news concerned the oil spill.

The president had announced a ban on any new drilling until the cause of the Horizon explosion was determined. This sounded like a good plan, said L.J., but it was a double whammy for coastal oil workers (like Janine Jett's boyfriend, the ill-fated Bobby). The gushing oil threatened their environment. The ban on drilling threatened their livelihoods. They were caught between a big, old rock and a very hard place.

"A terrible problem," agreed Charlotte, "But they're bringing in some sort of containment dome. Surely the well will be capped in a few days," she said and placed a bottle of beer in front of her cousin.

"So, anything new with you?" asked Liza Jane.

Charlotte didn't feel much like dredging up the whole, sad Harry and Abbie saga, but it was less depressing than discussing the oil spill. It seemed like the spill was all anyone talked about since the cousins' birthday when the deep-water well known as Horizon exploded. So Charlotte answered Liza Jane's fairly rhetorical question with a recitation of the afternoon's events.

"Say it ain't so! Lost-love Harry and Abbie-the-Pitt?"

Liza Jane paused long enough to taste her beer then began spewing questions like a fumbled Budweiser.

"And you sold him *The Gathering*? I didn't think you could part with it." Her eyebrows shot up. "You must still have a thing for him." She took another sip of beer and rolled those amazing green eyes of hers. "And he's engaged to that obnoxious Abbie? What's up with that? She's way too young for him. I mean, what could they possibly have in common?"

Charlotte bit her tongue before saying anything about pots calling kettles black or stone-throwers living in glass houses. Liza

Jane was fast approaching the middle of her fourth decade. In spite (or because?) of this, she had a soft spot for young men in T-shirts and cowboy hats who drove their pickup trucks like sports cars on the red clay roads of Creek County. She also had a serious thing for jazz. It was a bad combination, her tastes in men and music since the two rarely came in the same package.

The cowboys were straight-shooters, enjoyed changing strangers' tires and were as easy on the dance floor as they were in the deer stand. Salt-of-the-earth types, Liza Jane called them. But their interests never left the county. Their eyes sparkled too hard when they looked at Liza Jane. They acted their young ages. And they didn't care much for jazz.

But this conflict of interests was no more than she could expect what with a mother who'd sculpted, dabbled in the occult and named her only child after a song. And as everyone had predicted, the song and Liza Jane's daddy, Thornton Bradford IV lost their appeal about the time Liza Jane was beginning to crawl.

Thornton Bradford IV eventually cleared his soul of the emotional debris left by Liza Jane's mother and plodded forward. He married a CPA named Janice, produced two sensible, brown-haired CPA daughters and eventually moved to Decatur. In the crazy quilt of the Bradford family, Thornton, Janice and their two girls were a wide muslin border hemming in the little patch of crimson satin that was Liza Jane.

The opposing forces of Liza Jane's DNA together with her odd-man-out familial position and conflicting tastes in men made her prickly, wanting to take off like a bottle rocket one day and build a cozy-nest life the next. At forty-four years of age, she had long since given up on either, lacking the bravado for the former, the patience for the latter.

Charlotte, however, was optimistic about her beautiful cousin's romantic future. After much thought, she'd concluded that Liza Jane was simply a woman in transition. Transition to what? Charlotte had no idea. But she had a feeling it was something exceptional.

She had heard some of the younger women refer to Liza Jane as a cougar. They were as jealous as a runner-up in the Miss Cotton pageant, of course, but Charlotte had to admit they weren't far off. Liza Jane even admitted that she was starting to feel like a den mother.

"I'm tired of reminding them where they

left their boots!" she'd said.

Yes, the cubs were growing tedious. On the other hand, the few remaining intellectual types with more mature interests lacked the energy and the fun of the cowboys. Charlotte could only look on sadly as Liza Jane came face to face with the unfortunate reality. There wasn't an available man around who could keep her interested for more than a few months.

Charlotte had to give it to her indefatigable cousin, however. Instead of waiting around for Mr. Right, Liza Jane filled her time dating the high-spirited cowboys, decorating East Oyster's pricey real estate and keeping herself in extremely good shape. It appeared that she had decided to enjoy her life as it was and leave the fate of her love life in the hands of . . . well, fate.

Charlotte knew better.

While playing the unorthodox hand that nature had dealt her, Liza Jane had, out of necessity, learned to bluff with the best of them, giving the impression that she was as content as a clam with her unconventional love life. So instead of acknowledging the irony of her statement about the disparity in the ages and interests of Abbie Pitt and Harrison McMillan, she had characteristically changed the subject.

Though conveniently ignoring her own atypical dating agenda, where Charlotte's love life was concerned, Liza Jane thought fate could use a little help. She had come up with all manner of suitable and deliciously unsuitable guys for her cousin. Her latest match-making attempt was a rehash of Butler Finley's possibilities.

"I've got an idea," she said. "It would take your mind off of Harry McMillan, get you out of the house, and you could actually have a little fun for a change."

"I'm having fun. Really."

"Take it from me, sweetie, there's a lot livelier recreation out there than reading books and watching corny, old movies. You can do that when you're a hundred!"

"I'm not going out with Butler Finley."

Charlotte had been introduced to Butler at a yacht club party. When he'd learned she was a widow, he had adopted the expression of a funeral parlor employee and said, "Cancer?"

She knew what he meant but responded, "No. Sagittarius."

After all, she had just met the man.

"So why not give Butler a go?" said Liza Jane, flipping her hair to underscore the fun, carefree-ness of the notion. "He's fun, into art and loves to spend money. He's dying to

44

date you. And he's available!"

"He's just not my type." Charlotte laughed. "You have got to let it go, already. You go out with him!"

"I've been out with him." Liza Jane sighed sadly. "We just didn't geehaw." (Translation: he's too old). "But you . . ."

"No."

The twice-divorced Mr. Finley was a handsome, sporty, art-collecting piece of date bait who topped every party list and sat on every board worth sitting on in the town of East Oyster. He was the right age. He liked to travel. He could dance. He had a lovely boat sitting in the town marina.

He also had a too-easy laugh. He spent a lot of time on his hair. Charlotte knew an hour into a date with Butler she'd be thinking, *what am I doing here? I could be on my sofa in my bathrobe watching Grace Kelly chase Cary Grant around the Riviera!*

But she knew Liza Jane had a point. Escaping into the unrealistic world of old movies was probably not the best way of coping with loneliness. Of course it wasn't as bad as running around with a succession of men half one's age. Or was it?

To Charlotte's relief, Liza Jane decided to abandon the subject of Butler Finley. For the moment.

"Charlotte, is that what you were wearing? When the French hottie showed up in your gallery?"

Charlotte laughed. "He's not French." She looked down at her white, paint-smudged jeans and pale green T-shirt. "Oh, well, I did get my hair cut yesterday. And I am wearing makeup."

"You look great."

Charlotte made a little face.

"No, really. That short hair cut is fabulous on you."

Charlotte patted a blonde, shining curl and smiled.

"You're still in very good shape," Liza Jane continued. "And those jeans do a lot for your butt. Which is more than I can say for that praying mantis, Abbie Pitt."

Charlotte giggled. "She really doesn't have much of a rear end, does she?"

"I don't know how she sits down on that bony thing!"

"But you have to admit, she does look just like a model — a young model."

"Just because she's built like a pencil? And walks with that affected model walk? I don't think so!"

"Thanks, L.J."

"For what?"

"For making me feel better. You know,

46

when I saw Harry, I thought . . . well, I don't know exactly what I thought, but it was *extremely* disappointing to find out he's engaged to Abbie, and you've made me feel better about it."

"Everything I said is true. Besides, ever since Harry, you've played it safe — romantically speaking, that is. And since Dan died, you've hardly dated."

"I've had two men leave me for someone else. The other one died on me. Romance is risky behavior as far as I'm concerned."

"I don't blame you for being a little gun-shy, but honey, it's time for you to put yourself out there."

"Well," Charlotte sighed, "Even if I wanted to, Harry seems to be spoken for."

Liza Jane narrowed her eyes. "They ain't married yet. Besides, he was yours first."

"I think the statute of limitations has pretty much run out on that one. And I know that look. Don't get any ideas, okay?"

Liza Jane held up her right hand in a silent oath, and mentally crossed the fingers of her left.

"So how about another beer?"

As if in answer, Liza Jane's cell phone chimed, then chimed again. She fished it out of her bag and glanced at the messages.

"Sorry . . . drapery emergency over at

Nautilus Cay."

She hesitated, frowning at the phone, then added, "And I have to stop by the police station to see Foster."

"One of your cowboys need bail?" Charlotte teased.

"Very funny. No, but it's almost as ridiculous. Another one of Mama's pelicans has just self-destructed." She rolled her eyes and shook her head. "Like it's my problem."

"That is so weird," said Charlotte. "I mean they have been fine all these years and now they're falling apart?"

"Not falling apart. Exploding." Liza Jane sighed, and the nothing-bothers-Liza-Jane-Bradford attitude seemed to rush out of her. She bit her bottom lip in that way that the cowboys found irresistible. "That's the third one," she said. It can't be coincidence. And it's that big blue and orange one by the entrance to the park. One of Mama's best, in my opinion."

Charlotte pictured the statue. It was the largest of the Bradford birds, with dark, purplish blue feathers. It sat staring down at park visitors with oversized, crossed amber eyes. Its bronze webbed feet were crossed and stuck out comically over the edge of its brick pedestal. And though she would have described it in more artistic terms than her cousin, she agreed with Liza Jane. It was one of Lucy Bradford's best.

"I hope it was insured. It was probably worth a bundle."

"No, it wasn't insured, and you're right. It was worth a lot. But it was there long before the pieces became such collectibles, and I guess no one thought about it."

"What about the other two?"

"One was in St. Paul's courtyard. It was May Doody's. She'd let the church use it for their fund-raiser. When she came to get it, it was in pieces. The other one belonged to Butler. It disintegrated right there on his baby grand piano. But theirs — May's and Butler's — were insured at least. Unfortunately, they've disposed of the remains, so I don't know that we'll ever figure it out."

"Someone must be shooting them. Kids, maybe?"

"Nope. Foster looked for a bullet or rock, but didn't find one." She sighed rather dramatically, ran her fingers through layers of red hair and hopped off the bar stool. "Well, I'd better get going. Oh, I almost forgot." She reached into her bag and set a book on the table. "Maisy sent this."

"One Hundred Years of Solitude." Charlotte opened the cover. Alice Downy was scrawled on the title page. Beneath the signature was written, *Do you know another way to spell Ixtoc? Toxic!*

"Maisy suggested we read it, but I'm really busy, so I thought I'd give you first crack at it," said Liza Jane. "Do you have any idea what it's about?"

"I read it years ago. It's a strange book. As I remember, it's the story of this doomed utopia in South America."

"Doomed utopia — that's kind of a contradiction in terms, isn't it?"

"I guess it is. Interestingly enough, the name of the place in the book — the doomed utopia — is Macondo."

"Macondo," repeated Liza Jane. "Isn't that the name of the oil field where the spill happened?"

"Yes."

"Just a creepy coincidence, I guess."

"I guess," agreed Charlotte, but she knew that when it came to their Aunt Maisy, there were very few coincidences.

6.
FOWL PLAY

To keep her mind off the Harry-and-Abbie affair, Charlotte turned her thoughts to the bird statues created by Liza Jane's late mother, the notorious Lucy Bradford.

Why would anyone want to destroy East Oyster's beloved pelicans? Because that's what it has to be — vandalism. The statues wouldn't suddenly fall apart — or explode — on their own.

She looked at her watch. No wonder she was starving. Afternoon was now evening.

She made herself an omelet, toasted the last piece of ciabatta and threw together a green salad. She took this modest supper and a glass of chardonnay through the open French doors and onto her balcony where a spectacular sunset was in progress. A flock of a dozen brown pelicans returning home to roost were silhouetted black against the fiery sky. The breath-taking scene conversely conjured visions of the magnificent birds drowning in oil, and the image sent a shiver through her.

Charlotte's building — not just the building that housed her apartment, but her very own building — was situated on the corner of Palmetto and Semmes streets. Palmetto ran downhill to Palmetto Bay where the sun was just dipping its lower half into the water. Semmes Street ran along the edge of East Oyster's gentrified downtown.

Turner Gallery took up the bottom story of the building and Charlotte's sprawling apartment encompassed the top floor. The gallery entrance and the apartment's main balcony faced Semmes Street. As the balcony wrapped around to the Palmetto Street side and its remarkable view of the park and the bay beyond, it narrowed to a mere eight feet in width. This was Charlotte's favorite spot, quiet and cozy and seeming miles away from the busy activity of the Semmes Street shops.

She had furnished this space with a turquoise bistro table and chairs from Craig & Leon's, the shop three doors down. She'd made room for two aluminum chaises, decrepit but comfy with their rosy cushions, and a bougainvillea potted in terra-cotta. The bougainvillea flourished there where the balcony's wrought-iron railing made its elegant curve. The plant was so prolific with its thorns and delicate foliage and electric pink blooms splashed against the saffron stucco of Charlotte's building that many an artist had captured it in renderings of East Oyster's most charming street corner.

Charlotte popped the last chunk of avocado into her mouth and looked at her own Lucy Bradford original perched in all of its moss-green glory next to the bougainvillea.

"Please don't explode," she said aloud.

The bird simply stared out over Semmes Street. The crossed amethyst eyes invested her with a decidedly nerdy personality that Charlotte had grown attached to. She knew the bird was female since Lucy had named it *Dee Dee T.* This was in obvious reference to the pesticide Lucy blamed for the demise of so many of the birds.

Lucy Bradford had begun her love affair with the great, prehistoric-looking fowl when she discovered that due to hunting and pesticides such as DDT, Pelicanus Occidentalis (the brown pelican) had become all but extinct. Through her art, she'd hoped to encourage art-lovers and bird-lovers alike to aid in the protection of the magnificent creatures.

Though she did not live to see their return in the huge numbers East Oysterites enjoy today, her efforts had far-reaching results. Lucy's ceramic pelicans — comical, color-ful and at times surreal renditions of the real-life fowl — had been good to Lucy. Actually, they had been great to Lucy.

She'd sold them all over the world, and they had kept her in tequila and "meds" and airfare to exotic locales for years. The most famous, *First Love,* is actually two birds in flight, one atop the other, for which a grateful collector/suitor reportedly paid tens of thousands of francs (or yen or pesos, depending on who was telling the tale).

Another pelican purchaser/lover happened to be a "man in the movie business" who decided that funky, little, ol' East Oyster and Pitt Cottage were just the setting for his new project, *Midnight Charade.* The runaway success of the movie put East Oyster on the tourist map and ensured Lucy a permanent place in the hearts of the townsfolk.

For all of her artistic success and environ-mental sensitivity, Lucy Bradford bombed spectacularly as a parent. Liza Jane's father, stepmother, assorted relatives and the grate-ful souls of East Oyster had all taken a hand in shaping the girl's character. And it was a heck of a job.

When Liza Jane tore out of the house

looking like a red hot mess, and the poor, shell-shocked stepmother couldn't make her behave, great-aunt Maisy showed up in her micro-mini skirt, stilettos and bustier to testify in Liza Jane's behalf, her testimony being that the girl had inherited her impeccable taste from Maisy herself. To the dismay of the local thrift shop employees, Liza Jane immediately donated most of her wardrobe to them.

When Liza Jane threatened to drop out of middle school because she planned to become a comedienne (and face it, there's nothing funny about algebra), old man Warren told her the sad tale of his own drug-addled, dropped-out daughter. Liza Jane eventually dried her eyes and picked up her math book. And on and on it went. As you can see, it took everybody pulling out all the stops to get Liza Jane through puberty, much less high school and college.

It was about the time Mama Lucy decided she could no longer ignore the lump in her left breast that she became aware of the debt she owed the village who had raised her child. Once she'd accepted the doctors' grim diagnosis, she went to work, creating molds, pouring slip, firing and glazing through the chemo and chipping away at a lifetime of parental regret. Having watched the sausage being made, as it were, everyone was amazed at how good it was in the end. Because when Lucy died sixteen months later, all was in order — Liza Jane well provided for and valuable pelican statues and paintings bequeathed to almost everyone in town.

To this day, pelicans peek out from beneath hedges, spew water into ponds and grace great rooms and humble establishments alike. The friends and neighbors could have sold them, which is what Lucy no doubt had in mind. But most found it impossible to part with the pieces. And so Lucy's pelicans became a part of the colorful, eccentric fabric of East Oyster, Alabama.

The pretty little hamlet lazing beneath oaks heavy with Spanish moss and southern charm had always been a draw for artists and writers and therefore, tourists. Not surprisingly, the artsy/folksy denizens embraced their legacy as keepers of the clay pelicans and the various legends that attached themselves to the statues and paintings. These included everything from good luck to healing properties to libido enhancement. Of course, East Oysterites had also had their collective awareness raised concerning the real deal, Pelicanus Occidentalis. Following in Lucy's footsteps, the town became a forerunner in pelican habitat restoration.

They were well-rewarded for their dedication to the beleaguered brown pelican as well as their liberal-mindedness toward any and all art forms. To use Great Aunt Maisy's apt avian analogy, tourism took off "like a bird escapin' the snare." Things progressed to the establishment of The Lucy Bradford Museum of Natural Pelican History on the American Gulf Coast and an Annual Pelican Picnic and Regatta held on the second Saturday in April. The week leading up to the regatta/picnic was dedicated to showings of *Midnight Charade,* interviews with minor stars of the film and parties at Pitt Cottage. This, in turn, drew more tourists and their money to East Oyster's increasingly upscale boutiques, galleries and eateries.

Liza Jane had been devastated by her mother's illness and ultimate demise and unnerved by the hoopla surrounding her mother's bird bequests to the neighbors. But she'd gotten through it. And though she was now reacting in typical Liza Jane (see blasé) fashion, Charlotte knew her friend. The desecration of her mother's statues was getting to her.

The insult added to this injury was that the cousins had recently celebrated their mutual birthday. Though she was a decade older, Charlotte took the milestone in stride, but to Liza Jane each birthday distanced her from her beloved youth, reminded her that she was still a long way from getting her act together and put her closer to dreaded middle age. Sadly, she hadn't even admitted to herself that she'd likely achieved the status of middle age.

Charlotte could only shake her head.

Hope, unlike youth, springs eternal, she reminded herself.

As the sun dropped into the bay in an iridescent flash of chartreuse, Charlotte made a decision. Being Liza Jane's closest friend and cousin and East Oyster's most famous (living) artist, as well as owner of the town's best and biggest gallery, it was up to her to get to the bottom of the bird problem. Besides, it might even take her mind off gushing oil wells, tar-covered wildlife and out-of-work fishermen. Not to mention the impending Harry-and-Abbie nuptials.

7.
REQUESTS

While on her morning run down Palmetto Street, Charlotte decided to make a detour through the park. She stopped at the main entrance and surveyed the scene.

Scattered in the azaleas beside the brick pedestal upon which the park pelican had nested for thirty years were the colorful remnants of Lucy Bradford's fractured fowl. Getting as close as possible without compromising the "crime scene," if that's what it was, she slipped her phone out of a pocket and took several pictures of the sad remains.

She then picked up her usual route — a jogging path along the bay shaded by old oaks and cooled by breezes rippling in from the water. Dolphins breakfasting on a school of mullet broke the surface beyond the municipal pier. Closer in, a fisherman cast his line from a cherry-red kayak. It was a postcard morning.

The ritual of a run along East Oyster's

scenic bay front had become a necessary start to Charlotte's day. Over the years, she'd found that regular exercise and a daily dose of nature cleared her head like nothing else.

Painting was the main antidote for anything that ailed her, however. Investing her emotions in her work paid off in a settled psyche, exceptional art and a successful career. Between the run and the opening of the shop she tried to put in a couple of hours painting. The evenings usually found her watching one of her old movies or back in front of the easel, iPod blasting away and a glass of wine within reach.

As her muscles worked, the mantra of her breathing and footfalls cleared her brain. She visualized her latest work in progress. She had several old photographs of the house with its roses tilted toward the sun, but mostly she worked from memory. Charlotte smiled and picked up her pace.

After the summer of Harry, Charlotte had thrown herself into her work and quickly become well-known in New Orleans. Her fluid, shifting imagery was mesmerizing and sold like Saturday-morning beignets to novice and knowledgeable art collectors alike. Since Saint-Yves-Sur-Mer, she'd been infatuated with water and the magic that light worked on it. Her abstract portrayals of scenes in and around the river and lake and marshes of her native New Orleans were frequently veiled in mist, inflamed by a sunset or softened by the sunrise. More often than not, form and light dissolved into their reflections in the moonlight, turning them delicate and ethereal. C. Turners seldom stayed on gallery walls for any length of time. She rarely had more than one show a year. She didn't have to.

Thank goodness for the Schamms, she thought.

Laurie and Nevin Schamm were a couple of odd but talented potters who spent every weekend participating in arts and crafts shows around the southeast. When not on the road, they were rarely if ever seen. Liza Jane referred to them as the spooks.

But they were reliable if not amiable. Laurie kept Charlotte's books, and Nevin worked one or two afternoons a week in the gallery. Charlotte sold their plates and bowls and vases and mugs in Turner Gallery. The asymmetric pieces with their psychedelic glazes were so popular that Charlotte could hardly keep them on the shelves.

Yet even with the extra help, the balance between work and art was one Charlotte was finding increasingly difficult to maintain. The double-edged sword of a successful business had its trade-offs. For Charlotte, increased personal satisfaction and financial security was tempered by accompanying time constraints and mushrooming stress levels.

She found the latter to be a constant challenge to both her digestion and her right-brain sensibilities. The horrific disaster in the gulf along with the pelican vandalism — not to mention the invasion of Harry McMillan, affianced to Abbie Pitt — threatened to tip the precarious equilibrium she maintained.

In spite of her determination to put Harry McMillan in his place — which was at the bottom of her priority list — her mind kept returning to the quick smile, the mellow voice, the easy laugh . . . she was mid-way through a list of Harry's attributes when she became aware of a fellow runner closing in behind her. She moved to the right, but instead of passing, the guy stayed beside her. When she finally looked up, it was into the very eyes she'd been fantasizing about.

"It's you!" She stopped, aware that she was grinning foolishly at the man, but she just couldn't help herself. The dimple, the lovely white teeth, those adorable, slightly bowed legs. Who could blame her?

He wiped sweat from his forehead with his shirt sleeve and grinned back at Charlotte.

"You're very good at ignoring people," he said between labored breaths.

"Sorry. I was just thinking about . . . about the day ahead."

"Glad I managed to catch up with you." The grin intensified. "It wasn't easy." He gave her an appraising look, lingered a bit on her legs and said, "You're in good shape. You must run every day."

"Thanks." But she was thinking that Harry had also managed to stay in amazingly good shape.

"You, too . . . I mean, do you run every day?"

"I try to . . . Mind if I tag along?"

And so they set off down the path by the bay, adjusting their pace until they jogged in unison. To Charlotte it was as natural and comforting as the day's first cup of coffee, like they'd been starting their days together forever.

They ran in silence for a while, enjoying the views — and the companionship. Then Harry said, "So tell me about a day in the life of a gallery owner."

"It's not too exciting. Sure you want to know?"

"I'm sure." He smiled at her. "Even the boring parts. What will you do today?"

"Let's see. First I'll meet with a woman from Key West. She makes jewelry from shells, bits of coral, sea glass . . . that kind of thing."

"Interesting choice for a gallery."

"I like having a variety. Besides, her pieces are real works of art. Great-looking stuff."

"So they're expensive, I guess."

"No. That's the great thing. They're very affordable. And now that everyone's mind is on the oil spill, the jewelry is a reminder of the fragile beauty of beaches everywhere." Charlotte slowed her pace and gestured toward the bay. "Like this one. Can you imagine what an oil slick could do to this?"

"Unfortunately, yes. We've all seen the pictures of other oil spills. I heard that Louisiana has declared a state of emergency."

"Good grief," was all Charlotte could say.

They continued in silence, their thoughts mired in oil.

Finally, Harry said, "You know, in the short time I've been here, I've gotten kind of attached to this place.

Charlotte looked around her. "It's a beautiful spot," she said.

"It's not just the natural beauty — there's

plenty of that — but to the people here. It reminds me of St. Yves — a beautiful, quirky place full of . . . interesting characters, I guess you'd call them."

Charlotte laughed. "We definitely have our share of characters. But they're very nice for the most part."

"So what else is on the gallery agenda for today?"

"You really want to hear this?"

"I do. Over the years, I've thought about you and . . . you know, I wondered what your days were like. I pictured you in front of an easel, but that's as far as I got."

They slowed to a walk and Charlotte told him that like any business, hers involved a lot of non-creative busy-ness such as ordering invitations for an upcoming show. But she was excited about the artist, an emerging South American surrealist who went by the single moniker, Arcadio. Her Aunt Maisy (East Oyster's dearest eccentric) had introduced Charlotte to Arcadio's work, sending photos and articles until Charlotte was forced to take a serious look at him. She liked what she saw and promptly procured several of his paintings for Turner Gallery. Maisy's instincts were usually right on, she said.

"Arcadio . . . the name's familiar. Maybe

I've seen his work."

"Well, I hope you'll come to the show. I'll send you a card."

The rest of her day would be spent dealing with boxes of ceramics to be unpacked, priced and displayed. Several large abstracts by a Louisiana artist were waiting to be hung. And of course there was *The Gathering* — she'd need to wrap it up for him — if he still wanted it. *If your fiancée hasn't talked you out of it.*

"Absolutely, I still want it. I was planning to come by the gallery later today and pick it up."

He asked about her painting, and she told him that she'd recently begun something that had her almost as excited as when she was working on *The Gathering*. The project was invigorating, and had her snatching precious hours to paint whenever she could. But there was never enough time.

"I know what you mean. I don't know if you remember, but I'd planned on becoming an architect."

Charlotte remembered everything about Harry McMillan.

"Yes, I remember."

"Things didn't go exactly as planned. I ended up in real estate. It was a good living. But after my last landmark birthday, I decided there would never be enough time to run my business and do what I'd always wanted. I sold the real estate company and started drawing plans. So far I haven't regretted it."

And then they were back at Palmetto Street.

"Well, I guess I'd better get back," Harry said. "This was fun." He smiled at her, seemed hesitant to leave. "It's great seeing you again." He started back down the path, then turned and called, "I'll see you soon, right?"

He could have been standing next to her table all those years ago in Cassis, so hopeful that she would meet him the next day. *Don't forget, Charlie. Tomorrow, okay?*

"Okay. I mean, sure," she said. "See you later."

Charlotte headed up Palmetto Street, her mind on nothing but Harry. She shook her head. *You are not some school girl, she told herself. You are not in France. Harry McMillan is engaged. To Abbie Pitt. Agh!*

But it was all right to be happy to run into an old friend, wasn't it?

That's what all this emotion is about, she told herself. *It's just nostalgia or something.*

Or something, she could hear Liza Jane saying.

Which reminded her that the expensive avocado/cucumber scrub Liza Jane had talked her into buying was probably nearing its expiration date. And that she was in serious need of a manicure.

Once Charlotte had her fingernails free of oil paint and glistening with petal pink polish, her skin scrubbed to a painful but pretty glow (and smelling faintly like a green salad) and her new haircut blown out just like Honey the hairdresser had shown her, she found another pair of butt-enhancing jeans and an umber-colored T-shirt. Tawny sandals and new turquoise earrings had her ready for another day at the office.

Charlotte's first chore was to get *The Gathering* safely wrapped for Harry. She had just taken it down and propped it against the wall when the bell on the gallery door jangled. Charlotte sucked in her stomach, checked her reflection in a mirrored picture frame and adopted a casual, business-like smile.

Instead of Harry McMillan, however, Abbie Pitt, walking (and looking, Charlotte had to admit) like she'd just hopped on the fashion runway, strode toward Charlotte.

Charlotte freeze-dried the smile on her face and said, "Hi there, Abbie."

"Hi. Listen, I need you to come out to the

house — Pitt Cottage? I'm sure you know it. I'd like you to round up some things with aqua and pink colors in them. For my kitchen . . ." She actually smiled at Charlotte. "Our kitchen, that is." The smile vanished so quickly that Charlotte wondered if she'd imagined it. Abbie paused, lips pressed together, eyes to the beamed ceiling above — presumably thinking. "Maybe you should come out and take a look first. You decide."

Charlotte hesitated. But only for a second or two before curiosity won out over disdain. She just had to pick at that little sore place in her heart, had to see the future vacation residence of Mr. and Ms. Harry McMillan. Besides, the aloof but reliable Nevin Schamm was due to work the next afternoon. Charlotte wasn't exactly comfortable in his presence and sought excuses to be out of the gallery when he was there.

"Sure," she heard herself say. "How about tomorrow, say two o'clock?"

"That should work." With unAbbielike sincerity, she added, "I really appreciate it."

But she quickly recovered and said, "Charlotte, I don't want to hurt your feelings, but I don't think that ghost picture is going to fit in with my vision for the house. You'll understand when you see my colors. Bye."

Abbie had just turned on her fashionable heel when East Oyster's most eligible bachelor, Butler Finley came in. When in town, Butler was in the habit of dropping in once or twice a week for a "dose of art." Luckily for Charlotte, he was out of town quite a bit. According to Liza Jane, he'd just returned from a tour of top art museums and galleries in Houston.

He passed Abbie, then turned and said, "Excuse me, but you're Abigail Pitt, aren't you?"

"Why, yes, and you are . . . ?"

Butler smiled, threw back his shoulders and exhaled a cloud of charm at Abbie. "Butler Finley. I'm chairman of the Preserve the Pelican Board. We've heard you intend to donate the Pitt pelican to our little town."

"The Pitts are always happy to contribute to the well-being of East Oyster in any way," said Abbie in a bored, sing-song voice. But she was smiling right back.

"Well, we sure appreciate it. As a matter of fact, I'd be happy to come out personally and pick it up. Whenever it's convenient. Here's my card." His smile went into megawattage. "And call any time."

The Pitt pelican was indeed a Bradford original. Liza Jane had a photo of her mother painting it on the back door of Pitt

Cottage as a camera crew prepared for the shooting of *Midnight Charade.* The door eventually became a logo of sorts for the famous film. What it lacked in artistic merit, it made up for in popular appeal.

"It's kind of a shame," Craig Bloom later commented. "It drew a lot of tourists to the cottage, even though it was not Lucy's best work, by far. As you know, she was a ceramist first and a painter second. If I didn't know better, I'd say Ms. Abbie is trying to discourage interest in *Midnight Charade* and therefore Pitt Cottage."

Charlotte agreed with his assumption of Abbie's motives. But as far as the quality of this particular piece of art was concerned, she knew all too well that works of art are collected based on provenance (which this one possessed in the form of Liza Jane's photo), subject matter (the pelicans were universally loved), and rarity. Since Lucy was now partying in the great beyond, there would be no more Lucy Bradford originals. As for the fourth requirement of collectors — perfection? Well, Charlotte also knew that art's beauty does indeed lie in the beholder's eye.

Charlotte steeled herself for the inevitable conversation with Butler, but for the first time ever, he didn't give Charlotte so much as an insincere nod. Instead, he walked right out of the gallery with Abbie.

8.
JUST FRIENDS?

Charlotte looked at her beloved painting. *Ghost picture? Abbie has her nerve.* But now that she thought about it, the rising spirits seemed downright incandescent, more real than Charlotte had ever seen them.

Were the ghosts feeling as indignant as she? She smiled at the thought and decided it was just a trick of the sunlight streaming in through the window. She returned the painting to its place on the wall, but the intense luminescence remained. Maybe Abbie's description was an apt one after all.

Customers came and went, almost erasing Abbie's voice from Charlotte's head. She placed an order with the woman from Key West who created the fabulous yet afford-able beach baubles. Derek, her accident-prone, part-time help, unpacked a shipment of ceramics with nary a chip. The two of them hung the new paintings by the Louisi-ana artist. The abstracts' vibrant skies, shimmering seas and startling corals would sell quickly. To help them along, Charlotte and the artist pledged half of their profits to the Restore Our Gulf foundation.

Derek stood looking at the smallest of the paintings.

"Beautiful, isn't it?" asked Charlotte.

"I guess so, but I was thinking how Pup would go crazy over it. She loves colors like that."

"Isn't her birthday coming up?"

"Yes, ma'am. But no way I could afford that."

Derek was a bit of a bull in the china shop, but he was a good kid. His grandmother, Pup, cleaned houses — including Maisy's house, Charlotte's apartment and the gallery — to support herself, Derek and Derek's two younger brothers.

"Maybe I can get you a print," said Charlotte.

"Really?" But the grin vanished as quickly as it had appeared. "How much . . . ?"

"Something you can afford. No promises, but I think I can work it out."

"Sweet! Pup's got herself down over the oil, worried about eating the seafood. You know, we catch most of what we eat."

Charlotte didn't know.

"Try not to worry, Derek. They say the

seafood is safe." She gave him what she hoped was an encouraging smile. "I'll let you know about the print in a day or two," she said as Eunice Toowell entered the gallery.

Miss Toowell was the mayor of East Oyster and as conscientious as they come. There was just one drawback. Due to her excessive dieting — she'd been trying to lose twenty pounds for thirty years — and a serious shopping addiction, she doesn't do lunch meetings. Instead, those two hours were spent making the rounds of everything from the five-and-dime to Turner Gallery. This is done under the guise of "keeping up with the folks." Everybody knew the real story, but they figured as politicians go, it was a small thing.

On this day, Eunice bought a pair of hand-carved sconces, two picture frames and a toe ring. As she handed Charlotte her worn credit card, she shared the latest spill-related news. Oil had washed ashore on barrier islands off the coast of Louisiana.

"It's part of a national wildlife refuge, you know. The pictures of the beaches and marshes are terrible. There was an oil-covered baby dolphin —"

Eunice shook her head, collected herself and offered to spread the word about the newly-installed art and its subsequent donations to the gulf restoration group.

"At least it's something I can do. I feel so helpless!" she said, gathering her bags and heading for the door.

Charlotte managed to display most of the new ceramic pieces and put two large, white jugs aside for Liza Jane. A large oil painting and a set of Nevin Schamm's mugs sold to a couple from Canada. Financially speaking, the day was progressing nicely.

Craig Bloom, co-owner of Craig & Leon — Fine Antiques for the Garden and Home, stopped in with a tiny bouquet of violets from his garden. "From Leon," he explained, and popped the flowers into a miniature celadon vase which he grouped with some other pieces in the window. Leon, Craig's "partner in all things" was a quiet, handsome man who had been with Craig for as long as Charlotte had known him.

"Got some good news for a change," he said.

"Well, let's hear it," said Charlotte.

"You know Janine Jett's boyfriend, Bobby, was on the oil rig when it blew, right?"

"I thought you had good news."

"I do. Leon had a craving for a Pink Meanie yesterday so we took the boat out and docked it behind the Crab. According to Janine, Bobby is out of the hospital. She thinks he's going to be okay."

"Thank goodness."

Charlotte thought back to the night she'd looked out over the railing of Casa Crab thinking about the men on the oil rig.

"Liza Jane and I were in the Crab having a birthday Meanie when the Horizon exploded. I remember looking out over the gulf just as Janine was telling us how it was Bobby's birthday, too."

"Heck of a birthday. And it's going to be a heck of a summer if they can't plug that leak. I heard oil is washing up on Louisiana's barrier islands. What a mess!" He sighed and shook his head.

"I know. The mayor was in earlier. But I heard some sort of containment chamber is on its way. They'll get it fixed."

"They have to," said Craig. "Okay, change of subject. I saw Abbie Pitt come in here earlier. Couldn't help but be a little curious. Are you helping her with art? God knows she needs it."

"Yes I am, and yes, she does," Charlotte responded. Hoping to change the subject, she said, "Thank Leon for the violets. They're perfect against the green in that vase."

"Plenty more where those came from, my dear. All you want." Craig dropped onto a bar stool. It was painted in a rendering of Gauguin's Polynesian work. "These stools are fabulous. Comfortable, too." He sighed. "Way out of my league. Price-wise, that is."

This was completely untrue. Craig was as careful with his pots of money as he was shrewd a businessman. He never paid full-price for anything.

"Though they would be perfect in my kitchen," he continued. He smiled sweetly at Charlotte. "Did I hear you were giving discounts to old friends?"

"Now how did you know about that?"

But Craig was saved from a reply because at that moment the "old friend" himself came through the door. As Harry walked toward them, smiling his wonderful smile, Charlotte and Craig (though he is completely devoted to Leon) sighed simultaneously. After introductions were made and Harry promised to stop by Craig & Leon's, Craig excused himself, winked at Charlotte and fairly skipped out of the door.

His unorthodox departure apparently went unnoticed by Harry who wandered over to *The Gathering* where it was still propped against the wall.

"This painting is really something, Charlie," he said. "I know it's crazy, but I feel connected to it," he explained as if having a discussion with his practical side — or possibly practicing for the inevitable argument with Abbie. He pulled his gaze from the painting and said, "Can I get it today?"

She looked at *The Gathering* one last time and sighed. It would end up in an attic or resale shop if Abbie had anything to do with it.

Yes, but remember that your fiancée hates it, Charlotte wanted to say. But she'd learned long ago not to get in between a couple's opposing tastes in art. So instead she said, "Oh, yes. Yes, of course. I'll wrap it up for you right now if you have a minute."

"Sure. Here, let me help."

Harry picked up the big canvas and placed it on the framing table while Charlotte unrolled bubble wrap. They chatted about the oil spill, the weather and the deteriorating business climate in East Oyster as Charlotte wrapped and taped and grew a bit breathless at the nearness of him.

He asked about the famous East Oyster pelicans. Then, because he was so interested, Charlotte told him the story of her aunt, Lucy Bradford, the artist behind the pieces, and how much they meant to the community. How they'd assumed almost magical properties as the years went by and that the stories were embellished with each telling.

"I'm sure it all sounds pretty silly," said Charlotte.

"Not so much. I grew up on my aunts' ghost stories. Do you remember Simone and Marie?"

"Oh, of course. And I was raised in New Orleans, you know. Lots of ghosts and voodoo and everything. But I've never met anyone like your aunts. They were so . . . so authentically spiritual."

"That's a good description." He smiled at her. "They were very fond of you."

"I'm lucky I got to know them — if only for a short while."

"Your painting reminds me of them — and the ghosts they talked about. I thought maybe . . ."

"That they were the inspiration for the painting?"

"When I saw it, my first thought was, So that's what Marie and Simone were talking about. I had to meet the artist. When I found out it was you, well . . ."

The old connection between them was almost more than Charlotte could bear. She felt her face redden, her eyes prickling with tears.

"The painting is yours now," she said, almost in a whisper. "It's what you want it to be, what you see in it."

He pressed his lips together, accepting her answer, but disappointed.

And so she fought off the tears and told him of what she had seen in Marie's old face all those years ago, how she'd never forgotten it and had attempted to paint it a hundred times, trying to capture Marie herself. Then one night as she sat on her balcony watching a moon spilling its shine over the bay, the scene came to her. She'd stayed up all night getting the preliminaries done. A month later, *The Gathering* was finished.

"I never really planned on selling it. I certainly never thought I'd see you again."

"Sure you want to part with it?"

"Absolutely. I know it's what Marie and Simone would want. And it's what I want. I'm delighted you're buying it."

The mention of Marie and Simone had Harry and Charlotte remembering other aspects of that summer in Provence, carefree times at the Deux Rienes, lazy afternoons, moonlit nights . . .

The bell on the door jangled and several people came into the gallery at once.

"Let me know if you need help," Charlotte called to them.

"I'd better pay for this and get out of your way," said Harry. He handed Charlotte his credit card then lifted the canvas from the table.

When the sale was complete, Charlotte said, "I'll walk you out and get the door for you."

"Thanks." He looked around him as they headed toward the front of the gallery. He seemed to be taking in every inch of the high, beamed ceilings, the exposed brick walls, the arched, oversized windows and the wide planks of pine flooring. "This is a beautiful building. Did you have to do much refurbishing?"

Charlotte laughed. "I should show you the pictures of it before my sons and I got to work on it. It was a mess. Unfortunately, I haven't done much to the second floor, which is where I live."

"You know I sold my business recently. And I'm finally doing what I started out to do — designing and restoring places like this." A small, rueful smile passed over his face. "Like they say, better late than never. Anyway, I'd like to see your pictures."

"Sure," said Charlotte with more enthusiasm than she'd intended. After all, it meant more time with Harry.

As she opened the front door for him, he said, "I can't wait to hang this. I hope you'll come see it — and me . . . us, soon." He smiled self-consciously. "It's good seeing you again, Charlie. Really good. I want us to be . . . friends."

She attempted to respond in the affirmative, attempted to say *of course,* then *I'd like that,* even a flippant *oh, sure,* but the phrases stuck in her throat. So she just smiled, and as Harry McMillan and her beloved painting left the gallery she thought, *How can you be just friends with someone who melts your heart every time you look at him?*

9.
PITT COTTAGE

"The containment dome has failed. A fishing ban for federal waters in the Gulf of Mexico has been expanded and extended —"

Charlotte switched off the radio, opened the sun roof and headed down Pitt Ferry Road. Between tree-shaded beach cottages, the water flickered strobe-like in the afternoon sun. The air was salty sweet with the smells of spring and the bay — an afternoon too spectacular to listen to a radio announcer's voice of doom.

The houses along Palmetto Bay with their hand-painted signs and crushed-shell drives ranged from magnificent to modest, yet each held a promise of good times and memories to last the assorted inhabitants a lifetime. Many of the houses had been summer getaways for generations of the same families, with months or weeks allocated to various sets of cousins. But use as year round, single-family residences had increased exponentially with soaring property values. The last two decades had seen a rash of renovation and landscaping, and the fishing village atmosphere had slowly but surely taken on a resort ambience. One old-timer joked that things had gotten so uppity, his wife made him put on a coat and tie to check his crab traps.

In spite of the newly-established sophistication, however, Charlotte noticed several "for rent" signs. More fallout from the spill, she decided. Up until April twentieth, the few Palmetto Bay cottages for rent were snapped up as much as a year in advance. By spring, such signs were non-existent.

Pitt Cottage and its neighbors were situated on a wide waterway officially named Perdido Bayou by the Spaniards who discovered it. The bayou spilled into Palmetto Bay, which in turn spilled into the Gulf of Mexico. It was a twenty-minute boat ride from the rustic charms of the bayou to the pristine beaches of the gulf where condos, charter fishing, shopping and nightlife are tourist Mecca for those who took their vacations at a hotter, faster pace.

Another boost to the bayou properties' desirability was the undeveloped opposite side of the bayou known as Finley's Landing. This was rumored to be owned by a "black sheep" relative of the aforementioned Butler Finley. The property was composed of acres of pines ending in a point ringed with white oleander and surrounded by a sand bar that melted into Palmetto Bay.

At one time a spectacular beach house faced the point. It even boasted its own canal that meandered from the bayou through the property until it disappeared beneath the house. This unusual setup enabled the owners to drive their boats into lifts and walk directly into the cottage. Though the house had been lost in Hurricane Ivan, the strange, little canal remained.

Fifty years prior, someone had dubbed the area Cocktail Cove. This was due to the partying tendencies of the inhabitants who to this day are unsurpassed in their ability to turn any occasion into a celebration. Most people in East Oyster had never heard of the official name, Perdido Bayou, but everyone knew about Cocktail Cove.

At the end of Pitt Ferry Road, a freshly-painted sign informed Charlotte she had found the new-and-improved-by-Harry Pitt Cottage. She followed the familiar curves of the shell drive until suddenly, there it was. However, the vision looming before her barely resembled the house and rear guest quarters she remembered.

During the winter months, the main house's rear porch had been expanded to twice its original size. Through expansive windows Charlotte saw that it was being transformed into a large kitchen and breakfast room.

Touches of creamy paint freshened eaves and window frames. Bits of gingerbread trim and Bahama shutters in faded cerulean nestled against the silvered natural cypress of the house's exterior like they'd always been there. The guest house had been gussied up in the same manner so that it was a miniature reflection of the main house. And the famed back door upon which Lucy B. had painted a lavender pelican sitting on a nest of coral? It was nowhere in sight.

Key West casual, is how Charlotte would have described Pitt Cottage's new look. Containers of banana trees and palms (courtesy of Palm World?) sat by the porch. The parking area had been filled with fresh oyster shells, and a fence of elaborately carved pickets had been started. More Disney World than Key West, Charlotte decided. Definitely not what she'd expected. And so totally un-Abbie. But then Twiggy-on-steroids herself pranced across the porch in linen and espadrilles and a flowered scarf tied around her head. The whole scene screamed, see how relaxed and casual I am? And Charlotte realized that the house was, indeed, a reflection of Abbie.

The kitchen, almost finished, was pink and aqua alright, but fifties retro — not great, but not the horror Charlotte had expected. Yet like Abbie, it came off as insincere. It was a look-at-me room, lacking the sit-down-and-have-a-piece-of-pie feeling it was meant to evoke.

A large, framed poster advertising the house's claim to fame, *Midnight Charade*, hung on a wall in a butler's pantry. In it, a young couple embraced in the moonlight. Water shimmered in the background and the scene was framed by trees dripping with Spanish moss. The woman, who held a flashlight, smiled slyly over the man's shoulder and winked directly at the camera. It was kitschy but cool, especially because of its part in the house's history.

What a great poster, thought Charlotte.

Abby followed Charlotte's gaze to the poster. "Harry loves that thing," she said, punctuating her usual monotone delivery with a shrug.

The living area was almost complete. Venetian blinds had been removed so that the oversized windows opened up views of a deep lawn and the bay beyond. The bamboo furniture with its retro, banana leaf bark cloth was gone, as were the straw rugs and driftwood lamps.

The room's paneled walls now blushed with the palest pink paint. Everything else was white. White linen slipcovers. White lamps. A large, sisal rug the color of sun-bleached oyster shells. The old fireplace, painted igloo white now looked like it would surely melt with the first fire. The bare wall above the mantle soared between French doors and transoms that opened onto the porch.

Propped in a corner, face to the wall as if in punishment for its refusal to acquiesce to Abbie's whims, was *The Gathering.* Abbie followed Charlotte's gaze and rested there for a few seconds. But like the proverbial elephant in the room, neither of the women mentioned it.

Abbie led Charlotte upstairs and through the bedrooms simply and effectively freshened with paint. The master bath was finished except that there was a sheet over its large window. A king-sized bed swathed in pale blue linens sat like an oasis in the otherwise sparsely-furnished room.

Charlotte took photos of each and every

wall. She steeled herself for the inevitable signs of pre-connubial bliss — tangled sheets, photos of the betrothed grinning their brains out in romantic locales, his-and-hers toiletries co-mingling on the bathroom's new marble counter tops. But there was not one sign of cohabitation (or habitation, for that matter) — not a toothbrush, not an article of clothing, not even a lingering whiff of perfume. Or aftershave.

"Abbie," said Charlotte, "Have you moved in yet?"

"Yes. Why?"

Charlotte pictured dust bunnies the size of tumble weeds in the corners of her own place. "It's just that I've never seen a house this neat."

Abbie looked at Charlotte as if she were speaking Arabic.

"I'm impressed," Charlotte added with a chuckle. "Housekeeping isn't exactly my strong suit."

"Really," said Abbie, and headed back downstairs.

As they descended the newly stained and polyurethaned stairs, Abbie's cell began to chime. She plucked it out of her pocket.

"Yes. Pitt here." The words floated out on a tired, uninterested sigh. Then, "I'm fine. How are you," she said in a bored, singsong voice that reflected her impatience with the requisite niceties that began each and every conversation in East Oyster. She listened to the caller with lips pressed together, foot tapping the wasted milliseconds, then responded, "Yes. Tell him I'll be ready." She slipped the phone back into her pocket.

By the time they re-entered the living room, Charlotte had had enough of the woman's frosty attitude. Gesturing to the banished picture, she said, "Look, Abbie, art is subjective. I don't take it personally if you don't like this painting." Realizing she was headed into delicate territory, she added, "I'm afraid Harry has really connected with it, though. I'm sorry if it's become a bone of contention."

"Don't worry, Harrison and I will work it out. Now, I hate to rush you, Charlotte, but I have a plane to catch." She glanced at her watch. "I've got someone picking me up in a few minutes. Oh, and if you need to get back in, ask Butler. He has a key."

"Okay," Charlotte began. But Abbie had started up the stairs.

"Oh that's all right, Abbie, I'll just let myself out," Charlotte murmured, her sarcasm either unheard or ignored by Abbie.

As Charlotte passed the Pitt Cottage sign on her way out, she muttered to herself,

"Abbie should have it changed to Pitt Palace," and realized that she was developing what her Aunt Maisy referred to as an ill humor. So instead of continuing down the main road, she turned into the next driveway at a fish-shaped sign that read Downydew.

Downydew was the summer home of said Maisy Downy — the same Aunt Maisy who had sent her niece off to France decades earlier in hopes of mending Charlotte's broken heart. The old character whose hobby was telling fortunes and holding combination seance/cocktail parties was a favorite of the eccentric-loving East Oyster-ites. Her yellow and gold seer's tent and secret frozen margarita recipe were the main ingredients in successful functions and parties in East Oyster and beyond.

Along with an ancient malfunctioning ball unoriginally yet affectionately named Crystal, she'd inherited "the gift of intuitive powers" from her paternal granny who'd been a renowned fortune teller back in the day. In honor of this mystical granny, Maisy always dressed in full gypsy regalia complete with a flowing black wig. Crystal was toted to readings in a silver and purple bowling ball bag donated to Maisy by her late husband, Dubby. Crystal and the bag she called home were two of Maisy's prized possessions.

Maisy dispensed nuggets of remarkable wisdom and sips of her famous green concoctions while cursing and pounding the flickering Crystal. Though a few folks snickered at the old lady, they soon realized besides being a hoot and fixing the meanest margaritas in town, Maisy's predictions always rang true. Under the guise of Madame Maisy, she helped most of her neighbors see their way through the fog of their problems to clear solutions.

Charlotte decided a dose of Maisy's insight (and perhaps one of her famous cocktails) was just what she needed. According to Craig, Maisy had been in residence at Downydew for a few days — long enough to get settled and ready for drop-in guests, Charlotte told herself, and she turned into Maisy's drive.

As she did, she caught sight of a black BMW turning into the entrance to Pitt Cottage. Though the pines and bushes separating the properties were thick, she caught the glint of a silver pelican. It was the emblem of the Alabama Coastal Conservation Organization. As a proud board member, Butler Finley had the bird mounted next to the license plate of his BMW. Charlotte was sure that's what she'd seen. It had to be Butler Finley's car. If he was there to lay claim to the Pitt pelican, his timing was off since Abbie was on her way out of town.

Maybe it was the influence of the *Midnight Charade* movie poster with its sleuthing lovers. Maybe it was being in close proximity to her octogenarian auntie with a sixth sense. Or maybe it was just a need to figure out the enigma of the Harry-and-Abbie relationship. (What, besides youth, beauty, glamour and family money did he see in her?) Charlotte decided to do a little sleuthing of her own. She pulled the car into Maisy's parking area and walked through mammoth azaleas, camellias and a tangle of honeysuckle vines until she found a protected spot that had a good view of Abbie's back yard. She settled herself in the shadow of a palmetto and waited.

Several minutes later Abbie and Butler came out of Pitt Cottage's back door and headed toward the BMW. Butler, frowning and perspiring, juggled three pieces of hot pink luggage. Abbie followed, cool as an ice cube, carrying nothing but a Prada clutch.

Butler popped the trunk — yes, there was the silver emblem of ACCO — and wrestled Abbie's bags in next to a black leather suitcase. Always the gentleman, he opened the passenger door for Abbie. Before easing into the driver's seat, he turned and looked directly at Charlotte.

She'd forgotten she was wearing a hot pink blouse which even a mature palmetto can't camouflage. Butler squinted as if to make sure it was actually Charlotte crouched in the greenery. He frowned and waved hesitantly to her. She stood and gave a weak wave in return. But Butler was already getting into his car.

When Charlotte made her way back through the bushes and vines, she saw Maisy sitting on the back step of her porch. Her old auntie was wearing white jeans, a black, sleeveless Harley Davidson tank top that read, Born to Ride and silver stilettos that nicely accented shiny, aqua toenails. Her shoulder-length platinum-blonde hair was pulled into a tight ponytail which she claimed gave her an instant face lift.

Instead of asking what on earth Charlotte was doing stumbling out of her shrubbery, the old lady said, "Hey, sugar. You look like you could use a margarita."

The women had settled themselves on the porch, margaritas in hand, before Maisy said, "Okay, so what were you doing in the bushes?"

Charlotte sipped her drink, inhaled the

bay breeze and filled Maisy in, ending with, "Those two behaved like they were strangers in my gallery yesterday, but it seems that they already know each other. So why the charade? And it looked to me like they were going away together!"

"Or maybe he was giving her a lift to the airport because he also had a flight out," said Maisy.

Charlotte took a thoughtful taste of her margarita and sighed. "And maybe I'm imagining things."

Maisy gave Charlotte a pat on the knee, kicked off her shoes and propped her tiny feet on the coffee table.

"Trust your intuition, baby," she said. "Your first impression is usually the right one, in my humble opinion."

"You mean you think they're really going away together?"

Maisy wiggled her gnarly (but vibrant) toes around for a while then said, "I really don't know. But a lot of strange things are going on in our little burg." She sipped her drink and added, "A lot of things just ain't what they seem lately."

"You heard about the pelicans, I guess."

"Yep. Extremely troublesome. Between hurricanes, oil spills and a rotten economy, the folks around here have taken a beating.

Besides the pelican art attracting tourists, there's the town's emotional attachment to them."

"It's been tough on Liza Jane, too."

"So I hear." Maisy finished her drink and watched her toes some more. Finally she said, "You girls mean a lot to me. Like my own children. And you know what they say . . . 'You're only as happy as your unhappiest child.' " She reached over and patted Charlotte's arm. "Liza Jane told me about Harrison McMillan showing up engaged to Abigail Pitt." She shook her head. "What a kick in the ginnies."

10.
DINING AT DOWNYDEW

It took Maisy about twenty seconds to talk Charlotte into staying for supper. She then texted Liza Jane, who hadn't yet nuked her daily Lean Cuisine. An hour later the three women sat on Maisy's porch enjoying the best gumbo this side of New Orleans, French bread and a salad.

Maisy's dining table was large and round, its boards weathered to driftwood then polished smooth by years of use. A statue of clay pelicans served as a centerpiece. The birds, one alabaster with amber stones for eyes and one umber with mother-of-pearl eyes, snuggled together, the snowy and tawny feathers of their necks melded. This was Lucy Bradford's final — and finest — creation. And in a last nod to the glories of controversy, she'd titled it *Miscegenation*.

"So, Charlotte, what's the verdict on the Pitt house?" asked Liza Jane.

"I was just there this afternoon. How did

you know?"

"Craig, of course."

"I swear he is the Mata Hari of East Oyster! Well, the house is . . . it's lovely. Really lovely."

"But?" said Liza Jane.

"But it's not the house in *Midnight Charade* any more. And something tells me that Abbie knew just what she was doing, promising to keep the house open for tours. No one will want to come if it doesn't look like the movie."

"The locals won't be happy," said Liza Jane. "It's one more thing to discourage visitors." She turned to her aunt. "But you won't have to deal with noisy tour groups next door, Maisy."

"Or wayward travelers pulling in here all hours of the day and night," added Charlotte. "That's a plus."

"Not really." The old lady grinned at her nieces. "You can't imagine the interesting people you meet when somebody takes a wrong turn. Serendipity is hugely underrated." She sighed. "I'll miss the wayward travelers."

Charlotte gave a little snort. "Like I said, Abbie knows exactly what she's doing."

"Yes, I think she does," said Maisy wearily.

"You okay, Maisy?" asked Liza Jane.

"Got turtles on my mind."

"Turtles?"

"Sea turtles. They're coming in from the water to lay their eggs. Come July, those eggs will begin to hatch. Kemp's Ridley sea turtles are endangered already, you know."

They knew. They pictured the tiny hatchlings making their valiant trip by the light of the moon into the gulf. Would they be waddling through globs of crude into oil-fouled waters?

Charlotte gave Maisy's hand a pat. "They'll have the well fixed long before then," she said.

Liza Jane had stopped at the Big Oyster Bakery (aka The Big O) just before it closed. She'd snagged their last pineapple cheesecake. She now served this along with coffee to Maisy and Charlotte. They ate dessert in silence, enjoying the afterglow, listening to the rattle of a breeze in the palmettos and the murmur of waves on Maisy's beach. A banana shrub scented the air.

"Well, this is just about heaven," said Maisy. "Two of my favorite people sharing a good meal with me in one of my favorite places on earth."

But the mask of serenity on her pruney little face was suddenly replaced by a frown, and she sat up very straight in her chair.

100

"Now, what the hell is that?" she said and poked her fork toward the spit of land that jutted into the bay four hundred yards across the water.

Liza Jane and Charlotte followed the direction of Maisy's fork, but saw nothing except the outline of trees, black against the blushing sky.

"Now it's gone," said Maisy. "I thought I saw some headlights over at Finley's Landing — right over there behind the oleanders." She jabbed at the air again with her fork. "But the place is closed up tighter than a corset. No fishing signs are on what's left of the wharf and sawhorses with 'no trespassing' signs are blocking the drive. I drove over there and saw them myself. But someone is using that old shed."

"Now how would you know that? Unless you trespassed, that is," said Charlotte.

"Takes more than a couple of sawhorses to keep me out. Besides, I can always claim I got lost. People think everybody my age is demented. Anyway, I saw fresh tire tracks in the sand. And a shiny, new padlock was on the shed door."

"Have you consulted Crystal?" asked Charlotte, referring to Maisy's off-and-on crystal ball.

"She's on the blink again."

101

"Have you asked the Mata Hari of East Oyster?" asked Liza Jane.

Maisy shook her head. "Even our man Craig doesn't know." She grinned at Liza Jane. "But I've got him on the case. And Crystal is in the shop. She'll be glowing up a storm by next week."

Instead of asking where one sends crystal balls in need of repair, Charlotte said, "Well, we should know something soon, I guess." She stood and collected the dessert dishes.

As she headed back through the house, she saw headlights and heard a car moving down Abbie's drive at a suspiciously slow pace.

Like it's creeping, she thought.

Charlotte set the plates in the sink and went back to the porch.

"Now I'm seeing headlights, but they're headed to Abbie's," she said. "I don't like this, Maisy. No one should be over there, and with you here alone . . . Maybe we should call Foster."

"Chief Foster is up to his neck in oil worries and busted pelicans. He can't be bothered with nervous old ladies," said Maisy.

Charlotte knew that's exactly what Foster would think, too.

"Well, I'm not leaving you here by yourself until we make sure it's safe."

"So let's check it out," said Liza Jane, who wasn't one for sitting still and jumped at any excuse for a bit of excitement.

"I'm game," said Maisy.

"Only if you put on some sensible shoes," said Charlotte.

Maisy donned a pair of black, high-top sneakers, grabbed a flash light, and the three of them headed down to the bay where they could walk along the beach to Abbie's yard. They turned the light off and crept along a hedge of hydrangeas until they were next to the front porch. A light was on in the house. They all craned their necks in the darkness, hoping to get a glimpse of the intruder.

"Somebody's in there, alright. I'm pretty sure those lights weren't on when Abbie left for the airport," whispered Charlotte.

"Well, they're not winning any burglar awards, turning on all the lights," Maisy whispered back.

"Maisy has a point," whispered Liza Jane. "Maybe Abbie's flight was cancelled or something. And Charlotte, I really don't think you want Ms. Pitt catching you prowling around in her bushes."

Maisy snorted. "I'd like to see her talk her way out of that one!"

"Charlie?" The deep voice came from behind them.

They all screamed like banshees, and when Charlotte turned around, there was Harry. The look on his face was perplexed but amused."

"Who's Charlie?" asked Liza Jane.

"Oh, it's you," said Charlotte to Harry. "Woo, you scared me to death." She laughed a little fake laugh, tried to cover it by clearing her throat and said, "Gee, you're probably wondering what we're doing out here. I knew Abbie was gone and well . . . I should have thought about you being here. So silly of me. Uh, have you met my Aunt Maisy?"

"So this is Harry," said Maisy, her old eyes twinkling away. She introduced herself and Liza Jane, who flipped her hair like a friendly wolf hound and bestowed one of her warmest smiles on Harry.

"We thought you were a prowler," said Liza Jane.

"Or worse," added Charlotte solemnly. "Maisy lives over there by herself, and . . ."

"And I've got some gumbo on the stove," said Maisy. "Have you had supper?"

Harry laughed. "As a matter of fact I haven't."

"Well, what are we waiting for?" said Maisy.

"Lead the way," said Harry.

The women led Harry back onto the porch and sat once again around the table.

"Is this one of the famous pelican statues?" asked Harry.

"Possibly the most famous," said Liza Jane. "And one of the most valuable."

"I've accumulated a pile of possessions in my life," said Maisy as she walked back to the kitchen. "But this is one of my most prized. I bring it back to the city with me during the winter months. I'm very careful with it."

"I told Harry about the recent problems with the statues," said Charlotte. "We really need to get to the bottom of this."

"Maybe I can help," said Harry. "Do you think Maisy would mind if I took a picture of it?"

"Oh, I'm sure she wouldn't mi—"

But Harry had his cell phone out snapping pictures before Charlotte could finish her sentence.

Harry ran his hand over the birds.

"Where did your mother get her clay?" he asked.

"A white clay ravine not far from here. Creek Indians still own the land. The clay bed is very small, but they let mama take all she wanted. In return, a percentage of her profit has always gone to Native American causes and charities.

"After mama's pieces started selling, every potter and sculptor around wanted that clay. When the crazy superstitions about the birds having magical or healing properties started circulating, a whole other group of folks went crazy for it. The Creeks were willing to share the clay, but there were those who took advantage of their generosity — tore up the land and took big amounts of the clay to sell — that kind of thing, so that was the end of the Creeks' largesse. As far as I know, no one else has made use of what clay is left. Which also adds to the value of my mother's art."

Harry asked more questions — about Lucy Bradford's sketches and molds for her famous statues, and did Liza Jane still have them? About the amber and mother-of-pearl used for the pelicans' eyes. And did Liza Jane keep records of where all the pieces were now?

Harry must have realized that his interest in the pelicans was growing excessive, so he said, "I'm just trying to get a handle on what's behind the art suddenly coming apart." And he dropped the subject.

When Maisy set a bowl of gumbo and the last of the bread in front of Harry, Liza Jane said, "So you and Charlotte are old friends."

"Yes," Harry and Charlotte answered at once.

"We met in France," said Harry. "I was chasing a purse snatcher through the streets of Cassis, and Charlie here put out her dainty, little foot and voila, the guy was toast."

Maisy and Liza Jane exchanged a confused glance. "Charlie?" mouthed Liza Jane. Maisy made a little face and shrugged her shoulders.

"And Harry offered his services as a tour guide," added Charlotte, who was staring, doe-eyed at Harry and wouldn't have noticed if Maisy's hair was on fire.

"As it turned out Charlie was staying in Saint-Yves-Sur-Mer not far from a house I have there. It was my aunts' place back then."

"Oh, I'm so glad you have the house," said Charlotte. "You loved that place."

"Do you get over there often?" asked Maisy.

"Not often enough. My uncle — you remember him, Charlie — he takes care of things and has made a few improvements."

"I thought it was perfect just the way it was," Charlotte said with a little sigh.

"There's one improvement I think you'd be happy about. Do you remember the rabbit hutches?"

"Rabbit hutches?"

"How could you forget? You helped me repair the roof!"

"That's right! And the rabbits were so adorable with those big, floppy ears."

"I'll never forget the look on your face when you realized one of them was your dinner. But you cleaned your plate."

Charlotte grinned. "It was pretty tasty, I have to admit. But I've never had rabbit again."

"You'll be glad to know that we are out of the rabbit business. My uncle sold them all to Monsieur Blanchard."

"The nude sunbather?"

Harry and Charlotte both started laughing.

"One and the same," said Harry. "I always thought he was showing off for you."

"He was! Remember when he insisted on coming with us to Deux Rienes? He turned out to be quite a good dancer."

"He was terrible!"

"He was very good, and you were very jealous, if I remember."

The old stories, punctuated by their laughter, grew sweeter until their voices became husky with nostalgia. Before long, it was as if Maisy and Liza Jane had melted out of the room, leaving "Charlie" and Harry reminiscing about their perfect summer.

Maisy and Liza Jane slipped away to the kitchen on the pretense of preparing Harry's dessert.

"Are you seeing what I'm seeing?" whispered Liza Jane.

"If you're talking about the attraction between those two, well, whoa!" Maisy whispered back. She looked over her shoulder toward the porch and got the dessert out of the fridge. "Fix some fresh coffee, L.J. I've got to think on this."

They were silent for a few seconds before Liza Jane hissed, "What's up with his engagement to Abbie the Pitt? He's obviously still got a thing for Charlie . . . uh, Charlotte."

"I wish I knew. But something isn't right over there." Maisy nodded toward Pitt Cottage and slid a big wedge of pineapple cheesecake onto a plate.

Still whispering, Liza Jane said, "Like what?"

"I've seen Abbie and Harry together a few times. They don't act like any engaged couple I've ever seen. More like brother and sister — and a brother and sister who aren't especially close, either." The old lady sighed.

"I feel responsible in a way."

"Just because you gave Charlotte the trip to France?"

"Well, there's a little more to it."

"Maisy, what did you do?" said Liza Jane, forgetting to whisper.

"Shh," said Maisy. She placed the cheesecake and coffee on a tray. "You're getting ready to find out."

11.
MAISY COMES CLEAN

Maisy headed to the back of the house. Liza Jane returned to the porch. When she set the dessert tray on the table, Charlotte and Harry were literally gazing into each other's eyes. She cleared her throat.

"Oh, thanks," said Harry, "This looks delicious."

Charlotte watched Harry tuck into his dessert as if she were watching the Bolshoi Ballet.

As Harry was finishing up the cheesecake, they became aware of the sounds of doors and drawers opening. They could hear Maisy muttering to herself, obviously looking for something.

Finally, she called, "Found it!" coming in from the back of the house. She was balancing a fresh drink and what appeared to be a large photo album, which she opened and plunked onto the table.

"Uh, what's this?" asked Harry.

He was not yet accustomed to the unconventional behavior of Maisy Downy.

Maisy pulled a chair between Harry and Charlotte. "My late husband, Dubby and I traveled all over," she said. "And one of our favorite places was the area around Cassis. A beautiful area, not all uppity like the Riviera. Anyway, look at this."

She tapped a black and white photo on the right page of the album.

"Good Lord. Is that . . ."

"Yep. Your aunts with Dubby and me. We met them when we broke down outside their place. Not only did they help us out and invite us into their home, they gave us lunch while the car was being fixed.

"Marie and Simone and I . . . well, you wouldn't think it, us hardly speaking each other's languages and them being so much older than I, but we hit it off like sorority sisters. And, of course we had what I call certain sensibilities in common. You don't come across that too often. Their nephew took this picture of the four of us."

"Ah, sensibilities in common," said Harry, as comprehension dawned. "Talk about a small world," he said finally.

"No kidding. And I'll let you in on a secret. The older you get, the smaller it gets." Maisy sat back in her chair, took a long pull on her drink and continued. "As you know, you just about put the blue in the sky as far as your aunts were concerned. They talked about you in all their letters." Maisy hesitated uncharacteristically, as if unsure whether to continue. "Now comes the sticky part. Knowing of their . . . their intuitive natures, shall we say, I wrote to them about our Charlotte. Her heart had been broken, and she'd even stopped painting. The girl was miserable." She reached over and patted Charlotte's knee. "Well, I couldn't have that.

"Harry, no offense, but your aunts were very relieved when you broke up with the girl you'd been dating. Those old ladies were sure she was wrong for you and were afraid the two of you would get back together. They were really concerned about you, and like I said, I was worried to death about Charlotte. The three of us knew . . . not thought, mind you, but *knew* that getting you and Charlotte together was the answer to all of our problems. They assured me that if I could get Charlotte to Saint-Yves-Sur-Mer, the two of you would meet, and nature would take over from there."

"Good Lord," said Harry, shaking his head.

"Why didn't you just tell me you knew

Simone and Marie?" asked Charlotte.

"They asked me not to. It was their idea for the most part. But I went right along with it. So the three of us — Marie, Simone and I cooked up the whole thing. Your Uncle Dubby was against it, but I talked him into it. Anyway, he and I convinced Charlotte to head to that part of the world to practice her painting — gave her a ticket and enrolled her in that fancy art school. It was important that we got her painting again. That was the first thing. And what could be better than a summer romance to heal a broken heart?" She shook her head. "Or so I thought. But something went wrong, and Simone and Marie wouldn't — or couldn't — talk about it." Maisy paused, remembering it all.

"But why?" asked Liza Jane. "I mean why didn't they explain?"

Maisy shook her head. "I don't know, for sure. They were so old, remember, and I think they knew their time was almost up. The one thing they wanted in life was to see their Harrison happily married. Anyway, the next thing I knew, they had both passed away. I never knew what happened with Harry and Charlotte, why it didn't work out."

She looked expectantly at Harry who said

nothing.

"So Charlotte's trip to France was just a major fix-up?" said Liza Jane.

"Not exactly. As you know, Liza Jane, I do have certain insights — as did Simone and Marie. We weren't just a bunch of busybody matchmakers."

"But why didn't you tell me?" asked Charlotte.

"I didn't know what happened, and was afraid it would make things worse. And I have to say I didn't want to admit how I'd meddled. Then you fell in love again, married happily and had a family. What good would it do now? I thought. And remember, that was over twenty years ago. I regret my actions, but I have better sense now."

"Well, this doesn't seem very sensible," said Charlotte. Tears pricked at her eyes, and she felt herself blushing with frustration. "Don't you think you should have consulted me before bringing this up? I mean springing it on me? And on Harry?"

"Sorry, Maisy, but I have to agree," said Liza Jane.

"I'm kinda confused myself," said Harry.

"Secrets are like sores," said Maisy. "Keep the bandage on too long, and things start to fester." She took a big swig of her drink. "Mark my words, it is high time we aired things out around here. And I wanted the two of you to hear it together." They were quiet then, letting Maisy's revelations sink in, turning them over in their minds.

Finally, Harry said, "Charlie, Maisy's right about secrets. They can cause a lot of hurt." He took a deep breath and went on. "And I know I have a lot of explaining to do." He looked so miserable that the women almost felt sorry for him. But then he shook his head and pushed his chair back from the table. "I just can't get into it now. It's . . . it's complicated."

They all went silent again for a few minutes, digesting the evening's events, the women wondering, *Why can't you get into it, Harry?*

But they said nothing. Then Harry stood up, gathered his dessert dishes and took them to the kitchen.

When he returned, he said, "Good night, everyone. Maisy, thanks for having me over. Abbie and I look forward to returning the favor when she gets back in town."

He hesitated just for a second, then let himself out the screen door of the porch. The women watched the moon throw his long shadow across the lawn until he reached the beach and ambled off into the darkness.

12.

INPUT FROM CRAIG AND PUP

In the days that followed, Charlotte got in quite a few hours painting. The dipping roof lines and mullioned windows lent themselves to her technique. The more she painted, the more it came back to her — how the afternoon light washed the southwest corner of the house and sparkled in the splashing water of the fountain, turning the droplets into a cloud of diamonds.

She remembered Simone in the doorway. How her smile seemed to bubble up from deep inside and ignite the soft brown of her eyes. Just like Harry's. This thought was all it took to send Charlotte's mind slipping away to the mystery of Harry McMillan and the enigma of long lost love.

Who are you really, Harry? Could those old ladies and their "sensibilities" be right? Were we were destined to be together? Could it be that we are allotted one great love per lifetime, and we missed out on ours? She shook her head. *Ridiculous!*

When she stepped back from the canvas, there was a hint of melancholy there. She lightened the figures of the statue in the fountain and brightened the browns with white, but the aura of sadness remained. And sadness had not been a part of that gentle scene. Charlotte sighed and put down her palette knife. She was getting nowhere. It was time to tend to other matters, anyway.

She managed to procure a print from the Louisiana artist for Derek's grandmother, Pup. The painter, who was also a friend, gave Charlotte a good price, which Charlotte reduced a bit further so that it might meet Derek's budget. She'd been meaning to start Derek on some simple framing jobs, so she decided to throw in the framing which Derek, under her tutelage, would assemble himself.

Since Pup had started working in the gallery, she'd become somewhat of a connoisseur. Like her grandson, she had an eye for color and form. The thought of Pup unwrapping the print on her birthday had Charlotte humming away as she prepared for Arcadio's upcoming show.

She decided to serve South American appetizers as well as daiquiris and mojitos. Columbian surrealism could be a bit of a hard sell in East Oyster, she realized. A little alcohol would foster a deeper appreciation of the art and lessen the apprehension when it came time to fork over the credit cards. Also, all profits would go toward protection of pelican nesting sites — a big incentive to East Oysterites. Maisy had agreed to set up her tent in a corner of the gallery, and she always drew a crowd.

Via the laptop, Charlotte placed orders for the food as well as a couple of flower arrangements, and she was done.

"What's got you in such a delightful humor?" It was Craig. She hadn't heard him come in.

"Oh, just happy to be tying up loose ends. What's up with you?"

Since Craig and his sidekick, Leon, had been enlisted by Maisy and were now officially "on the case," Craig had been coming into the gallery with daily reports for Charlotte. These were interspersed with updates on the oil disaster and tidbits of gossip about Harry, Abbie and other persons of recent interest.

He pulled up one of the Gauguin-esque bars tools that he'd been coveting and said, "Oh, by the way, I just delivered two of the most charming garden benches you ever saw out to Pitt Cottage," he said. "They are now in repose beneath the big oak in the front garden."

"Really?" mumbled Charlotte, clearing her desk. It occurred to her that she sounded a bit like Abbie, so she added, "Sounds like the perfect spot for them."

"I agree. I just wish you could be sharing one of them with Harry the handsome architect. After all, he was yours first. According to Liza J, that is."

"Some things just aren't meant to be, I guess," said Charlotte with a grim, little smile. "Okay, oil spill news first."

"The well's still spewing. I heard from the mayor that the government is going to nearly double the no-fishing zone. According to Eunice, that will extend it to almost twenty percent of the gulf. That means no fishing, no shrimping, no charters. Nothing. And I heard one of the government guys say it appears the explosion was due to a cascade of technical, human and regulatory errors. All the bigwigs are blaming one another!"

"Like Lemony Snicket," mused Charlotte.

"You've lost me, sweetie."

"You know — a series of unfortunate events."

"Yeah, right. Very unfortunate," said Craig.

They commiserated over the plight of the fishermen for awhile, then Charlotte asked wearily, "What's the latest on the pelican mystery?"

"Well, our fashion-challenged mayor has called a meeting. By the way, did you see what she had on yesterday? I didn't know they still made polyester. And the hair — well, it's just an embarrassment to East Oyster."

Charlotte laughed. "I saw her. That hairdo is definitely dated."

"Dated? Good God, that woman put the boo in bouffant!"

When Charlotte stopped laughing, she said, "Okay, so tell me about the meeting."

"It's gonna be a long one. First on Mayor Toowell's agenda is the oil spill, of course. But Chief Foster will be giving a report on how the pelican investigation is progressing thus far. Which, in as much as I can tell, is nowhere."

"Who's going?"

"To the meeting? Well, the City Council and the Protect the Pelican board, both of which include Butler Finley; Liza Jane and, of course, Maisy; yours truly and Leon, who really doesn't care one way or the other, but wants to keep me happy. Very sweet, really. Oh, and Ms. Abigail Pitt and her fiancé will be in attendance — if Abbie gets back in town, that is. I'm assuming you will be there. I mean you are East Oyster's primo artiste, and besides, anyone who owns a Lucy Bradford would be wise to attend."

"Then I'll be there."

Just then Derek's grandmother, Pup, came in from the back room. Pup was tall, slender and muscular — like a runner, though she got her exercise cleaning houses during the day and serving at the occasional cocktail party at night. The woman had the energy of three twenty-year-olds. As usual, she was dressed in jeans and a T-shirt and had a striped scarf tied around her head. Elaborate earrings dangled from her ears. No one would guess she was a grandmother — until she opened her mouth, that is. Her views leaned heavily toward the old-fashioned. And she wasn't opposed to sharing them.

Example: Upon seeing a portrait of Maisy as a beautiful young brunette she asked who the woman in the painting was. "Why, that's me," said Maisy proudly. "Dubby had it done when we were first married."

Pup's mouth dropped open. She looked at the portrait then back at Maisy and shook her head.

"Lord, ain't time a wrecker?" she said.

"Yes, it is," agreed Maisy, sadly. But she

had to laugh.

Pup now gave Craig a cool nod. She didn't approve of Craig and Leon at all, and referred to the couple as "them boys." Behind their backs, of course. And though Craig had offered Derek lucrative pay for some after-school work, Pup refused to let Derek work for them.

Craig, on the other hand, had been raised plantation-style and tended to have a bit of a superiority complex when it came to "the help." He referred to Pup as "the Swahili maiden." Behind her back, of course.

Being fond of them both, Charlotte was determined not to get in the middle of this sociological phenomenon. She observed her friends' exchanges with good humor, careful to respond to any negative comments with positive remarks. Craig was a great guy — a great gay guy. Pup was a remarkable woman — a remarkable black woman who stood steadfastly by her beliefs and principles.

"Okay if I start in the back, Charlotte?"

"Sure. I'm about to close up."

But Pup walked over to the new oils. "Them colors looks like fire, don't they?" she said. "Ooh, honey, it must be something to paint like that."

"Why don't you try it, Pup?" said Craig.

"Hah! Like I got time." She headed toward the back, then turned.

"Charlotte, ain't you worried about your bird up on the balcony? I hear them things is coming apart all over town. Maybe we ought to put it in a closet or something."

"You might be right. I'll think about it," said Charlotte. "Pup, you knew Lucy. What do you think is going on with the pelicans?"

"We was discussing that subject after church last evening. You know we got one in the fellowship hall. But it's a painting, not a statue. Anyway, the preacher's worried about it, been praying over it to beat the band. Sister Johnson said she thinks it's Ms. Lucy Bradford herself behind all this mess."

"Now that's an interesting supposition," said Craig with a smirk, but Pup ignored him.

"We got to admit that girl was cursed with a restless spirit, that's for sure," Pup went on, "And now with the poor real pelicans getting stuck in oil. You know she had a thing for them big old ugly birds, and Liza Jane with no man and Pitt Cottage being done up like a condominium, well . . . who knows? It's enough to rattle bones."

As Charlotte was mulling Pup's theory over, the gallery phone rang.

"Charlie?"

"Yes. Hi, there."

"I was wondering if I could stop by and see those pictures of your building sometime soon and maybe get a tour of the place."

"Well, sure," Charlotte said, tucking a stray curl behind her ear. "After I close is best, obviously. So any day after work is fine."

"Are you busy today, in say, an hour?"

"No. I'm not doing anything right now."

"Oh, really?" mouthed Craig, pointing to himself.

When Charlotte put the phone down, Craig said, "As much as I'd like to stay and observe your date with the dreamboat — who is betrothed to another, remember — Leon and I have yoga in an hour."

"It is not a date," said Charlotte. "And how do you even know who I was talking to?"

Craig hopped off the stool. His face became serious — a rare occurrence. "It's painfully obvious, my dear. Look, I don't like playing the part of the fuddy-duddy downer. I just don't want you to get that big heart of yours broken. Again."

"I'll be careful. I promise."

"That's my girl," he said and sauntered out the door.

Charlotte knew Craig was right. And if it was "painfully obvious" to Craig that she was talking to Harry, then was it also obvious to Harry how she felt? As she raced upstairs to shower and change into her butt-enhancing jeans, she vowed to heed Craig's advice.

"Careful, careful, careful," she repeated to herself as she flipped through blouses in her closet and tried on various shoes and earrings. But her big heart, as Craig referred to it, felt like feathers in her chest. And she hadn't had that feeling in so long that perhaps it was worth the risk of having it broken all over again. As Craig said, Harry was betrothed to another.

Though he wasn't married to Abbie, Charlotte had strong convictions about taking someone else's man. She'd been on the receiving end of that sad scenario. As difficult and dangerous as it was, she would accept the relationship on Harry's terms — as a friendship.

"You going out?" asked Pup when Charlotte came down to pay her.

But just then Harry came through the door.

Pup looked from the smiling Harry to the grinning Charlotte. She folded the check Charlotte had just given her, stuck it in her bra and murmured, "Girl, you better watch yourself. Last I heard, that man is taken."

Charlotte frowned and rolled her eyes as if Pup were completely off base. She introduced Harry to Pup. They shook hands, and Pup took off like the proverbial scalded dog.

"That Pup, always in a hurry," Charlotte said in answer to Harry's confused expression.

Harry sat on the stool vacated by Craig, and Charlotte pulled another to sit beside him. She put the before-and-after photos on the desk in front of them. As Harry examined each picture, Charlotte explained what he was looking at. Several times she got up to point out where improvements had been made. She was aware of Harry's eyes on her architectural details as much as the gallery's.

In the final shot, Charlotte and two attractive young men stood in the courtyard behind the building. The threesome looked dusty and tired. They wore pained expressions as they leaned into one another.

"Oh, those are my sons, Mark and David. We had finally finished the job. Craig brought us champagne to celebrate." Charlotte laughed, remembering. "He asked us when we were going to start on the upstairs, then took the picture. As you can see, that was the last thing on our minds."

"Your sons take after you. They have your eyes."

"They're great boys. And very close. They're off at school, but both hope to end up here. Growing up on the water, seeing it every day — it's hard to be away for long. Maisy says we just can't get the sand out of our shoes."

"I know what you mean. As a kid, spending summers in Saint-Yves-Sur-Mer . . . well I'm always a little homesick for it. And those sweet old aunts of mine. Simone taught me the dead man's float when I was three. Marie showed me how to bait a hook."

"Maisy taught me how to swim and cast a net," said Charlotte. "And to get up on one ski, believe it or not."

Harry smiled at Charlotte. "No wonder East Oyster reminds me of St. Yves."

"They're both such pretty little towns."

"It's more than that. Their personalities are the same."

Charlotte thought back to her summer on the Mediterranean — the incredible light, the sweet, salty air, the sun on the water, the slow-paced locals and happy tourists. Sharing it all with Harry.

"That's a good way of putting it," she

agreed. "The same personality. Yes, that's exactly it."

She looked back at the photograph. "So anyway, I'm keeping my fingers crossed that both of my sons end up here in East Oyster. Maybe then I'll get on with the renovations."

"So you never got around to the upstairs?"

"I can't decide what to do with it. Come on, I'll show you."

She wondered briefly if this was a good idea, but quickly rationalized, *I'm inviting him as a friend and professional. Surely there's nothing wrong with that!*

Harry followed her through the gallery into the courtyard, all the while admiring aspects of the building and the garden. There was the slate patio secreted behind jasmine-covered brick walls, the corner fountain tucked into a nest of palms and azaleas and the fabulous wrought-iron gate discovered in New Orleans and procured for her by Craig Bloom.

"Okay, now for the negatives," said Charlotte, leading him up the stairs. "This is the only entrance, and it opens into the kitchen. But I can't afford to tear out the kitchen and relocate it. Besides, I like where it is."

When they'd entered said kitchen, Charlotte said, "You see, it's such a big space."

There was a wall sectioning off the bedrooms and adjoining baths, but the rest was one cavernous room, partitioned into kitchen, dining room and living areas by groupings of furniture and a scattering of rugs. In the oversized master bedroom, a flimsy wall with a cheap, hollow door had been erected to close off Charlotte's "painting mess" as Pup referred to the easels and brushes, paint tubes and pallet knives, stacks of art books and canvases. It was a beautifully chaotic space, but in an inconvenient, hastily-erected room.

"It needs walls," Charlotte said. "I have all of this art that needs hanging! But I want it to flow. I like the openness of it and don't want to lose that. And I love the big windows and the light." She gestured toward the walled-off corner of her bedroom which was framed by tall windows looking out toward the bay. "It's a great place to paint, but the wall is so . . . so shabby. And I have to walk through my bedroom to get to it. You see my problem."

He laughed. "I think I do. I also think you could keep all the positive things you mentioned and still make it more like a traditional living space."

"Really? I wouldn't know where to begin."

"Well, think of it as a blank canvas." He

looked around him. "Really, Charlie, it's a great space. The high ceilings and these windows! You don't come across this too often. If you don't mind, I could take measurements and do some basic plans."

Craig's and Pup's admonitions blinked like caution lights in Charlotte's brain.

"Oh, I don't know . . ."

"You wouldn't be under any obligation, no charge or anything either."

"That is very generous, but . . ."

"I'm just about finished with Pitt Cottage and don't have another job lined up, nothing to keep me busy. Not having a project . . . well, it's driving me crazy. You would be doing me a favor."

She laughed and said, "I don't see how I can say no to that."

Harry retrieved a tape measure and a legal pad from his truck. Charlotte helped him measure the space. They discussed her thoughts in more depth. She showed him magazine clippings she'd been collecting. She was so excited by Harry's suggestions that she hardly noticed the light growing dim.

She turned on a lamp and said, "I can't thank you enough. Your ideas make perfect sense!" It was about this time that the caution lights in her brain dimmed and went out. "Harry, would you like a glass of wine?"

They took their wine and some crackers and cheese out onto the balcony where they watched the comings and goings on Semmes Street. They talked about Charlotte's sons and Harry's daughter. They talked about fishing and the weather. They discussed East Oyster's restaurants and laughed about getting older.

They did not talk about the plight of the local pelicans — real or otherwise. They did not talk about that long-ago summer in Saint-Yves-Sur-Mer, or elderly, matchmaking relatives with "sensibilities." Charlotte did not ask Harry why he had broken her heart or what "complicated" circumstances prompted him to walk out of Maisy's porch with merely a vague promise of explanations and atonement. And she did not ask him why, when he was engaged to be married to Abigail Pitt, he was here making her fall in love with him all over again.

When she walked him to the door, he took her hand, and smiled at her — a little sadly, she thought — and he said, "Thanks for the wine, Charlie." He kissed her lightly on the cheek. "I'll have the plans done soon."

"I can't wait to see them," she said as lightly as she could. She watched him go down the stairs and cross her little courtyard until he passed through the Palmetto Street gate and out of view.

13.
EAST OYSTERITES UNITE

"Good Lord, I had no idea there would be a turnout like this," said Craig when he and Leon and Charlotte walked into the ballroom of the East Oyster Inn.

Charlotte loved the room. It was an oddly appealing mix of crystal and cypress, mirrors and palm, leaded glass and bamboo. Attendees packed the space, and when it could hold no more, they spilled out onto the patio and croquet lawn where a stellar spring day seemed to mock the gravity of the proceedings.

Dolphins played as a breeze ruffled the endangered waters in which they swam. A blue heron poked its bill into the still-plentiful supply of fish, speared a croaker and took flight, its great wings gliding through soft, pure air. Pelicans, oblivious to their possible fate, dived into the bay. Seagulls whirled and laughed at the recklessness of humans who couldn't or wouldn't see the tsunami of trouble unleashed by their inattention, disrespect and greed. The mirrored walls of the ballroom caught and reflected these scenes as if making sure they escaped no one's notice.

Beyond the activity of the bay, where the humans gathered, there were proprietors of shops, restaurants, hotels, bars and bait shops along with their employees — the assistants, servers and cooks, most of whom lived paycheck to paycheck. There were shrimpers and charter boat captains and their crews, and old Pete, who sold them their ice and repaired the locals' nets. Mary Louise and Jan, sisters who (up until the spill) had a booming beach-wedding business, were there along with the florists and caterers and photographers who depended on them for their livelihood.

There were owners, sellers and rental agents of the beach condos and beach houses together with the people who cleaned them and tended the gardens and kept them in repair. There was Gladys Bingle who'd come to the gulf coast of Alabama from Wales to see the hatchling turtles make their way into phosphorescent waves by the light of the moon. She'd helped plan the transport of a subsequent generation of eggs to safer waters off of

Florida's east coast, wondering if it was the end of the turtles' life cycle on her Alabama beach.

Bankers, envisioning even higher mountains of defaulted loans were there. Folks who lived on little, but lived well because of the climate and the beauty and because after generations of life on the coast, it was part of their DNA — they were there. There were the lawyers, defense and plaintiff, good and bad who mingled through the group, alternately soothing and inciting emotions depending on whose side they represented. And there were the inevitable bottom-feeders looking to make a dishonest buck off the troubles of their honest neighbors.

At the podium, the mayor, wearing her big hair with great authority, introduced a panel of officials, including Chief of Police Foster. Maps of the gulf and diagrams of the Macondo oil field and the Deepwater Horizon well had been set up on easels. These were used extensively in various explanations and strategies. The lifespan and volatility of oil going from sheen to mousse to tar balls were explained. As the good folks of the coast were scratching their heads over this one, it was announced that the oil had been flowing at a rate two and a half to five times higher than previously estimated. Tar balls had come ashore in West Oyster, a town to the west of East Oyster.

"Not to worry," said one official, informing the group about the "Vessels of Opportunity" program in which "fishermen or other boat owners whose earning capacity has been diminished by the Deepwater Horizon Oil Spill, will become the backbone of the nation's ocean-going response, performing critical functions such as boom deployment, skimming oil and rescuing oiled wildlife."

The locations of the four-hour course to become a Vessel of Opportunity, aka VOO, and the pay scale (depending on size of vessel, etc) would be posted in the lobby.

An official with the oil company spoke, assuring the audience that they "would be made whole again."

A couple of lawyers spoke. The mayor (who was sporting her new toe ring, Charlotte noticed) spoke, catching them all "up to speed." The containment dome had been a failure, she said, but they all knew this. There was a back-up plan, however — a complex maneuver known as a top kill. By this time, not only "containment dome," but "boom" and "dispersants" and "junk shot" had been added to the lexicon of East

Oyster. Finally, the mayor introduced Foster.

As he began talking about pelican art, most of the attendees made a fast exit. The tried-and-true East Oysterites, bleary-eared as they were from the previous info-overload, stood firm. They weren't about to abandon Lucy Bradford or her birds.

It was then that Charlotte noticed a non-Oysterite who nevertheless seemed extremely interested in Lucy's ceramic pelicans. As a matter of fact he was so far out on the edge of his seat, Charlotte thought he might fall off. The man was small and pale, thirtyish — a nondescript fellow in every way except for his hair. It was thick and curly and as fiery red as an East Oyster sunset.

Sadly, the police chief had nothing much to say. Reading from a piece of paper, he stated, "There have been some note-worthy developments, but it would compromise the investigation to go into the particulars at this juncture."

He folded the paper, placed it in the breast pocket of his khaki shirt and returned to his spot at the far end of the stage.

"That's what you think," murmured Maisy.

Due to Maisy's usual outlandish attire (capri pants, silver espadrilles, crab earrings and a Save our Gumbo T-shirt), Charlotte had managed to find her quite easily in the crowd.

"I used to change Foster's diapers, and I'll be darned if he's going to keep the particulars from me!" she said, punctuating the statement with a head-nod that set the Crab earrings bouncing and reflecting sunlight into Charlotte's eyes. "Charlotte, see if you can get hold of Liza Jane — she's got to be around here somewhere. Grab us a private table out on the patio, and order a couple of platters of fried crab claws." Maisy sighed. "If they can still get them, that is. This blasted oil spill is ruining my digestion, to say nothing of my disposition, so you better order me a screwdriver. Foster and I will be right out. And order him a root beer. He's still on duty." She started in Foster's direction, then turned. "And while you're at it, Charlotte, check out the love birds," she added, nodding to the large mirror beside Charlotte.

Reflected in the glass were Abbie and Harry. Abbie was being unusually conversant and extremely flirtatious. With Butler Finley. Harry stood next to them. A small, approving smile — *an adorable smile,* thought Charlotte — lit Harry's eyes and tugged at the corners of his mouth. He looked every bit the lovebird. But he wasn't looking at Abbie. He stared at Charlotte herself. She could see it in the mirrors. When she turned her gaze back to the room, and their eyes met, Harry's smile broadened into that heart-melting grin, and he waved to her. She returned the smile and the wave, and for a few seconds it was as if no one else was in the room.

Then Abbie followed Harry's gaze. When she saw Charlotte, her eyes narrowed for a second before she proffered a limp wave. She looked at her watch, pointed out the time to Harry and they left, leaving Butler alone, looking confused and very disappointed.

Charlotte got Liza Jane on the cell, and she arrived at the table just as Maisy and Foster did. Minutes later the server arrived with their drinks, plates piled with steaming crab claws (from Florida waters) and the horseradish sauce the inn was famous for.

When the waiter left, Maisy said, "Foster has agreed to let us in on the developments he mentioned in the meeting. But only after I assured him that he could count on our complete —" She looked at Craig for a few seconds before continuing. "— discretion."

When everyone had assured Foster that

they could keep whatever he was about to divulge under their respective hats, he checked over first one shoulder then the other, grabbed a couple of claws, took a manly swig of his root beer and began.

14.
THE FRENCH CONNECTION

"Well, first of all, this bird caper's turnin' into a first-class pain in the neck," said Foster, speaking so low that the others had to lean in to hear. "It looks like that pelican of Miss May Doody's — the one that was smashed in the church yard? And remember the big blue and orange one in the park?"

They all nodded.

"Well, both birds have turned up in top-notch condition. In France."

"France?" they all said at once.

"Yep. Marseille, France."

"But how . . ." they all began, but Foster closed his eyes dramatically and held up a hand which silenced them all immediately.

"I'll try to explain. Several tapestries were stolen from a collector, and when they were recovered, Miss Doody's bird, Butler's bird and the town's bird were with them."

"Wow," said Leon, who was a man of so few words that they all stared at him.

"So who stole the stuff?" asked Maisy.

"And how does a smashed statue turn up in one piece in Marseille?" asked Craig.

"And what possible connection could there be between Marseille and East Oyster?" mused Liza Jane, as if she were thinking aloud.

Charlotte's and Liza Jane's eyes met and widened as the same thought occurred to them.

Harry is a connection! Harry, who owns a home in a town near Marseille. Harry, whose arrival in town with Abigail Pitt coincided with the beginning of the bizarre statue explosions.

"Well, that's the problem," said Foster. "I don't have many answers to a whole lotta questions. First of all, the perp flew the coop . . . uh, so to speak. Anyway, the stolen art was found in an abandoned garage behind a café. A waiter chasing a cat found the stash, thought it looked valuable, called the local constabulary and as they say over there, walla, walla."

"How on earth did they connect the pelicans to East Oyster?" asked Craig.

"A guy from New Orleans has a house in Marseille and saw the story in the French papers. He knew about the Lucy Bradford statues, so he contacted the gendarmes —

that's what they call themselves — and they contacted us asking if we were missing any statues. It was pretty coincidental, our pelicans being vandalized, so I had them send us pictures, and they look exactly like the pictures of Miss May's bird and Butler's bird that I got from them. I got a photo from the archives when Lucy presented the other one to the town. It matches up, too. And they all have Lucy's signature thumb-print under the foot."

"That's right," said Craig. "I'd forgotten she marked all of her work with her thumb-print."

"As to how the birds got themselves back together, I have no idea," said Foster.

"What happened to the pieces of May's pelican?" asked Liza Jane.

"No one knows," said Foster. "May collected them, said she was planning on gluing the thing back together, but now she can't find the pieces anywhere. I was derelict in not 'confiscating the evidence before it was lost,' according to Butler. Like I knew a crime had even been committed." He sighed dramatically. "Butler's got some nerve. But I guess as president of the Preserve the Pelican board, he feels like he's got to throw his weight around. You know how he does."

They all nodded which encouraged Foster

to go on at length about decreased revenue, inadequate staff, an increase in meetings and his involvement in oil cleanup.

"I won't even get into the increased drug abuse and domestic violence because this oil disaster has got everybody out of work, scared to death and mad as heck."

"What about the pieces from the park?" asked Craig, changing the subject for which everyone was grateful.

"Oh, they're at the station. Butler insisted I confiscate the evidence since according to him I botched the first one. He was waiting on me in the park when I got there. Of course, the pieces of his bird are gone — said the housekeeper threw them out. That's the problem. No one knew that his or her statue falling apart was anything but an accident."

Foster drained his root beer, stifled a small burp and stared out at several real pelicans, each perched on a piling of the inn's pier. He looked tired.

"Have you said anything to May or Butler about the birds in France?" asked Maisy.

"Nope. Just the mayor."

"Good," said Maisy. "Be sure and remind the mayor not to breathe a word to anyone."

"Do you know something, Miss Maisy? Because this does happen to be a police

investigation involving some very valuable . . ."

"I only know what you've told me, Foster.
Would you like another root beer?"

Three root beers later, they had talked the
whole thing to death and gotten nowhere.
Or so it seemed. But each one of them had
ideas forming in the shadowy corners of
their minds. Maisy could feel it. *Let them
sleep on it for a few days,* she thought. She
suggested they meet at Downydew in a week
or so. They were assured margaritas would
be involved, so they all accepted.

15.
MUSICAL CHAIRS

Like the bad penny she was, Abbie eventually turned up in the gallery to see what Charlotte had selected for the Pitt domicile. With the exception of two or three really good pieces, Abbie was pleased with the paintings and signed prints. Charlotte reluctantly agreed to help her hang everything.

Why on earth would she agree to spend more time with her nemesis, Abbie the Pitt? These are the reasons: Charlotte was charging Abbie for her time away from the gallery, and all profits were going to the victims of the oil spill; for the first May ever, trade at Turner Gallery had slowed down; and because Charlotte lowered her standards for no one — not even Abbie. In other words, Ms. Pitt was a patron — a disliked patron, but a patron, nonetheless and deserved the same respect and attention as any other customer. And besides, Nevin

Schamm was due in. It would be easy to get away.

Nevertheless, dealing with Abbie always put Charlotte in a funk. Even before the woman had become engaged to Harry, Charlotte found it difficult to be in her presence for long. Abbie was a walking gray cloud. And once she'd vacated the premises, along with traces of her expensive perfume, wisps of gloom trailed in her wake.

In addition to the blue pall left by Abbie, the latest news on the oil spill was depressing as usual. The "top kill" maneuver (pumping stuff into the well shaft and sealing it with cement) had failed. It was announced that the Deep Water Horizon oil disaster in the Macondo oil field is the worst in U.S. history.

To top off this pile of gloom, Charlotte was missing her ghosts something terrible. She'd tried several different things in the space where *The Gathering* had hung, but each paled in comparison to the soaring spirits that kept Simone and Marie — and Saint-Yves-Sur-Mer — alive for her.

Finally she dragged a step ladder over to the back wall and hung one of the vivid Save Our Gumbo posters there. She set an aqua and lavender half-moon table beneath the poster and placed a large conch shell on it.

A shrimp-pink sign reading Donations finished off the space. She was placing a crisp ten-dollar bill in the shell when the bell on the gallery door rang.

Why do people come in at five minutes to closing? She asked herself for the millionth time, and turned to greet the latecomer with a tired smile.

"Hey, Charlie. I just finished these and thought you'd like to look at them." It was Harry, carrying a cardboard tube and looking extremely attractive in jeans and a creamy linen shirt. "I'll just leave them here if you're busy, though," he said.

An hour later, when they'd collaborated on a few minor changes, Charlotte said, "It's perfect!"

"You're not just saying that, are you?" Harry teased.

"Absolutely not. I love it. Moving the kitchen door and adding a wall is such a good idea. It makes the kitchen more functional."

"And look at this," said Harry. "We'll just rebuild this wall to your painting area with a pocket door — a nice one opening into the living area. When we get around to the second phase — the outside, you'll have an outside entrance from the balcony which will extend around the back porch."

"You are a genius, Harry. Really. You've given me actual rooms and yet kept all the great light up there. It looks simple now that I see it on paper, but I could never have figured it out."

The gallery bell rang again, and this time it was Liza Jane.

"Hey, whassup?" she said.

And so they went through the plans again with her. She too was impressed with Harry's ideas and added a few of her own. "If we could move this closet over a foot, I have the perfect linen press for that space. It will hold a good-sized, flat-screen TV that can be hidden when you're not watching it."

She and Harry, decorator and architect, went to work on the changes, their creativity playing off one another. Charlotte watched them thinking how fine it was her two old friends got on so well. Friends. Not friend and boyfriend. *Just friends,* she reminded herself. She sighed. *I will be content with that.*

As if underscoring Charlotte's thoughts, Harry's cell began to ring. He picked it up from the desk and said, "Hi, Abbie. Yes, we're just about done here. Sure. Charlie's . . . Charlotte's cousin, Liza Jane is here, so why don't we all grab a bite to eat?" He turned to Charlotte. "You up for a celebratory burger?"

"Sure."

"I'm in," said Liza Jane.

He turned back to the phone. "How about the Backyard Grill?" A look of annoyance passed over his face. "I'm sure they have salads or something. Okay. We'll meet you there. Who?" Another look of annoyance, then. "Okay, sure. See you in about fifteen minutes. Bye."

As they walked the several blocks to the restaurant, Harry explained that Abbie was bringing a business associate who happened to be staying at the East Oyster Inn.

"Hope you don't mind."

"The more the merrier," said Liza Jane.

"It's fine with me," added Charlotte.

They had ordered beers and were looking over the extensive burger menu when Abbie and a pleasant looking man entered the restaurant.

Abbie made introductions and instructed the man whose name was Grant James to sit next to Charlotte. Charlotte scooted down the bench seat so that Grant was between Liza Jane and her. Abbie positioned herself on the opposite bench next to Harry. She smiled warmly at Charlotte, which of course had Charlotte suspicious from the get-go.

"Grant," she said, "Charlotte is a wonderful artist. Charlotte, Grant is very interested in art. Aren't you, Grant?"

Oh, brother, thought Charlotte. *I knew something was up. This has fix-up written all over it. But why would Abbie want to fix me, whom she can't stand, up with her friend? Certainly not to keep me away from Harry. She doesn't consider me — at my advanced age — a threat to anyone!*

"Well, yes. Yes, I do enjoy art," Grant was saying while watching Charlotte who was apparently in the throes of some heated inner dialogue. "Though I don't know much."

The waiter appeared, snapping Charlotte out of her reverie and saving Grant from embarrassment, since he didn't know the first thing about art. The group placed orders for two cheeseburgers, two hamburgers and one salad with diet dressing on the side. Four beers and one Perrier.

Grant looked to be a little older than Charlotte. He was just under six feet, had a pretty sizable bald spot and a bit of a stomach, but he possessed a killer smile and what Maisy called enjoyment lines around his blue eyes that gave them a perennial twinkle. The easy smile and laid-back self-confidence made him way more attractive than his physical stats.

"Grant is single," Abbie explained, continuing her subtle-as-a-sledgehammer matchmatching maneuvers.

Surprise, surprise, thought Charlotte, but she liked it that Grant didn't react to Abbie's proclamation and that he didn't feel the need to explain why he was single. She'd spent many an hour "out on the town" listening to war stories from divorced men and sad, often horrific tales of chemo from widowers.

Grant did explain that he was in the insurance business, which he claimed to enjoy very much. Charlotte glanced at Liza Jane to see if she was yawning yet, and this is where it got interesting. Liza Jane was listening attentively to the man.

He lived on his family-owned cattle ranch in Florida. He'd stopped in East Oyster on his way home from the New Orleans jazz fest.

"Oh, I had to miss it this year," said Liza Jane. "Was it fabulous?" She actually batted her eyelashes at the man.

"Definitely fabulous," said Grant, smiling and with the hint of a tease in his voice. He was obviously warming up to Liza Jane. "Even if you don't love jazz, it's a heck of a good time."

As previously mentioned, Liza Jane is an

outrageous flirt. Maisy explains it this way. "People like to do what they're good at." And Charlotte had to admit, Liza Jane was the Rembrandt, the Mozart and the Einstein of flirting. As an example, when the subject of music came up with one of the cowboys, the conversation might go something like this.

Cowboy: "Jazz, huh? What kind of jazz?"

Liza Jane (with just the hint of a wicked grin): "Are you familiar with . . . Fourplay?"

Cowboy (with a very big grin): "Baby, I invented foreplay."

Liza Jane: "Really? Because I thought I invented it."

Cowboy: "Whoa! Where have you been all my life?"

Liza Jane: "Actually, I'm talking about the contemporary jazz quartet known as Fourplay." But having surmised that there would be no musical connection between herself and the adorable cowboy, she would have flashed him another wicked little grin and added, "I love Fourplay."

Contrast this with the conversation she was now having with Grant.

Grant: "So who do you like, jazz-wise?"

Liza Jane (with just the hint of a wicked grin): "Fourplay."

Grant (with a twinkle in his eye): "We are

154

still talking music, right?"

Liza Jane: "Right."

Grant: "I'm more of a purist when it comes to jazz, but yeah, if you like it laced with a little R & B or pop, Fourplay's great."

Charlotte figured that Grant might possibly be the first straight man Liza Jane had ever discussed Fourplay with who not only wasn't drooling all over himself, but knew what she was talking about.

"Charlotte, Grant plays the saxophone," said Abbie, trying to steer the conversation back to Charlotte. But it was no use.

"The sax? That's my favorite instrument," gushed Liza Jane. Charlotte assumed Grant had either been told or figured out that Charlotte was his intended fix-up because after he and Liza Jane had discussed great sax players for a few minutes, he changed the subject to Turner Gallery.

What he lacked in knowledge about art, he made up for with a genuine interest in the business end of a gallery. He was easy to talk to, interesting and had a dry, contagious sense of humor. Charlotte and Grant were soon laughing and chatting like old friends. The man was impossible not to like. The only questions in Charlotte's mind were, *Why is he friends with Abbie?* And *Why is Harry scowling at him?*

155

Once the subject of gallery business had been thoroughly discussed, Charlotte asked, "So how do you know Abbie?"

"She worked on an advertising campaign for my company. I'm staying at the East Oyster Inn and just happened to run into her this afternoon. She kindly suggested I join her and her fiancé for dinner." He smiled at Charlotte. "I'm glad I took her up on it."

Abbie smiled happily at this mini-flirtation while Harry frowned and chugged the rest of his beer.

Butler Finley was making his rounds through the place, speaking with everyone — servers and patrons, locals and tourists, friends and enemies. Charlotte had to admit that if Eunice Toowell ever stepped down, Butler would be prime mayor material. When he strolled up to their table, Abbie insisted he join them. After the tiniest bit of encouragement by the others, he acquiesced. Abbie patted the chair at the end of the table which was closest to her, and Butler slid into the unoccupied seat.

By the time the burgers — and salad — were consumed, the group had jelled. Grant was charming, funny and interesting, even winning over Harry who nevertheless looked miserable every time Grant and Charlotte smiled at one another. Liza Jane was always fun in her outrageous way. Butler could talk to a possum, so he was easy. Abbie, thrilled that Grant and Charlotte were hitting it off, decided to go crazy and indulge in a lite beer, taking her uptightness down a notch.

All too soon they said their good nights. Charlotte and Liza Jane insisted on walking back to the gallery. Butler moved on to a table of latecomers. Grant caught a ride back to the inn with Abbie and Harry.

"Well, that was fun," said Liza Jane when she and Charlotte started down Semmes Street.

"I guess. The idea of Abbie and Harry playing cupid for me is pretty depressing, though."

Liza Jane sighed. "I think it was all Abbie's idea. But as far as what Harry's up to in general? Well, the jury's still out, as far as I'm concerned."

"I think the jury's in," said Charlotte. "The verdict is guilty. I'm just not sure of what."

"So what did you think of Grant?" asked Liza Jane. "He sure seemed to like you."

"Oh, he's very nice. Really interesting. Great personality." Her voice trailed off.

"But he's not Harry."

Charlotte started to protest but couldn't

muster the energy. Besides, she couldn't fool Liza Jane.

"No. He's not Harry."

"So you're not interested in Grant at all?"

Charlotte laughed. "He might be the only mature, charming, jazz-loving — not to mention, available — cowboy on the planet. He's all yours, L.J."

"You're sure?"

"Absolutely, totally sure."

"Oh, and Charlotte, let's not mention this to anyone."

"Don't want it getting back to the cowboys?"

"Well, there's that, but also — just in case you missed it — Harry was so jealous I thought he'd pop. It's exactly what he deserves. Let him stew for awhile. See you tomorrow."

As she waved goodbye to Liza Jane, Charlotte remembered the renovation plans left on her desk and decided to pop into the gallery before going up to her apartment. The interior took on the appearance of one of Charlotte's abstracts in the glow of the two low lamps she'd left on. The shadows of statues and vases dripped over hanging paintings, diluting color and shape and turning them into ghostly renditions of themselves.

She involuntarily sought out *The Gathering* and was momentarily surprised to see the Gumbo poster in its place. She'd loved how her ghosts glowed and swayed in the half-dark of the gallery after everything on Semmes Street was closed.

She sat behind her desk, hands on the plans for her new and improved digs. But instead of picking them up, she closed her eyes, just for a second, and *The Gathering* materialized before her.

Charlotte saw every brushstroke, remembered applying each subtle layer of color that produced the dusky shadows and white iridescence of the ghosts. She saw the joy that Marie had seen as the spirits conquered doubt and despair. And she saw the joy again, reflected in Marie's face that enchanted afternoon in Provence so many years ago.

She heard the old woman's voice describing the scene for Charlotte, her young visitor. And then Charlotte saw Marie herself sitting before her, right there on the Craig's favorite bar stool. Simone occupied the one next to her.

"Marie? Simone?"

But the old sisters only smiled, held up their thumbs and faded into the gloom of the gallery's dim light.

Charlotte jerked her head from the desk. She looked at her watch. She'd been asleep for over an hour. The weird dream starring Marie and Simone seemed to have lasted but a few minutes. Charlotte took a deep breath, blinked the sleep from her eyes, picked up the plans and exited through the back door to the courtyard. But she couldn't erase the comical picture of two old ladies sitting on Gauguin bar stools smiling smugly and holding up their thumbs.

Once in bed she snuggled herself into the sheets and concentrated on a soft rain that had started. It pattered on the roof, dripped on the balcony tiles and whispered in the Bougainville lulling her back into delicious unconsciousness. She was smiling at the memory of Marie and Simone as she gave in to the waves of sleep washing over her. Her last conscious thought was, *What a delightful, ridiculous dream.*

16.
COASTAPHOBIA

Charlotte had placed the artwork selected by Abbie into the gallery van. Later, when she thought about it, she couldn't say what had prompted her to grab Arcadio's small oil painting and add it to the collection. In his surrealist interpretation, a scarlet sun setting in an aqua sky threw its final rays onto white-washed Century plants.

It was not something that Abbie would have chosen. But Charlotte thought it would add needed interest to the monochromatic living room in Pitt cottage, and once Abbie saw it in the room she might want the painting.

What the heck, she thought. *It's worth a try.*

Abbie busied herself upstairs. *Probably shooting ice water into her veins,* thought Charlotte — while Charlotte hauled the stash of art into the house. She noticed that *The Gathering* was still in its place of banishment in the corner by the fireplace. The space where it should be hanging — above the fireplace — remained blank. She felt her face flush with indignation, but headed back out to the van for another load.

By the time she'd finished, she was hot and perspiring. She caught a glimpse of her frowning self in the glass of the new kitchen door and noted that the humidity had transformed her sleek, blonde do into a fluff of sweat-darkened waves around her head. Unattractive half-moons showed under each arm of her pink T-shirt. She irrationally blamed all of this on Abbie before finally realizing that it was nothing but her own doing.

Why have I put myself in this house I once loved and now hate only to be bossed around by a woman I can't stand who is involved in a weird relationship with the love of my life?

As she had long ago learned to do, Charlotte stopped herself in mid-tizzy, closed her eyes and took a deep breath. She put herself mentally on the chaise on the balcony of her apartment. A breeze and a glass of chardonnay cooled her as she turned to the first page of *The Great Gatsby* (one of her best tranquility inducers) and stepped into the beautiful, shallow lives of the Buchanans.

Now that she thought of it, Abbie reminded her a bit of Daisy Buchanan. Self-absorbed and delicate. Rich and beautiful. She had to admit it. Abbie was beautiful.

She heard her mother's words echoing from her teenage years. *Pretty is as pretty does.* And she felt better.

In spite of the similarities between Abbie and Daisy Buchanan, the scene she'd conjured up calmed her. She could stomach Abbie and the transformed Pitt cottage for a few hours, and since she was donating the proceeds, the Save Our Gulf volunteers would be all the better for it. Yes, she'd made the right decision after all, she decided.

She checked her watch. Liza Jane had promised to "pop in" to make last-minute suggestions on the exact placement of the art, but was thus far a no-show. While waiting for uptight Abbie and relaxed-to-the-max Liza Jane to make their appearances, Charlotte placed the paintings against the walls where they would hopefully soon reside.

The living room was mostly windows, and she didn't want to disrupt the spare, cool ambience of the space, just set it off, give it some interest, for God's sake. She placed the Arcadio against a narrow, blank wall. Perfect. Next she picked up *The Gathering* and carefully propped it on the mantle. As she stepped back to get a better perspective, she heard a gasp.

She turned to see Abbie, her brunette beauty set off in the palest green silk. To Charlotte's horror, Abbie's lip began to quiver. She clasped her hands tightly against her chest, accentuating her perfect bosom. The mega diamond in her engagement ring sparked at Charlotte atop knuckles gone white with the pressure.

"What. Is. This?" Abbie croaked.

"Oh. I was just trying different . . ."

"Just stop, Charlotte. Surely you know that I'm doing everything I can to get all of this creepy stuff out of here, and you keep bringing it back in! Why are you doing this to me? Answer me, Charlotte."

"Abbie, I . . . You don't have to keep any . . ."

"Why are you trying to fill the house with ghosts?"

"Look, Abbie, I didn't bring *The Gathering* here. And this." She gestured to the Arcadio. "This is really good art by an up and coming artist. In my opinion his work is a worthwhile investment. And frankly, I thought the room could use some color. That's all."

Abbie had the decency to look embarrassed.

"It's just that I don't like scary things," she said. "I hate *Midnight Charade.* Hate it!" She paused, closed her eyes dramatically and took a deep breath, as if to calm herself. Which in Charlotte's opinion was a very good idea. The woman was close to losing it.

"If you must know," Abbie continued, "I'm having a hard time adjusting to this house, to this area. I don't know how you people stand it. My God, you have alligators here! And the oil . . . None of my friends will come here now — they're afraid oil is ruining the beach." She clasped and unclasped her hands. "Not to mention the thing with that ridiculous pelican art . . ." Her voice rose, once again dancing along the edge of hysteria. "And that painting." She waved toward *The Gathering.* "It seems to glow. I just won't have it in my house."

Charlotte froze in indecision. Like a rookie cop talking a jumper off a ledge, she dare not say the wrong thing and set Abbie off again. Because she was obviously in the throes of an excruciating bout of . . . what? Homesickness? Buyer's remorse? Engagement remorse? *Now there's a happy thought.* Coastaphobia? Charlotte felt a tiny smile creeping around the corners of her mouth. Was Abbie's hysteria contagious? She gave

165

herself a mental slap. Where was her compassion? This was not funny. There was something very wrong with Abigail Pitt.

Finally she said, with as much nonchalance as she could muster, "You know, Abbie, I shouldn't have even brought the Arcadio. It's not what you like. I don't know what I was thinking. And *The Gathering*? I'll be happy to take it back or swap it for something else, something happier, less intense. Look — redoing a house is stressful."

"Just be quiet!" yelled Abbie.

Charlotte opened her mouth to apologize then wisely closed it. The two women stood as if captured in a photograph. Abbie's outburst had startled them both.

"I've had a bad year," Abbie said. "I lost my older brother recently. It was terribly traumatic. I've had to take a leave of absence from my job. My nerves . . . I'm not usually like this. I would appreciate it if you didn't mention any of this to anyone."

"Of course," said Charlotte as quietly as possible.

Good Lord, the poor girl is deranged with grief. Charlotte couldn't help but feel sorry for her. Still, Abbie was scaring her. The mood swings, popping in and out of town, the engagement to Harry that didn't seem

166

real somehow.

The loss of her brother could explain the frosty attitude and mood swings, I guess. The leave of absence does explain all the free time spent in East Oyster, thought Charlotte. *But where is she going when she leaves here if not to her job? Think about that later! Abbie has just told you she has lost her brother.*

"I'm very sorry about the loss of your brother," Charlotte said.

"Yes, it's been terrible. But also, it's . . . well, it's very complicated."

Those were the words Harry used.

These people and their complications are really getting tiresome, she thought.

Charlotte's musings were interrupted by a knock on the back door.

"Anybody home?" called Liza Jane, walking right in.

She came into the living room, looked back and forth at the two women and said cheerfully, "Okay, then. Let's hang some art."

Charlotte started to object, but when she looked back at Abbie, the Pitt princess was as cool as an ice cube. Plus, there was no way Charlotte was coming back to this house. Besides, Abbie would probably think twice about murdering Charlotte while Liza Jane was there, so she jumped right in as if

167

nothing had happened.

"We were just discussing the Arcadio," Charlotte said.

"It's great," interrupted Liza Jane.

"But not really Abbie's taste. And neither is *The Gathering.* So why don't I just get these out of here."

She picked up both paintings, one under each arm, and propped them by the back door. She turned their offending faces to the wall lest Abbie get a glimpse and have another melt down.

In less than two hours all the art was in place. Liza Jane happened to have an enormous shell mirror in the back of her SUV which Abbie loved for the spot above the mantle. The space where the Arcadio was meant to go was left to be filled at a later date by Abbie.

In a final attempt to rid the house of its ghosts, Charlotte took the *Midnight Charade* poster in trade for the two hours of work hanging art. Harry probably wouldn't like it, but at this point, she really didn't know or care what Harry McMillan liked. She would write a generous check to the Save Our Gulf foundation out of her own account since she had pledged the profits to them.

When the Arcadio, *The Gathering* and the

168

movie poster were stowed safely in the van and Abbie out of earshot, Liza Jane said, "Wonder what old Harry's gonna do when he learns that you have absconded with *The Gathering* as well as the *Midnight Charade* poster."

"I imagine he'll wonder what in the heck is going on." Charlotte shrugged. "So let him be the confused one for a change. At this point I really don't care. I'll reimburse him for *The Gathering,* and that should be the end of it."

"Now, why do I doubt that?" muttered Liza Jane. "I've got to run, and my calendar is double-booked all this week, but we're going to lunch soon. I'm buying, and you're going to tell me what exactly was going on in there when I walked in."

17.
ARCADIO

In spite of Nevin pulling an extra shift in the gallery, Charlotte was swamped with last minute details for the Arcadio event. (Too busy even to think about the strange behavior of Abbie and Harry.) As a result, Maisy was putting in lots of overtime in the gallery. Due to the increased demand on her time at the many fund-raisers going on to help oil spill victims, Maisy often showed up in her work clothes. A few customers were taken aback at being helped by a tiny octogenarian pseudo gypsy, but for the most part her eccentricity added to the genteel yet oddball ambience of East Oyster.

By mid-afternoon on the day of the reception, Charlotte sent Maisy home to rest. The old girl didn't seem herself, somehow. Not only did she appear tired, the sparkle had left her eyes, the spunky, irreverent conversation was absent. Maisy had always been incredibly tough, despite her frail appearance and advanced years. Most people wouldn't think anything of an eighty year old having a sinking spell, but it worried Charlotte.

The gallery closed at five. Two hours later, Charlotte had turned down the a.c. and propped open the front door to Turner gallery. Though invitations were sent to regular patrons, the reception was open to everyone. Arcadio's strangely enthralling paintings were juxtaposed so that they complimented one another to the fullest, each one in its best light.

They're all so simple, yet so intriguing, thought Charlotte again and again as she looked at them.

There was one that especially captivated her. It was titled *Pescar.* On the eight-by-ten canvas, two white figures stood in leaf-green water. They seemed to be holding or sharing one hot pink fish beneath an even hotter yellow sun. The scene was set against a lavender sky. The fish was disproportionately large and vibrant, giving it prominence and imbuing it with deeper meaning. Besides the juxtaposition of objects and the hues Arcadio had chosen, Charlotte couldn't say why the painting held such appeal for her, but she confided to Liza Jane that if it hadn't been bought by mid-evening, she would claim it.

A table of south-of-the-border finger food and two bars had been set up. Brazilian music (it was the closest thing to Columbian Charlotte could find) floated out of a hidden CD player. The young artist himself arrived by hotel car from the East Oyster Inn. Thankfully, he seemed delighted with the paintings' placement, the music and the choice of food. He immediately snagged a shrimp empanada and a margarita, proclaiming both "delicioso."

Maisy's tent was set up in a corner with a sign offering five-minute mini-readings at ten dollars each. She claimed she didn't want patrons' minds wandering from the art, but Charlotte figured Maisy just wasn't up to an evening of intense readings, and this was a way to honor her commitment without exhausting herself.

The gallery was soon packed to overflowing with locals, area artists and tourists. Liza Jane was attired in a green dress that looked to have been painted on her perfect bod. She breezed over to Charlotte and said, "I'm not really in the mood for small talk. Why don't I work the front desk so you can talk up the art."

Derek, looking very grown up in a striped dress shirt and black trousers was assigned the job of assisting her.

Charlotte figured men would be throwing credit cards at Liza Jane in that dress, and everyone liked Derek enough to put up with his occasional snafus, so it was a good combination.

Maisy appeared to have benefited from her afternoon rest and an abundance of patronage in her teller's tent. Though she still wasn't in top Maisy form, she happily introduced Arcadio around, telling everyone that as far as she and Crystal (ball) were concerned, Arcadio was someone to watch. Craig and Leon circulated and reported back with comments they'd overheard.

"There are elements of magical realism all through his work," the paper's art editor had said to Eunice Toowell.

"Yes," agreed the mayor. "Note how a simple object like that bird takes on almost supernatural proportion by its placement above everything else. And the surface of the painting looks almost photographic!"

"Yes, he uses layers upon layers of paint to achieve that — much like the old masters did," said the art editor who'd obviously done his homework. Charlotte had read those exact words in a catalog from an exhibit of Arcadio's work in California.

The shopaholic mayor declared the bird

to be a pelican, the symbol of her beloved town. She purchased the large painting for her office. Craig was impressed by the mayor's artistic insight as well as her willingness to back it up with such a pricy purchase, so he made only one unkind comment about her "appropriately surreal attire."

Maisy, who by this time had become quite chummy with Arcadio, made the next purchase. The subject was a school of fish swimming above the water. Done all in shades of blue, it lightened from pastel sky to electric turquoise fish to inky water. Maisy decided that it projected great optimism about the future of Cocktail Cove. It would hang in her living room between windows that faced the water.

Leon, who was looking especially spiffy in a dinner jacket sans tie and buttery loafers sans socks, fell in love with a small, vibrant rendering of what appeared to be the moon melting over an oil rig. It was titled *Offshore* and cost as much as the coveted Gauguin bar stools. Craig, softie that he is, bought it for his "partner-in-all-things."

Chief Foster even showed up, munching on empanadas and rolling his eyes at each successive painting he viewed. But Charlotte was glad for his presence. With the art vandalism and theft going on, Foster was a welcome sight. Besides, a shock of red hair had caught her attention. It was the stranger from the town meeting who'd been so interested in the Bradford birds.

"Who is that guy?" she asked Foster.

"The one looks like his hair's on fire?"

Charlotte nodded.

"Says he's here on vacation — staying at the hotel. Looks harmless," he added, dusting crumbs off his stomach.

That everyone saw facets of the oil spill in Arcadio's work and that much of the profit was earmarked to remedy the ramifications of the spill resulted in the largest sale of Columbian surrealism the town — and possibly the state — had ever seen. Of course, the open bar and that dress of Liza Jane's hadn't hurt.

Ninety percent of the sales had transpired in the first ninety minutes of the exhibition when interest in particular paintings spurred competition to own them.

"It's amazing how an object's desirability increases when it's about to become the property of somebody else," noted Maisy.

Butler Finley had his picture taken with Arcadio. He partook robustly of the appetizers and mojitos and schmoozed with everyone worth schmoozing. But he didn't buy so much as a postcard.

Charlotte checked the receipts, breathed a sigh of relief and gratitude, and realized she was starving. A server had just placed a platter of crab fritters and cheesy arepas on the food table. Charlotte had two of each, all the while accepting positive comments on the show. The little fried cakes were almost as delicious as the effusive compliments.

Next she checked on Arcadio. She found him in deep conversation with Maisy and none other than Harry McMillan! Harry was so handsome in a tie and linen sport coat that Charlotte almost choked on a hot fritter. And yet, the bizarre episode with Abbie had all but erased the pleasant feelings she'd had when Harry helped her with plans for her apartment. There was something so strange about his engagement to the unbalanced Abbie, that Charlotte was beginning to get a bit creeped out herself. She headed to the bar for a well-deserved, well-needed libation.

"Congratulations, cuz, you've done it again!" It was Liza Jane who, after working the busy desk, was in need of a drink herself.

"Thanks for manning the desk. It was a lifesaver. By the way, that dress is fabulous on you. I think a couple of guys bought paintings just to talk to you."

"Oh, this old thing," Liza Jane said, waving away the compliment. "I guess you saw Harry the heartthrob. He came in just a while ago." She raised her eyebrows as high as they would go. "A-lone."

Charlotte remembered Abbie's aversion to the Arcadio in her living room. "I'm not surprised," she said. "Abbie thinks Arcadio's work is scary, remember?"

"How could I forget?" said Liza Jane. "Which reminds me, you still owe me the scoop on whatever weirdness was transpiring during the picture-hanging at Abbie's."

"Now that this show is over, I've got some free time. Can you fit in a quick lunch tomorrow?"

"Sure. And speaking of this show, I've got good news and bad news."

"Good first."

"Harry bought a painting. But I'm afraid it's the one you had your eye on. The one called *Pescar.*"

"The fishermen?"

"Yep. And you know what? It was right after Craig told him *Pescar* was your favorite. Odd that he would buy it when he knew you wanted it."

"Everything Harry does is odd!" She sighed. "It is a bit more cheerful than the

177

others. Maybe Abbie will allow it in the house."

"Or maybe you'll end up with it like you have the rest of Harry's art. Has he said anything to you about *The Gathering* and the poster?"

"I haven't talked to him." Charlotte arranged her face into a mask of exaggerated nonchalance and added, "And really don't care to." She dropped the façade and added, "The scene with Abbie, which you will hear in lurid detail, was just too much. There is something, I don't know . . . unbalanced about her — and her engagement to Harry."

"So you haven't talked to him at all tonight?"

"No."

Liza Jane glanced over Charlotte's shoulder. A wicked smile played across her pretty face. "That's about to change," she said. "Here he comes."

Charlotte groaned, but turned to face Harry with what she hoped was a neutral expression.

"Hello, Harry," she said flatly. "Thank you for coming. Sorry Abbie couldn't make it," she lied.

"Abbie is not feeling well. As you probably know, she's delicate. We owe you an apology concerning the art at Pitt Cottage."

"Apology accepted. Art is subjective. And emotional. Thanks for making a purchase tonight. I hope you enjoy it." Charlotte's tone was businesslike, almost cold.

"Thank you," Harry responded just as stiffly. "After all, it's for a good cause."

"Yes, it is."

As the conversation ground to a halt, Liza Jane slithered off to talk to Maisy. Harry and Charlotte stood there looking at one another.

Finally, Harry said, "Congratulations on a successful event. I guess I'll be going. Goodnight, Charlotte."

Charlotte? Did he say, Charlotte? He'd never called her Charlotte. What happened to Charlie? It was always Charlie.

She felt as if she'd been slapped. Tears stung her eyes as she remembered how she and Harry had stood in this very spot, and he'd called her Charlie and she'd thought . . .

"Ms. Turner, are you okay?" It was Derek.

"Yes. Yes, of course. These spicy appetizers have my eyes watering, that's all. Have you had anything to eat? Come on, let's get you a plate."

Charlotte rattled on numbly as she led Derek to the food table and handed him a plate. Derek looked concerned, but as is typical of the adolescent male, he quickly shifted his attention to the plate of fritters and empanadas.

Charlotte found Arcadio and they made the rounds of those who were having one last drink or dessert cake before heading home. The mayor walked up, her beehive hair-do swaying precariously as she snacked on a cocoa cake.

After showering Charlotte and the artist with praise, she turned to Arcadio and said, "I hope you don't mind me asking you, but I'm curious about your name. Surely you have more than one."

Charlotte thought this was a bit intrusive, but since she'd been dying to ask the same question, she smiled expectantly and said nothing.

"Oh, yes. I have other names," said Arcadio. He smiled good-naturedly, but did not elaborate. Finally, he shrugged his shoulders and said, "I am named after a character in a book. The author is an ancestor, I think. My father chose to name me after a famous character rather than the creator of the character."

"One Hundred Years of Solitude," said Charlotte.

"Yes," said Arcadio.

"Do you know the oil field where the well

exploded is called Macondo? Like Arcadio's doomed utopia?"

"Yes. It was Columbians who named it." He looked at her steadily and said, "A co-incidence, though. Merely a coincidence."

"And your paintings? The prominent images of the triumph of nature? Are they also coincidence?"

"It is fulfilling for me when I paint nature. I thought these paintings concerning the resilience of nature would do well here where it is on everyone's mind." He smiled. "I was correct."

Mayor Toowell had been jerking her head back and forth as Charlotte and Arcadio spoke. The tower of tease wobbled comically as she did so, but she didn't seem to notice.

"Keep going," she said. "This is interesting."

"It was Senora Downy who first had the idea. It was she who first contacted me," said Arcadio.

"Maisy Downy?" asked the mayor.

"Yes. She called me at my home in Columbia right after the oil well exploded. She, too, spoke of Macondo and the strange co-incidences we discussed. Maisy Downy is a very unusual woman."

"I'll say," said the mayor, bobbing her

head for emphasis and sending the whole coiffure forward.

Arcadio and Charlotte held their breaths, but Eunice simply reached up and pushed it more or less into place as a fascinated Arcadio looked on. Remarkably, the mayor's do stayed aloft as she bade them good night and headed for the door.

When it closed behind her, Arcadio said, "Your Aunt Maisy said something else to me. I think it would be okay for me to share with you. Her husband . . . Dubby?"

"Yes, my Uncle Dubby."

"He is in the oil business, I believe."

"Yes. Well, he was. He became very rich in the oil business."

"I thought that must be. Well, Maisy said it was your uncle's idea that I should come here. But he is unable to be here tonight?"

"Yes. He would have enjoyed meeting you, I know."

Charlotte just couldn't bring herself to tell Arcadio that Dubby had been dead for four years.

18.
REVELATIONS OVER LUNCH

Charlotte practically skipped into the gallery the next morning. She felt as if she'd been holding her breath until the previous night's show was over. Now she could exhale and look forward to a relaxed schedule, a nice check for oil spill victims and at least a day's worth of compliments on the show, the party, Arcadio and his amazing art. The seven paintings — out of twenty-three — that had not sold were a nice addition to the gallery. Charlotte would have them on display for a month and was confident that most would sell.

It was mid-morning when a delivery man entered carrying what was surely a painting wrapped in brown paper. A note was attached.

Oh, no, not a return!

All sales from the show were supposed to be final. But Charlotte didn't like unhappy customers. She opened the note. It read,

Thought you might like this memento of good times in St. Yves. Harry. It was *Pescar.*

Charlotte smiled, remembering fishing excursions with Harry during that long ago summer. Yes, she'd keep the painting. The smile faded. *But is it time to lose Harry?* She knew the answer to that one. If she didn't hop off the emotional roller coaster he had her on, she was apt to end up as unbalanced as Abbie.

By noon, word of the successful show had gotten around town. There was lots of interest in the Arcadios left from the show and other art as well. So when Nevin Schamm came through the door, Charlotte happily turned the gallery over to him and headed to her luncheon date with Liza Jane.

"I can't believe Abbie yelled at you," said Liza Jane through a mouthful of onion rings.

"It was scary."

Charlotte had filled her cousin in on the events preceding Liza Jane's arrival at Pitt Cottage, but not before swearing her to secrecy. After all, she had promised Abbie not to tell anyone. But surely that didn't include Liza Jane, her closet friend, confident and cousin?

"I don't guess you mentioned that *The Gathering* was not actually hers to return. I mean it does happen to be the property of her fiancé."

"Are you kidding? I'm telling you, Liza Jane, Abbie is emotionally unstable. Seriously. Emotionally. Unstable." Charlotte sighed. "I can't help but feel sorry for her. I mean with the death of her brother and everything. Grief is a tricky thing."

"Especially when it's suicide."

"What? How do you know that?"

"Grant told me."

"The jazzman?"

"Yep. He called the other night."

"Just to talk?"

"I guess. One of his horses had just foaled, and he was all excited about it."

"And he called to share it with you. Very interesting."

Liza Jane waved away the comment and continued. "He had to deliver this foal himself. He really is an amazing guy," she added, more to herself than Charlotte. As if suddenly realizing that she might be going on a bit about Grant, she changed course. "So anyway, we eventually got on the subject of Abbie. According to Grant, Abbie's brother, Tim, died about a year ago in an accident with a gun that a lot of people believe was not an accident at all. Evidently, he was very despondent. Grant doesn't know any other details except that Abbie and her brother were both single and very close. He was her only family."

"Poor thing. No wonder she's so shaky."

"Yes," agreed Liza Jane, "She has every excuse to be . . . shaky. But . . ." She shook her head. "I don't know."

"But you don't know what?"

"Look, you lost your parents, then your husband — the father of your two young sons. You were devastated, but you never acted like Abbie. I know people handle things differently, but I'm telling you, Abbie has other issues going on besides grief. And I hate to say it, but I'm thinking Abbie is not a very nice person. She's even been giving Maisy a hard time."

"Maisy? How so?"

"She told their neighbor that Maisy was giving the children alcohol. Turns out she fixed them virgin margaritas."

Charlotte had to laugh. "I'm actually glad to hear she's up to her old tricks. She hasn't been herself lately," said Charlotte. "I'm worried about her. She seems tired. Kind of depressed, even."

"She has seemed tired. But Maisy depressed? That is worrisome. You don't think it has anything to do with Abbie's accusation, do you?"

"No." Charlotte smiled, thinking about

her aunt and all the controversial stunts she'd pulled. "Maisy has been doing out-landish things her whole life. Negative comments about her behavior roll off her back. I think she actually enjoys them in a way. It's something else. Something a lot more important than Abbie Pitt is bothering her."

"Maybe it's just old age," suggested Liza Jane. "She is in her eighties."

Charlotte shook her head. "I'm worried that it's more than that. She told Arcadio that Dubby had suggested she get in touch with him and bring him here."

"That's just vintage Maisy. Goes along with the whole sixth sense thing."

"Maybe. Well, we know the oil spill has her upset. She cares so much about all the people around here. I think that's it, more than anything," said Charlotte.

"And she's definitely been overdoing it with all the fortunetelling gigs. Why don't we drop by with lunch and have a talk with her?"

"Good idea. You call her, and I'll have Big O fix one of those mushroom quiches she loves."

"We'll have a good visit. We'll talk to her about overdoing things."

"But gently — we need to cheer her up, remember."

"Right," said Liza Jane. "Relax. She'll be fine."

They were silent for a few seconds sorting through this latest assessment by the eternally optimistic Liza Jane.

"Okay," she said. "So back to Harry. Any late, breaking ideas to explain what's going on with him?"

"No. And I'm done thinking about it." When Liza Jane smiled condescendingly at this pronouncement, Charlotte said, "I mean it this time. Things have gotten way too strange. The Harry McMillan I knew would never be involved in something as weird as this . . . this sham engagement.

"If he is contemplating marriage with someone like Abbie and all the while looking for ways to spend time with me, giving me paintings." (At this point she explained the gift of the Arcadio.) "Then he really isn't the Harry I thought he was. Maybe that Harry never existed. Maybe he's even involved in the pelican business," she whispered. "Maybe he's being nice to me because I have a gallery full of art that he would like to steal!" she added with a bit more volume. "Maybe he just wants a roll in the sand for old time's sake!"

In her indignation, Charlotte had forgotten where she was. A silence like you never heard came over the restaurant. The place was full of chatty women who sat up like a bunch of well-dressed prairie dogs stopping mid-sentence and/or mid-chew to listen. Charlotte felt her face heating up with embarrassment. Liza Jane pressed her lips together to stifle a giggle.

Charlotte closed her eyes for a moment, composing herself. The other patrons of the Backyard Grill went back to their meals and conversation, happier somehow after hearing Charlotte's outburst. Charlotte leaned toward Liza Jane and said at a much lower decibel, "Obviously you were right. I should never have gotten involved in this . . . this Bermuda love triangle. I really didn't know him at all. As Holly Golightly used to say, 'He's a super rat.' "

"Who's Holly Golightly?"

Sometimes Charlotte forgot that her cousin was a decade behind her and didn't share her love of vintage movies.

"You know, Audrey Hepburn, Breakfast at Tiffany's . . . Now, I'm tired of talking about Harry. So I take it you're going out with the jazzman?"

"Yes. He has business in New Orleans. He's stopping in East Oyster, and we're going to dinner." Liza Jane grinned in spite of herself. "But let's not make a big deal over this, okay?"

"Okay," Charlotte agreed.

But something told her that this might turn into a very big deal, indeed.

19.
PUTTING THE PIECES TOGETHER

It was about eight o'clock that evening when the long days of preparation and nervous energy surrounding the Arcadio art show caught up with Charlotte. She stayed awake long enough to eat a scrambled egg and brush her teeth before collapsing into bed.

She felt positively unburdened. She could relax. The show was behind her, *The Gathering* back at home where it belonged. When — and if — she got around to implementing the plans Harry had drawn up, and she had actual walls in her apartment, *The Gathering* would find a permanent place.

It had been a mistake to sell it, even to Harry. Simone and Marie would understand. She thought again about the odd dream she'd had when she'd fallen asleep in the gallery. How real it had seemed, like the two old ladies were actually there with her, sitting on the Gauguin bar stools like a couple of strange, old-lady hitchhikers holding up their thumbs. Their thumbs?

"The thumbprint!" she said aloud and threw back the sheets.

Finding her cell phone in the bottom of her purse, she flipped through the pictures until she came to the ones she'd taken of the shattered pelican in the park. She zoomed in on the pelican's huge webbed foot, now in several pieces. There on the bottom of the largest piece was the indentation that was Lucy Bradford's signature — her thumbprint. Charlotte wasn't sure what she was looking for exactly, but tomorrow she would check out the remains of East Oyster's prized pelican. She climbed back into bed, sent up a quick message of thanks to Simone and Marie and fell into a dreamless sleep.

Early the next morning, Charlotte called the police station. Wanda, who was on phone duty most mornings, put her through to the chief.

"Foster, I know you're busy, but could I come by the station and take a look at the pelican pieces from the park?"

"Why?"

"I'm not sure, but I have a picture I'd like to compare with the actual pieces."

"Come on over," said Foster wearily. "What else do I have to do but fool with clay pigeons?" she heard him mutter as he hung up the phone.

Charlotte laced up her shoes, grabbed her phone and headed out, but instead of her usual route, she headed away from the bay toward the East Oyster police station. Most of the area shop keepers were already busy tending to plants (East Oyster's vendors are downright competitive about the mini-gardens surrounding their places of business), setting up displays on sidewalks, unfurling umbrellas or enjoying a coffee while chatting up their neighbors. The Oysterites waved and called good morning to Charlotte as she passed.

Though the Big O and Hawkins Hardware are across the street and halfway down the first block, the aroma of the bakery's just-baked almond croissants and perking coffee mingled with scent rising from pots of gardenias and trellises of jasmine in front of the hardware store. The toasted almond and baking pastry smells were so alluring that Charlotte decided she had time for a croissant and café to go. As she waited for the light to change, she saw the bakery's screen door open.

Out stepped Harry wearing shorts, a yellow, tan-enhancing T-shirt and running shoes. He smiled at a small boy holding a large doughnut. Harry looked very good. When he saw Charlotte, he waved and the smile broadened. Then, as if suddenly remembering how they'd left things at the gallery, the smile faded. The wave faltered. But his eyes stayed on hers. And as it always did, the very sight of him filled her with such delight and such longing that she almost couldn't catch her breath.

Seconds later Abbie, wearing a white pencil skirt and heels, came out of the bakery. She carried two coffees. Charlotte had to admit, Abbie also looked very, very good.

They look good, she thought. *Together.*

In the upscale, relaxed atmosphere that was downtown East Oyster they looked like just another good-looking, prosperous couple — handsome, older man and beautiful, young trophy wife. She heard Maisy's voice in her head.

"All cats look gray in the dark, honey."

(Maisy was full of quotes, and Ben Franklin was one of her biggest resources).

Charlotte smiled, returned the wave and resumed her run toward the police station. She'd seen Abbie's stripes in the light of day — she was not your average trophy wife-to-be, and even though Charlotte was still very suspicious, a little jealous and completely bewildered, she just couldn't stay mad at Harry.

The coolness of early morning was already succumbing to the building humidity. Come July, as the day progressed, any spot not in deep shade and facing the bay's constant breeze would turn into a sauna.

And hurricanes love saunas, Charlotte reminded herself. The thought of even a tropical storm in the midst of all that gushing oil gave her a chill in spite of the warm air. She offered up yet another silent prayer that the monster well would soon be capped.

"Had your coffee yet?" asked Wanda when Charlotte entered the station.

"Yes, thanks."

After a few minutes of obligatory small talk, Charlotte asked if Foster was available.

"Go on in. He's got the busted bird all ready for you."

So much for keeping my little sleuthing mission quiet, thought Charlotte, who had vowed to keep a lock on her lips.

"Mornin', Charlotte," said Foster, getting to his feet behind his desk. "Had your coffee yet?"

"Yes, thanks. So how's the investigation going?"

She knew Foster preferred "cutting to the chase" as well as the use of professional

195

and/or cop lingo whenever possible.

"The bird statues haven't been returned yet. I don't know any details, but from what I hear, the Frenchies invented bureaucracy, so I ain't worried. And what I do know . . . what I have told you is just between you, me, Maisy and Liza Jane — y'all being family to Lucy Bradford and all. A loose lip can sink a ship, as you well know." (Like Maisy, Foster was full of quotes, though his were usually approximations of the originals.)

"You can count on me, Chief."

"Good."

Foster nodded to a cafeteria table set up in a corner of the room. The shattered remains of the park pelican lay in the center of the table in a shallow cardboard box. The pieces seemed to have been placed as they had been found in the park.

"There's the bird," said Foster. "Figured out what you're looking for yet?"

"No." She smiled sweetly at him and said, "I thought you might help me with that."

His face softened into a smile. "Okay, whatcha got?"

Charlotte took her phone from the pocket of her shorts, flipped to the photo of the bird and held it up for Foster.

"When did you take this?"

"The morning after it happened."

196

Foster actually seemed interested. He took the phone from her and studied the picture, then the clay shards, then the picture again.

"I'll be a . . ." His voice trailed off. He shook his head, looking tired. And it wasn't even nine AM yet.

"What?"

Charlotte took the phone from him, looked back and forth as he had. She saw it. The piece of the pelican's foot with Lucy's thumbprint was missing from the fragments in the box. She zoomed in on the piece in the picture.

"Foster, there's something strange about this picture."

"No kidding. There's a piece in it that's not here." He looked embarrassed. "We never thought to put it back together."

"But there's something besides the missing piece. I need to go home for a minute and check on something," she said.

As she started for the door, Foster said, "Why don't I drive you?"

The tone of his voice and the look on his face told her it was not a suggestion.

Within a few minutes, Charlotte and Foster were on her balcony, gently turning over her own Lucy Bradford original. Charlotte took several pictures of Lucy's signature thumbprint with her phone, but it was

197

obvious that the two thumbprints — the one on the park pelican and the one on Charlotte's pelican — did not come from the same thumb.

"Lucy's print is much smaller," said Foster. "I think the print on the park bird was made by a man."

"So the park pelican is fake?"

"It would seem so."

"But I saw Lucy present the pelican to the town. It's been there ever since that day."

Foster scratched his head. "I don't think so. What I think is, somebody switched birds."

"What does that have to do with the birds falling apart? And turning up in one piece in Marseille?"

"And now there's the missing piece," said Foster.

"Who would have taken it?"

"A better question is when?"

"What?"

"When. And why."

"Lord, Foster, we're starting to sound like an Abbot and Costello routine."

Foster actually chuckled. "What I mean is, when was the piece taken?" He continued. "We just assumed all the pieces were there when we collected them. I brought them here myself, so it didn't get lost, if that's what you're thinking."

"Oh, no," said Charlotte even though that's exactly what she was thinking. But the police chief had enough problems without her doubting his professionalism.

"Listen, I've got to get back to the station," said Foster. "Let's keep this between us, okay?"

She sent the photo of the bird pieces to his cell, which he put in his shirt pocket. She hoped he wouldn't accidentally delete the park picture before making it back to the station. She knew the aromas floating out of the Big O had a way of seducing Chief Foster. He headed back through her kitchen, but stopped at the door.

"By the way," he said. "What made you think to compare the photo and the bird?"

Charlotte remembered Simone and Marie sitting on her bar stools smiling like a couple of cats full of canaries while holding up their thumbs.

"I really can't say," she said.

20.
POINTS OF VOO

Before you could say VOO, vessels of opportunity in all shapes and sizes had descended upon the waters. Their main job consisted of deployment and maintenance of floating plastic barriers known as boom. Boom was placed across inlets and passes, around marinas and marshes — anywhere the dreaded oil might do damage. Which was pretty much everywhere. Folks were so afraid of the oil that even homemade boom consisting of net-covered straw and hair — human and animal — sprouted up like kudzu.

The VOOs, as they became known, were comprised of just about anything that could float and become motorized. Air-conditioned charter boats as well as skiffs rigged with ice chests and umbrellas or tarps qualified as vessels of opportunity. Captain Little's boat painted bow to stern with mermaids atop leaping dolphins and signs advertising dolphin cruises reminded them of happier days. Would they ever again wave at sunburned tourists in search of dolphins as Captain Little passed Maisy's pier? Would there even be dolphins when this was all over?

The VOO flotilla had to be the oddest, most comical assortment of watercraft ever assembled on Palmetto Bay. Yet the VOOs and the folks who worked on them (VOO crew?) were easily recognizable due to the regulation life vests and long pants that they were forced to wear. These rules were implemented with safety in mind, but as Maisy pointed out, drowning or even sunburn might be an easier way to go than heat stroke.

VOOs of every variety patrolled the gulf, bays, bayous, and streams. The program provided free gas and good pay that was much-needed and well-deserved by those who'd lost income because of the spill. But when non-spill victims smelled money, they headed south, too.

Maisy referred to them as scalawags. Though they hadn't lost a penny due to the catastrophe, they were determined to cash in on the VOO program. Many bought anything that could pass for a boat, hired a crew and collected the big bucks. And when

Butler's forty-six foot yacht, *Air Apparent,* became a VOO, there was some grumbling.

Maisy's boat along with those of her neighbors was high in its lift because the inlet had been closed off with boom. There would be no shrimping and little fishing, skiing or tubing the kids in the foreseeable future.

Charlotte, Liza Jane, Foster and Maisy sat on Maisy's porch drinking margaritas after an early supper of crawfish pie, cheese grits and cornbread. Due to a plumbing emergency, Craig and Leon had begged off at the last minute though Craig (who was a big Perry Mason fan) insisted on a full report regarding the "case of the purloined pelicans," as he now referred to it.

When Charlotte asked Craig how he deduced that the pelicans had been "purloined" as opposed to vandalized or even detonated by feisty spirits, he'd replied, "Simple, dear. The broken ones are fakes. It's the only explanation if you don't believe in poltergeists, which I don't. And things simply cannot be in two places at one time. The original statues are intact in Marseille, ergo, the ones whose remains have so conveniently been discarded, are fake. I just haven't figured out why yet."

Of course, Foster and Charlotte had come

up with a similar theory. But the pieces to the puzzle were swirling around in her brain like roof shingles in a hurricane. She needed to think them into place, then maybe a concrete explanation would also fall into place.

As the little group of friends sat at Maisy's table, the neighbors' children — twin girls and a younger brother — played along the beach, their shadows growing long in the afternoon light. They splashed and laughed and ran along the soft sand, oblivious to the peculiar flotilla of VOOs returning from a day fighting oil.

"Good Lord," said Maisy, pointing off to the distance. "Somebody tell me I'm hallucinating."

The mayor's pontoon boat, *Landslide* was cruising down the bay. Riding tall on the deck were two sunny yellow porta-potties.

"Do you suppose they're there to service the VOO crews?" asked Charlotte.

"Yep," said Foster. "The mayor turned *Landslide* over to the VOOs. You know, you gotta give it to her. That boat is her pride and joy. She'll never look at it again without seeing those johnnies settin' up there." He shook his head. "It went from a party boat to a potty boat overnight."

"On top of having her boat turned into a

floating restroom, Craig told me that she's using the money she earns from the VOO program to set up a pelican washing station," said Maisy.

"To the mayor," said Liza Jane, raising her glass.

The others did likewise.

"To the mayor," they said.

For as Craig had recently remarked, "Eunice is a shameless shopping addict and tacky as a tarball, but she's one heck of a mayor."

"Now, speaking of pelicans," said Maisy, "I believe Foster has some news."

Foster filled Maisy and Liza Jane in on the latest news from France and the matter of the mismatching thumbprint signatures since Charlotte had done as instructed and not breathed a word.

"The good news is that the busted birds are fakes," said Maisy. She reached over and patted Liza Jane's knee. "Your mother's birds — and her legacy — are still in one piece, thank the Lord."

"So someone stole the real statues and substituted fakes so no one would notice," said Liza Jane. "But who broke them?"

"The thief? Or maybe it wasn't the same person," said Maisy. "Or maybe the fakes were inferior and came apart." She sighed.

"I don't know."

"But why now?" said Liza Jane. "I mean the statues have been here for years without anyone bothering them. We all know they're valuable. So what's changed?"

"The oil spill, the economy," said Maisy.

"Right," said Charlotte. "So it must be someone desperate for money," she continued. "Unfortunately, that could be half the folks in East Oyster."

"Including Abigail Pitt," said Liza Jane. "If the old grapevine is to be believed, Abbie is seriously down on her luck, and the pelican trouble started about the same time she came to town."

And about the time Harrison McMillan showed up in town, Charlotte reminded herself, but of course, no one brought this up.

"Abbie's already ticked us all off by taking over Pitt Cottage, one of our biggest tourist attractions," Liza Jane continued. "If you ask me, she doesn't care about East Oyster or the pelicans or anything but Abigail Pitt."

Murmurs of agreement went round the table.

"Somebody's been poking around Lucy's old clay bed, too," said Foster.

"Oh, I know," said Liza Jane. "I ran into Eddie Hillman the other day. Since the clay bed is on his family's property, the subject of the broken statues naturally came up. Eddie said someone has been helping him or herself to clay from their property — you know, where Mama got her famous white clay. He's got someone patrolling the area now and hasn't had any more problems, so I don't know . . . it might just be a coincidence."

"Whole lotta coincidences lately," mumbled Foster, who was making notes with his phone's tiny keyboard.

"Pup says some of the people in her church think it's Lucy herself, unhappy about . . . well, about things in general," said Charlotte. She dared not mention Pup's comment about Liza Jane being without a man.

Liza Jane and Foster rolled their eyes, but Charlotte noticed that Foster added this little detail to his notes.

"Seeing real pelicans dripping in oil might be enough to wake the dead," said Maisy. She shook her head. "I'm reminded of the story of Midas. We need the oil — some folks call it black gold, you know — but now it seems everything we touch and love is turning to crude."

Foster looked at Maisy. "I seem to remember Lucy was into a lot of hocus-pocus for a while . . . uh, no offense, Maisy. We know that you've got the gift, sure do. But are you actually giving credence to the idea of Lucy Bradford throwing temper tantrums from beyond the grave?" he asked.

"Maybe." She smiled sweetly at Foster.

Charlotte thought about Harry's aunts and their talk of ghosts, how Marie was transformed by a memory on that summer afternoon in Saint-Yves-Sur-Mer.

Yes, maybe, she thought.

"Well, that's just . . . just completely ridiculous," said Liza Jane, with such intensity that Charlotte knew she was talking to herself as much as to the rest of them. Could Liza Jane actually be worried that her mother's spirit was in the throes of other-worldly unrest? Or was the dredging up of her mother's unorthodox life on this plane the thing that upset her? She knew one thing. All of this angst was getting everyone seriously out of sorts!

Other than Abigail Pitt (because nobody liked her) and Lucy Bradford herself (because it was so outlandish), the group was reluctant to voice suspicion of any of their neighbors. If Foster had any suspects in mind, he wasn't sharing. He did say he was following up on the missing clay and was in contact with Eddie Hillman.

"So who's the art collector whose stolen tapestries were with the birds?" asked Maisy.

"Some old guy who wasn't fond of locking his doors," said Foster. "He has absolutely no connection to East Oyster or Lucy Bradford though."

"What about the big fingerprint? The one in the picture Charlotte took. Can't you match it to its owner through some fingerprint database or something?" asked Liza Jane.

Foster sighed. "We're trying, but I don't think it's clear enough," he said, scooting his chair back from the table. "Now I've got to go. Thanks for the supper, Maisy." He patted his stomach and added, "Nothing like home cooking for an old bachelor."

Reminding them once more of the perils of loose lips, he got up to leave.

The darkening sky was shot through with the afterglow's purples and pinks, reflecting itself on the still water of the cove, so Charlotte and Liza Jane decided to take their drinks out onto Maisy's boathouse. Maisy was tired, she said, but insisted her nieces stay as long as they wanted.

"Just lock up on your way out."

The old lady blew them goodnight kisses as she plodded off to her bedroom.

21.
PHANTOMS IN THE NIGHT

Maisy's boathouse was quite grand as boathouses go. There was a large covered area rimmed with wooden seats, a picnic table and benches, and a large closet for boating equipment. This part of the setup was pretty much par for Cocktail Cove. With so many storms coming out of the gulf and pier insurance so high that it was impractical, most folks learned keeping to the basics was best.

But Maisy's late husband, Dubby, had added a large bar with refrigerator and ice machine. He'd installed a TV for watching sports, a sound system, subtle lighting, ceiling fans and fabulous, comfy furniture made to Maisy's specifications. There was room to dock a dozen boats because until Dubby died at ninety-two, he and his eighty-year-old wife threw the best parties around. And in Cocktail Cove, that was saying something.

Charlotte and Liza Jane got comfortable on twin chaises, sipped fresh margaritas and watched the sky fade from pink to black. To the south, lights from condos on the gulf glowed like an Emerald City in the distance. Familiar constellations filled the sky overhead.

The cousins discussed the latest developments in the "purloined pelican" case (Craig had Charlotte thinking of it as such). When the conversation turned to Lucy Bradford, Liza Jane said, "You don't think Mama's spirit is restless, do you? I mean she was so restless in life, I've always comforted myself with the thought that in death she finally found peace."

"Of course, I don't think that. Besides, I think Lucy found her peace in being a good mother to you in the end."

"Thanks," said Liza Jane who nonetheless found herself blinking back tears and feeling compelled to change the subject.

"You won't believe who I'm going on an actual second date with," she said.

"Grant, the mature yet jazzy cowboy?" teased Charlotte.

"One and the same."

"Details, please."

"He's coming back through town next week, and we're going to a benefit for West

Oyster." Liza Jane frowned. "The town's whole economy is based on seafood."

"Most of the workers are from southeast Asia, right?"

"Right. And so many of them don't speak English. Many of them have always been paid in cash . . . some lost what little paperwork they had in Hurricane Katrina, so they can't prove they're out of work due to the oil spill."

"So the money you raise will go to what exactly?"

"Basic needs — food, money for electric bills, etc. And job counseling. All some of them know how to do is pick crabs. And now there are no crabs to pick. I'm telling you, Charlotte, this oil spill could literally wipe West Oyster off the map."

Charlotte sighed. "Poor West Oyster. She's always been like East Oyster's ugly sister."

"I know. For being fifty miles up the coast, the difference between the two is night and day."

"It's a shame West Oyster never had a Lucy Bradford to put it on the map," said Charlotte.

"I feel so sorry for them. I'm hoping this benefit will bring some attention to the desperate situation they're in. And I think we'll have a good crowd. There'll be some jazz musicians to entertain. I'm donating some things from the shop for the silent auction. I was planning to go anyway. Might as well ride over with Grant."

Charlotte knew that Liza Jane's offhand attitude toward the date was a sign that she had high hopes for its success.

"So what's the latest on handsome Harry?" she asked.

"Nothing."

"You haven't seen him?"

"Only in passing. I saw him coming out of Big O the other morning. With Abbie. They both looked great."

Liza Jane swung her feet off the chaise, sitting sideways, in order to face Charlotte, who could barely see her in the dark.

"Listen, cuz. I have no room to give advice to the lovelorn."

"Who says I'm lovelorn?" interrupted Charlotte.

"You're lovelorn. I know the look. I've seen it in the mirror."

"No, you haven't. On every guy you date, maybe."

"Okay, okay," laughed Liza Jane. "I just haven't met anyone worth getting lovelorn over."

"And the advice?"

"Do I have to say it? Be careful. Be very

careful."

"I know. I mean, I know! For starters, he's engaged to someone else. But it's like that disappears from my brain whenever I see him — unless he's with Abbie. Which is always a shock, because when I'm with Harry it's like it was when we first met, like he feels the same way. But he obviously doesn't because he's . . ." Charlotte's voice caught. "He's marrying someone else. Again."

Liza Jane reached over and gave her cousin's hand a pat. It reminded Charlotte of Maisy.

"Oh, I sound ridiculous, even to myself. But I don't know what to do. I make up my mind to put him out of my thoughts, and it works for awhile. But then . . . the truth is I've fallen in love with Harry McMillan all over again."

"The weird thing is that I don't think you're imagining his feelings for you," said Liza Jane. "Good Lord, he goes all gaga every time he's around you. So why is he still engaged to Abbie?" Liza Jane paused, considering her next words. "I wasn't going to tell you this, but there's something else. When I talked to Eddie Hillman the other day, he said that just about the time he discovered someone had taken some of the clay, he caught Harry poking around the area. Harry claimed he was just walking through the woods and happened upon the clay bed, but he asked Eddie a bunch of questions." Liza Jane pressed her lips together then added, "Kind of like he did at Maisy's the night he came over for gumbo."

"You think Harry is mixed up in the pelican vandalism?"

"I don't know. What I do know is that a lot doesn't add up with Harry. We don't know anything about him — or Abbie — for that matter. Just because Maisy was buddies with his old aunts doesn't mean Harry is okay. And really, how well did you ever know him? You were together for a summer. And his behavior back then was just . . . just reprehensible. And now he's doing it again with some vague assurances of an explanation? And isn't Cassis and St. whatever-it-is near Marseille? Where the stolen statues turned up? That went missing about the time Harry and Abbie blew into town? Harry's the only one in East Oyster who has a connection with France, who has a house there. I'm sorry, Charlotte, but I'm starting to get a bad feeling about Harry. I don't care how charming he is."

Following Liza Jane's outburst, Charlotte said nothing for a few minutes, but in her heart of hearts, she felt there was an explanation.

Finally Liza Jane said, "Sorry, honey, but if anything bad happened to you, and I hadn't voiced my concerns I would never forgive myself."

"It's okay. I count on your brutal honesty."

"Then why do you have anything to do with him?" Liza Jane asked softly.

"I guess it's because I never got over him." She sighed. "And I have to take the risk because I know that this is my only chance at finding true love — the kind of corny, all-encompassing love I've been looking for since that summer in Provence. Is that so crazy?"

"Well, sort of. But incredibly romantic. We have to consider, though, that if the worst of the Harry scenarios turns out to be true, there could be a lot more at stake than heartache. If he and Abbie are involved in something illegal, it could be dangerous."

The cousins sat digesting Liza Jane's words in the darkness. The slight breeze picked up, tinkling barely audible wind chimes on a neighboring pier. Small waves rippled against the pier's pilings. A mullet jumped. Dolphins surfaced somewhere close, blowing air that sounded like soft sneezes before submerging again with a gentle stirring of the water. So it took a while for the rhythmic splash of a paddle to register.

"Somebody is out there," whispered Charlotte, remembering Foster's admonition concerning loose lips and sinking ships. Though they'd been talking quietly, she knew how sound carried over the water at night. How many times had she heard entire conversations from a boat or neighboring pier?

"We discussed all the details of the pelican case," whispered Liza Jane. "Foster will kill us if they get out."

"And I will kill myself if anyone heard me talking about Harry," said Charlotte.

The sound of a paddle moving through the water was just beneath them now. Then there was the hollow thump of fiberglass against a piling.

"Hi, there!" called Liza Jane.

"Hey! Who's up there?"

Could it get any worse? Charlotte asked herself because the voice below them was none other than Harry's.

"Liza Jane and Charlotte," Liza Jane called, and made an omigod! face in the semi-darkness.

She got up and turned on the light. There was Harry, looking as innocent and friendly as a puppy, seated in a sunny, yellow kayak.

How could this adorable man be guilty of anything!? Charlotte searched his face and based on the innocuous expression on his face, decided that he couldn't have heard their conversation. It also appeared that he, like Charlotte, had abandoned the unfriendly attitude they'd adopted the night of Arcadio's art show.

Besides the guiltless expression, Harry wore a pair of ratty, khaki shorts. The top of blue boxers showed at the waist. On his feet were the biggest pair of brown crocs Charlotte had ever seen. He was shirtless.

Strapped to the kayak was an ice chest, a gig and an old-fashioned floundering lamp. Charlotte hadn't seen one like it in years. It reminded her of nighttime adventures with her dad, tiptoeing through the shallows in the moonlight, looking for a vague oval outline on the bay's bottom and those two weird flounder eyes peeking out of the sand. Charlotte had always thought the fish looked like it was designed by Picasso.

"Since one side of the flounder is always on the bottom, both of their eyes are on the top side," her dad had explained. "At night it buries itself in the sand lying in wait for its dinner. But guess what? Tonight Mr. Flounder is going to be our dinner."

A quick thrust of his gig behind those eyes brought up a flapping, brown-speckled pancake of a fish.

"You tickle a flounder and he's gone," he'd said. "Quick and hard with the gig as soon as you see him. That's the only way." Her dad put a hand beneath the fish until it landed in the ice chest. It wasn't long before Charlotte was catching as many as her dad. The sight of the old floundering lamp made her downright nostalgic.

"Where in the world did you get that lamp?" asked Liza Jane. "I haven't seen one of those in years."

"I found it in a storage shed at Abbie's. The guy at the hardware store told me how to use it. He filled it with kerosene and put new mantles on it, so it ought to be easy."

"Have you ever been floundering before?" asked Charlotte.

"No, but I hear conditions are right, so I thought I'd try it." Harry was right. An incoming tide, calm, clear water and a dark night in spring and summer are the ingredients for successful floundering. Charlotte looked up at the sliver of a moon floating behind a cloud.

"It's a perfect night, all right, but be careful. It's easy to get a burn from those old lamps. And look before you gig. I know a

218

guy who gigged his own foot, thinking it was a fish."

"Sounds like you know your way around a flounder," said Harry.

"Well, I used to go with my daddy, but that was years ago."

"You wouldn't consider showing me the ropes, would you?"

"Oh, I don't know . . ."

Liza Jane gave her cousin a look that said, *Are you kidding me?*

"C'mon, Charlie," said Harry. "There's a little room left in this kayak." When she didn't answer, he added, "You could be saving the life of an inexperienced gigger."

It was a perfect night. And Harry probably would do more damage to himself than the fish if left on his own. And she was wearing shorts and her oldest running shoes.

"You have a light, right? In addition to the antique floundering lamp?"

"I have two flashlights, and there's reflective tape all over this thing. If I was a boy scout, they'd be giving me a safety badge."

Charlotte laughed. "Okay, but just for an hour or so — til you get the hang of it."

Liza Jane rolled her eyes, but all she said was, "Call my cell when you get in. I want to know if I'm having flounder for dinner tomorrow night."

Charlotte climbed down Maisy's ladder and eased herself into the kayak behind Harry. The soft night air and the salty smell of the water, being with Harry — it could have been a summer evening in St. Yves when they were Charlie-and-Harry, the couple so perfect that even crusty old fishermen would smile and give a wink when they passed on the quay.

With Harry in front, she was free to check him out in the last light from the pier. His shoulders were just as broad as she remembered, tapering down to a waist only slightly thicker than it had been in his youth. The dark hair was thinner on top and was flecked with gray, but still curled boyishly at the nape of his neck. He dipped the paddle into the water and the muscles in his back and arms flexed. He smelled like soap and well . . . like Harry.

"Do you remember when we used to go fishing in St. Yves," asked Harry.

"Of course." She laughed. "I remember we never caught anything." She sighed and added, "It was fun, though, watching the sunrise from that little beach."

"You know what I loved about it, Charlie?"

"I have no idea, Harry."

"That you liked it as much as I did. You're

the only woman I've ever known who got excited about getting up in the dark and meeting a guy on the beach to fish. It was . . . romantic."

It was such a funny, guy thing to say, but she had to agree. It had been romantic. What she said was, "Everything is romantic on the Cote d'Azur, I guess — even fishing."

As they slipped farther into the darkness, Harry switched on the flashlight, strapped it under the kayak's bungee cord and headed across the cove toward the shallows around Finley's Landing. The light put out a single, non-reassuring beam in the darkness.

"Man, it's dark out here," said Harry. "Kinda spooky."

Charlotte laughed. "That's part of the fun. I know how you boy scouts are, though. You better hand me the other flashlight."

It was over four hundred yards across the cove. Before the oil spill, boats of every size and shape might be cruising up the bayou at all hours, but with the waterway boomed off, there was little chance of traffic. Still, Charlotte swung the light in a circle. It didn't illuminate much, but would make them visible to any oncoming boats.

The kayak glided through the water, and soon she could see the bottom. They were about ten yards from Finley's Landing. Three flat, dark shapes took off at the sound of Harry's paddle.

"Were those flounders?"

"Sting rays."

"Whoa, remind me to watch my step."

"Watch your step."

"I love a funny fishing guide."

Charlotte laughed and gave him a little poke in his back. "You get what you pay for. But don't worry, I've never stepped on a sting ray, and I've never known anyone who has."

"Good to know."

"Of course, crabs are a different story."

"Are you still kidding?"

Charlotte laughed. As they floated into the deeper shadows of oaks and pines towering above the oleanders, she added, "I'm kidding about the crabs, but you're right. It's a good idea to watch where you walk."

"Okay, guide, we know where the rays are. Where are the flounder?"

"Probably all around, but they're hard to see." She held the flashlight close to the water. "Oh, look there. See that shape?"

"I'm not sure."

"See the eyes?"

"Yeah, at least I think I do." He looked

222

around at Charlotte and grinned. "Now what?"

"We need to be in shallower water. We'll beach the kayak and light the lamp. It works a lot better than a flashlight."

Just then an outboard motor cranked up. Charlotte and Harry looked up in time to see a dark blue hull emerge from the canal at Finley's Landing. Charlotte aimed the flashlight in the direction of the boat, but instead of continuing at idle speed so as not to swamp them, the boat sped up. It was on a collision course for the kayak. Charlotte waved the light above her, but the boat had not planed off, and she wondered if the driver could even see the light. The boat flew by the kayak, its prop grinding in the sand, then turned into the deeper water. The kayak and everything in it, including Harry and Charlotte, were tossed into the wake of the disappearing boat.

Charlotte's ankle bone cracked into one of the metal fittings on her way over the side. Remembering the gig with its deadly barb, she made her way carefully toward the beach, sputtering and coughing. When the water was about a foot deep, she sat on the sandy bottom, blinked the salt water out of her eyes and tried to catch her breath.

Between coughs she tried yelling to Harry,

which came out as frantic croaks.

He didn't answer.

Had he been hit by the boat, sliced up by the boat's propeller? She pictured him floating face down in the dark water, his body a mass of gruesome injuries.

"Oh, my God! Harry!" she called, her voice turning shrill and ending in a sob.

22.
SHIPWRECKED

Charlotte heard water moving and looked toward the point. But the splashes had obviously been made by a dolphin, because all she could see was the faint shape of the kayak. It looked like a midget ghost ship floating where the sand bar suddenly dropped off into deep, dark water.

Charlotte choked back another sob and limped toward the kayak. But then she heard a moan.

"Oh, Harry! You're alive!" she sobbed with relief.

Next came more splashes, some coughing and a string of expletives. Charlotte wiped her face with her hands, slightly embarrassed about her loud and emotional display of concern for Harry. She took a deep breath and attempted to regain her composure. Harry was alive and breathing. That was the main thing. But where was he?

As she hobbled through the shallows

toward their empty kayak, the crescent moon edged out from behind a cloud. Its puny glow illuminated the scene somewhat. Harry, who had been using the kayak as a kick board, reached the sand bar and stood up. Like a wet version of the rising Phoenix, his six foot three frame emerged dripping not ashes but the brackish water of Cocktail Cove. Though her brain was awash in relief at the sight of an intact, upright Harry, when the moon's pale shine caught the wet boom floating in the distance, she had to wonder.

Where did the homicidal, blue-hulled boat go?

Harry, pulling the kayak behind him like a yellow toy, hurried toward Charlotte.

"You're limping! When I get my hands on —"

"I'm okay. Really. I just bumped my ankle."

"He could have killed you, Charlie."

"Us, Harry." She shivered, and her voice cracked. "He could have killed both of us."

Harry wrapped his arms around Charlotte, and a shaky sigh escaped him. She rested her face against his warm, wet chest and could hear his heart pounding. He held her tighter, kissed the top of her head and stroked her back. She relaxed into him, feeling right at home snuggled in his arms.

The next thing Charlotte knew, he was kissing her, not on the head but on the mouth, gently at first, then with all the passion of a young man in the throes of a summer romance. Charlotte's arms went around his neck, and he pulled her even closer. And out of that blissful mist of love and lust and gratefulness to be alive, something blinked in her brain. And blinked again. It was that little caution light ignited by the warnings from Craig and Maisy and Pup and Liza Jane.

Charlotte pulled away.

"You're engaged," she said quietly.

Silence. Then . . . "No, I'm not. Not really."

Not really?

In the previous minutes, Charlotte had pretty much run through her repertoire of emotions. The one she hadn't yet tapped into on this crazy night was anger, and it came boiling up out of her.

"Not really? Not really?" she said in such a low growl that she was scaring herself. Empowered by the sound of her new, menacing self, however, she continued. "Well, I think Abbie really thinks you are. I mean she's really wearing a really large diamond, and you are really living with her, aren't you? In Pitt Cottage that was a big part of this town's bread and butter. Not that you and Abbie care. Not really."

"But I thought . . ."

"What? That people will still come to see it when it looks like just another slick condo and bears no resemblance to the house in *Moonlight Charade*?" Her bottom lip started to quiver. "Which happens to be one of my favorite movies." This final sentence was punctuated by a sob.

She knew she had completely lost control of her temper and had insulted Harry's masterpiece of a redo, but she was completely unprepared for his reaction. He took off out into the water. Then she realized he was going after the kayak which was drifting toward the bay. Not that it would do them much good without a paddle.

Harry returned, dripping wet yet again, pulling the recalcitrant kayak behind him.

"I guess we should look for the paddle," he said. "I'll head down toward the bay. If you're sure your ankle's okay, look around here."

His voice was distant and quiet and sad.

Charlotte was instantly remorseful, of course. Harry was proud of his work with Pitt Cottage. And rightfully so. It was a beautiful transformation — stylish, modern

228

and functional. Charming, even.

But a reduction in the revenue generated by fans of *Midnight Charade* would be another blow to the town's struggling economy. As far as Charlotte was concerned, Harry and Abbie had effectively erased a piece of East Oyster's history, which was an even greater loss. With the transformation of Pitt Cottage, the connection between East Oyster and *Midnight Charade* had been severed, and the setting for one of the most popular films of the seventies now existed only in its dimensionless movie form, as flat as a DVD.

After searching for a good half-hour, Charlotte and Harry decided it was time for plan B.

"I'll swim across, get a boat and come back for you," said Harry.

It was a brave, gallant offer, but it was said in that distant tone that had Charlotte fighting back the tears.

"That's too dangerous, Harry. A boat would never see you. And what if our friend in the blue boat decides to come back?" She looked across at the necklace of lights from houses ringing the cove's east side. She easily picked out the light burning on Maisy's pier. *So near and yet so far.*

"I could walk, but I'm down to one shoe,"

said Harry, "and it's a long way through the woods to a house."

"I have both my shoes," said Charlotte. "I could go."

"There's no way I'm letting you do that," Harry said, his voice softening a bit. "You've been through enough, and it's my fault."

They both knew he was referring to more than the ill-fated fishing expedition.

Charlotte said, "I didn't have to come along. The only one at fault is that idiot who almost ran us over. And speaking of the phantom boat, where did he go? The last I saw of him, he was headed out to the bay, but he couldn't have gotten through the boom without it getting caught up in his prop."

"There's a section of boom missing. I saw it when I was looking for the paddle. That's the way he came in and left."

"What was he doing at Finley's Landing? And why the fast exit? He was in such a hurry I don't think he even saw us."

"He saw us, all right."

"But why . . . ?"

"I don't know. But I promise you, I'll find out."

They were tired, out of sorts with the situation, themselves and each other and had had the life scared out of them. As they

230

stood in the shallow water, out of ideas, their toes turning to prunes, something bumped against them. Charlotte looked down, and there it was. The paddle.

"Well, look who's back," said Harry, sounding a little more like himself.

Charlotte voiced a few half-hearted concerns about crossing the cove without a light. But when Harry said wearily, "Okay, I'll cross, get a light and come back for you," Charlotte hopped in the kayak.

"Paddle fast," she said.

Harry didn't respond, but started paddling.

Soon the kayak bumped gently against Maisy's piling.

"I guess Harry and Charlie's big adventure is officially over," Harry said.

Charlotte sighed. "I guess it is. And we never even went floundering."

"Rain check?"

"No. No more rain checks, Harry."

Charlotte reached for the ladder.

When she'd climbed up and was standing on the pier, Harry said, "Charlie, I am not marrying Abbie. And Abbie is very aware that I'm not marrying her. It's complicated, but I promise you there's an explanation."

"Well, I'd love to hear it, Harry. I really would."

Charlotte turned toward the house, intending to put some distance between herself and Harry and his rain checks and promises of clarification and reparation. But before she made it across the boat house, Harry had tied the kayak to the ladder and climbed up.

"It's been a long night, Harry."

"You said you'd love to hear an explanation."

"You have an actual explanation?"

"Yes."

"Okay. But it better be good."

"It is. I promise."

Charlotte found two thick beach towels in a cabinet. Then she went behind the bar and opened two beers. She wrapped a towel around her, tossed one to Harry, handed him a beer and sat on a chaise. Harry sat on the other one. "Thanks," he said.

Charlotte sipped her beer. "I'm all ears," she said.

Harry sipped his beer, trying to decide where to start. He looked at Charlotte sitting there in the gentle light of Maisy's boathouse and thought how she really hadn't changed much in all the years. The lines were smile lines, for the most part, adding character and definition to her pretty features. But the thing that got to Harry, that tugged at his heart was her spirit, the sparkle in her eyes, the easy laugh, her desire to see the good in people — in him. In other words, the things that made her Charlie.

He was breaking the most solemn of promises if he told her what he and Abbie were up to, but now that he'd found her again, he couldn't . . . he wouldn't upset her any further. He would not take a chance on losing her again.

He took a deep breath and began his story.

"As you know, I have been married. It didn't last long. Therefore, I have dated plenty of women. And most of them have been very nice. But sooner or later I would find myself comparing them to you. So things usually ended on a sour note. Not one of them came close to you, to what we had.

"When my marriage went from bad to worse, I went to a therapist. He convinced me that I was exaggerating my memories of you, that I had put you — or this unrealistic version of you — on a pedestal. This was because of my innate fear of commitment, according to him.

"It sounded like a bunch of bull, but I half believed it. Until I saw you again. The day I walked into your gallery, I knew. I was right.

You were the one I should have been with all this time."

Charlotte dabbed at her eyes with the corner of her beach towel and said, "Then why did you marry someone else?"

"Do you remember me telling you that summer in St. Yves that I had just broken up with someone?"

"Yes, you said it was an immature relationship or something to that effect."

"Yes. It was. But after you left, I got a call from her. She was pregnant. Her parents were adamant that we marry. They were very conservative, lived in a very conservative, tight-knit community and so they told everyone that we'd eloped before I left for France. You know how people were back then. I was sworn to secrecy. I felt so bad about the predicament I'd left Annie in. While she was at home trying to hide her morning sickness from her parents, I was having the time of my life in Provence. And falling in love with you."

"I always thought it must have been something like that," said Charlotte, her voice barely above a whisper. She sighed. "And then it happened again. With Abbie. Can you imagine how I felt?"

"Yes, I can. I felt every bit as terrible about it as you. Worse, probably. Before, I made a stupid mistake. It resulted in a beautiful daughter, but I lost you. This time, it's just a strange set of circumstances."

"Please tell me Abbie isn't pregnant." She was only half teasing.

"No, I assure you. At least not by me. But I made a promise to Abbie and even more important, to someone else. To Abbie's brother, Tim."

"I'd heard that she'd lost her only sibling . . . her only family. So sad."

"Yes. Very sad. Unbelievably sad." He pressed his lips together and shook his head. "Tim and I had been friends since he moved to Nashville years ago. He was a great guy. A great friend. But he was always in over his head financially. Always going to make it big with some scheme. Long story short, he got in with the wrong people and did something illegal. These people, they used him, set him up. They got away with everything, and Tim ended up facing prison. His girlfriend left him. As you said, he had no children, no parents — only Abbie — his younger sister.

"I was convinced that his death was suicide because he called me the week before he died and asked me to look after his sister if anything happened to him. Then he shot himself. He was a hunter. He knew guns and had always been careful with them."

"How awful. I'm so sorry, Harry."

"It was awful. Abbie was going through some tough times of her own, Tim had told me. I didn't know Abbie, but I knew from things Tim told me that she was kind of . . . kind of high-strung is the impression I got." Harry shook his head again at this bit of understatement. "With Tim facing a prison sentence, I told him Abbie could call on me anytime. I had no idea that he was contemplating anything so . . . so drastic.

"After the funeral . . . and it was the worst thing, that funeral . . . because other than Abbie and me, there was hardly anyone there. Tim's friends all disappeared when he got into trouble. And for the most part, Abbie's buddies aren't the kind to fly across the country to be with a grieving friend.

"After the service, Abbie asked for my help in finding the people she holds responsible for Tim's death. She had this idea that if she could find them, she could figure a way to make them pay for what they'd done."

"Good grief," said Charlotte.

"I know. It was crazy. But to her credit, she'd traced one of the people involved to East Oyster and felt sure she could get proof of his guilt. And it just so happened her family owned a house in East Oyster."

"Pitt Cottage."

"Right. Pitt Cottage. It needed renovating. There was a guest house I could use rent-free." He frowned. ". . . which, by the way, I retire to each and every evening. My daughter was in St. Yves for the summer. I had gotten into renovating old buildings. And I'd promised Tim. Besides, I wanted to see those guys held responsible almost as much as Abbie. And Abbie was determined. She would have pursued it on her own. I couldn't let anything happen to her."

"So you agreed," said Charlotte. "And got engaged along the way?"

"It wasn't until after I had made all the arrangements to come here that Abbie insisted we pretend to be engaged. It was necessary to her plan, she said. When I balked at the idea, she got so distressed — hysterical, really — that I went along with it. The hysterics were my first inkling of just how . . . how troubled Abbie is.

"Besides, I thought, what difference would it make? It would save me the trouble of the inevitable fix-ups. I could concentrate on my work, help Abbie, fulfill my promise to Tim and be on my way.

"I had no idea I would like it here so

much . . . certainly never dreamed that I would find you again. Can you imagine? I walk into your gallery, find that you'll actually speak to me after what I did to you in France, that you're single and I'm engaged? But not really engaged, and I can't even tell you?" He shook his head. "It was a nightmare."

"Tell me about it," said Charlotte.

He looked at her and said, "I know. I am so sorry."

"Well, that's some story."

"Unfortunately, there's more." He took a deep breath and let it out. "It turns out Abbie wants this engagement to be real. And lately she's gone from dropping hints to acting as if we really are getting married. She's more than just delicate, as they say. She's unstable."

"So what are you doing about it?"

"She's taken a leave of absence from her job. That has helped. When she goes back to New York it's to see her doctor — a psychiatrist. I've even gone with her a few times. With this doctor's help, I've tried to make her understand that I am not marrying her. I'm telling you, it's the craziest thing I've ever been involved in. But she's following the doctor's orders and taking medication now, which has also helped."

"So who is the person Abbie traced to East Oyster?"

"I can't say."

"Because you promised Abbie."

"Yes. And some other people, too. Not police, exactly, but authorities. The whole thing is . . . it's complicated."

"Everybody keeps saying that."

He smiled at Charlotte. "Because it is. Very complicated. But nearing the end, thank God. I know I don't have the right to keep asking you to trust me, but I'm asking. Abbie and I have to keep on as if we are engaged. We've come this far. I took a big chance when I told you that we're not getting married. No one else can know. I mean no one, Charlie. Not Maisy, not Liza Jane."

"Okay. You have my word. No one."

Charlotte smiled innocently at Harry, but inwardly she cringed. Because really, how long would she be able to keep this bombshell from Maisy and Liza Jane?

23.
SHARPS AND FLATS

In addition to Harry's profession of love (though he hadn't actually used the L word, had he?) and the president's reassurances concerning the well from hell, the weather in L.A. (Lower Alabama) was spectacular and holding. Every day was dressed in the leaping green of the season and set against a dream of blue sky.

The soreness and bruise on Charlotte's ankle was fading so that she hardly noticed it. Abbie was back in the Big Apple supposedly doing whatever associate directors of sales at fancy ad agencies do, but in actuality tending to her sick psyche. Her absence was like another fresh breeze sailing in from the bay.

After seeing what Charlotte was working on, Maisy proclaimed it a "masterpiece in the making." She'd insisted on coming into the gallery several mornings a week so that her niece would have extra time to "make magic on the canvas." The old thing still wasn't herself, but Charlotte decided it would be good for her to be around people — and Turner Gallery. Maisy loved the place and referred to it as an oasis of repose.

For the first time in a long time, Charlotte felt some control over her life. Harry had explained himself. The explanation was farfetched, but an explanation none the less. She felt a burden had been lifted. The seeds of optimism were taking root in her heart!

On top of this good fortune, a tourist with an unlimited line of credit popped into the gallery. Being an admitted A-type, she was being driven crazy by the decelerated pace of East Oyster. In two hours, the woman had done a year's worth of birthday and holiday shopping and commissioned a painting of the bay at sunset for her husband. And the lagniappe (little something extra, as the Cajuns call it) was that Charlotte would have almost a year to complete the painting.

The upswing in Charlotte's business and personal life was almost enough to erase the effects of weeks spent stressing over gushing oil, busted pelicans and shattered dreams of former lovers. She felt better than she had in quite some time. But lucky streaks have a way of ending or at least losing steam, and this one was no exception.

Gooey brown globs of oil — like chocolate, but tacky and toxic as roof tar — had come ashore at Creek County's gulf state park and the national wildlife refuge where the beloved pelicans roosted and fed. It stained the pristine white beaches rated as some of the most beautiful in the world. It fouled the clear green water where dolphins had thrived.

There was another development in the case of the purloined pelicans. A really disturbing development. The pelican painting in the fellowship hall of Pup's church had gone missing — not self-destructed or exploded like the statues, but simply disappeared off the wall.

It was a small church with an old preacher and a poor congregation. Stealing from these folks was the lowest of the low and had everybody even madder and more depressed than they had been. Butler Finley suggested a reward for any info leading to the return of the missing painting. He was reportedly so ticked off that he put up the first five hundred dollars.

Now that Charlotte had the plans for the renovation of her apartment, there was no real reason for Harry to stop by. And he hadn't. It was her move, so to speak. If she wanted to move forward with the renovation plans, then she should call him. But besides the trepidation over dismantling her home — she'd been through renovation misery when redoing the gallery — was it a prudent move to get so involved with Harry? In spite of his assurances that she was "the one," doubts started to rear their ugly little heads in his absence.

What if he made the whole fantastic story up just to keep me from finding out some dark, dastardly scheme hatched by Abbie and him?

The fact that Liza Jane kept voicing her very valid suspicions about the man didn't help. In spite of all the misgivings and suspicion, however, Charlotte missed him more than ever. Her lovely disposition of the previous week had turned as dark as the oil plumes snaking their way through the gulf toward East Oyster. And in a sort of ripple effect, this blue mood once again snaked its way into her painting. It had her using too much umber and black. She was losing the light and the mood of the place.

In an attempt to cheer Charlotte up, Liza Jane and Maisy appeared at her door on a hot Saturday morning.

"I've got a cold beer and sandwiches and two rods. It's a beautiful day! We're going fishing."

243

"No arguments," said Maisy. "I'll take over the gallery for as long as you need."

They headed to Maisy's where they swam and laughed and fished like children. Several speckled trout were caught. Liza Jane filleted them on the spot and put them on ice.

"Do you suppose they're okay to eat?" asked Charlotte, her gloomy mood returning.

Her question had them both thinking about the future of the Gulf Coast's vast seafood industry, not to mention the billions in tourist dollars.

"They've been testing the seafood. You know that. Everyone says it's fine," said Liza Jane irritably. She sighed. "I'm sorry, Charlotte, but if we doubt the safety of it, how do you think the rest of the country is going to feel about it? It's fine!"

"But that's the double-edged sword, isn't it? We want the rest of the country to know how devastating to everyone this oil spill is, but we don't want to scare them away from the seafood, away from the beaches that are still beautiful."

"It makes you wonder," said Liza Jane. "Is it possible for the gulf coast to have the oil industry as its number one industry and tourism as its second? Do we destroy the fragile beauty of the gulf for the sake of the oil that we all need?"

"I think we know the answer to that — stricter regulations on the oil companies. And why aren't we drilling more in Alaska than in the gulf? Hurricanes and deep water drilling don't mix. It seems like cleaning up tundra would be a lot easier than cleaning up a gulf!"

"I don't know," said Liza Jane. "I'm sick of hearing about it and talking about it and worrying about it." She sighed and ran her fingers through her hair. "What do you say we change the subject?"

Other than this little bump in the road, the morning on the water did the job of raising Charlotte's spirits. By the time Liza Jane opened the picnic basket, Charlotte was laughing and so hungry she would've eaten oil-soaked sushi.

"So how was your date with Grant?" she asked, handing her cousin a sandwich.

"Very good, actually. We made eight thousand dollars for West Oyster, and I got a decorating job out of it. Grant knew all the guys in the band. They talked him into sitting in for the sax player for a set. He's really good. And the saxophone does happen to be my favorite instrument."

"Nothing makes a date like great sax."

Liza Jane laughed. "We had a really good time. Lots of sax, but no sex, of course. I have my standards."

"What about chemistry and all that? Did you two hit it off? Are you going out again?"

Liza Jane pressed her lips together in thought, then said, "Do you have a fantasy guy?

"I thought we weren't going to talk about Harry."

"Oops. Sorry. Well, I think most single females — and a lot of attached ones — have a guy in mind that fills all the requirements."

"If they're lucky, it's the one they're with."

"Right. But sometimes it's a real person that is unattainable or inappropriate or something, like you-know-who. Sometimes, as in my case, it's a vague figment of the imagination that is kind, interesting, smart, funny and since we're dreaming him up, extremely good-looking and down-to-earth."

"When you fantasize, you don't fool around, do you?"

"There's more. He gets me."

"And Jazzman gets you?"

"He seems to. And I get him. Not only do we like the same weird combination of things, we understand why we like jazz and driving pick-up trucks down country roads. We both know that the other is . . . uh, a bit outside the norm, shall we say. But like Grant says, it's the sharps and flats that make the music beautiful."

"Wow. A poetic cowboy. When's the wedding?"

"Very funny. Now you're going to hex it."

"Okay. I take it back. So, what about the extremely handsome part of your fantasy?"

"I love his looks! Besides, I just threw the good-looking part in for fun. And yes, we are going out again. He'll be in town next week, and we're going out to dinner."

"This calls for a celebration," said Charlotte. "How about another cupcake?"

"Oh, why not? I'll work out an extra half-hour. That should cover it."

Charlotte looked at Liza Jane's amazing figure, her gorgeous red hair, those flashing green eyes. A cupcake — even one with chocolate cream cheese icing from the Big O wouldn't put a dent in those looks.

And now it seems she may have found Mr. Right, thought Charlotte.

She was happy for Liza Jane, but couldn't help feeling a tiny bit jealous. She sighed and decided that she would just have to live vicariously through her beautiful, younger cousin's good fortune.

After depositing a couple of fillets in Maisy's fridge, she and Liza Jane headed back down the drive. As they were getting ready to turn onto Pitt Ferry Road, a black BMW exited Abbie's drive. It was Butler Finley.

"Butler is getting pretty chummy with Abbie, don't you think?" said Charlotte.

Liza Jane shrugged as she pulled out onto the road behind Butler. "Probably something to do with the Pitt pelican."

Charlotte didn't say anything.

"What? You think there's something going on between Abbie and Butler?" Her voice softened. "Maybe you have a little wishful thinking going on?"

After swearing Liza Jane to secrecy, Charlotte told her cousin all about the floundering expedition with Harry. Told her everything. With doubts about Harry creeping back into her consciousness, she just had to have someone to talk it over with. And if she couldn't trust Liza Jane, who could she trust? When she got to the part about the kiss, she paused, searching vainly for the words to convey the absolute, unbelievable fabulousness of it. Just thinking about it had her back in his arms, her face against his chest. The next thing she knew, she was feeling that gentle, grateful kiss in her hair, on her neck, on the corner of her mouth.

"What is wrong with you?" asked Liza Jane. "You're all flushed and breathing hard. Omigod! Maybe it's the oil after all!"

"It's not oil, L.J. I was just thinking about how Harry and I were almost killed in the cove."

"Good Lord, I didn't realize it had been that harrowing. You're not having some kind of post traumatic episode or something, are you?"

Charlotte sighed. "Sort of," she said.

And as the bay cottages on Pitt Ferry Road flickered by, she related the rest of the story, including the kiss. When she'd finished, they were parked on Palmetto Street just outside the gate to Charlotte's courtyard. Liza Jane gave a long, low whistle.

Finally she said, "Must've been some kiss."

Charlotte sighed. "It was a dream kiss, Liza Jane. Like all of Harry's kisses. And if it turns out that Harry McMillan is a dirty, rotten scoundrel and has been lying through his beautiful teeth to me, that kiss was almost worth the heartache I'm in for."

"Wow," said Liza Jane, wondering how long it had been since her cousin had been kissed before Harry planted the record-breaking smooch on her. "Well, it *was* kind of like being marooned on a desert island," she said. "And you and Harry thinking each other might be maimed or dead!"

"But L.J., I think he was telling me the truth about not marrying Abbie. No, I take that back. I'm sure of it. I'm sure he was telling the truth. But I can't help wondering if he is stringing me along so I won't interfere in whatever is going on. Oh, this whole mess is giving me a headache."

Liza Jane was quiet for a few minutes before saying, "Unless our Harry is one heck of an actor, he has genuine feelings for you."

"I think so, too."

"But that doesn't mean Harry McMillan isn't a fraud and isn't playing all of us." Liza Jane sighed. "It comes down to trust. Do you trust Harry? More importantly, do you trust your instincts?"

"Maisy says I have good instincts."

"True. Remember, though, unrequited love can be a bear. And thinking about Harry, seeing Harry, kissing Harry is just feeding the monster."

24.
SOOTHING THE SOOTHSAYER

The consistently agreeable weather of May soon surrendered to the southerly breezes of June. The increased humidity that had the air feeling soft and dewy was still a long way from the saturation points of July and August. Summer had arrived in East Oyster.

Folks exercised outdoors earlier, donned sun hats and pulled their chairs into the shade. Windows were closed, and air-conditioning units began their constant hum. Children made for the water and stayed in bathing suits all day long. Geraniums and petunias sagged and drooped in their pots and their hot-weather replacements — begonias and crotons and bougainvilleas — made their appearance. And though the daily convective thunderstorms that East Oysterites could set their clocks by hadn't yet begun, showers increased so that sprinklers and hoses lay idle in gardens. Hurricane tracking maps were printed up though they had not yet made an appearance in newspapers and at check-out stands.

One of those odd, spring/summer breezes that are warm yet somehow feathered with cool, was drifting in off the water. It was enough to stir the yellow daylilies and white oleanders that had lived beside Maisy's porch as long as Charlotte could remember. Maisy had the ceiling fan on. A wisp of silvery hair, sticking up from her unbrushed head, floated in the circulating air.

She, Charlotte and Liza Jane sat around the table on her porch. Charlotte passed a wedge of mushroom quiche and some sliced tomatoes to her aunt who stared vacantly out over Lucy Bradford's pelican statue to the water.

Though Maisy was in her eighties, she enjoyed relative good health. She was generally energetic, upbeat, and despite weighing in at less than a hundred pounds, had the appetite of a woman half her age. Remarkably, she took no prescription medicine.

But you would never know it looking at her on this day. Charlotte thought she'd lost weight. Craig had mentioned that Maisy seemed tired — "off her game" was how he'd put it. Mayor Toowell was concerned. She'd stopped by the gallery with some "miracle vitamins hot off the shopping channel" for Maisy. Charlotte noticed that they sat unopened on Maisy's kitchen counter.

"You girls spoil me," Maisy said as Charlotte placed a glass of tea next to the plate. "I just have a little cold."

"Maisy, we're concerned," said Liza Jane. "You're not yourself lately. And it's not just a cold."

"People my age have a right to feel puny once in a while."

"That's true," said Charlotte. "But L.J. and I have been talking. We're afraid that you've been overdoing it with all of these fortune-telling gigs." She smiled at her aunt. "It's not like you to be this puny."

"You have single-handedly raised a ton of money for the oil spill victims," said Liza Jane. "Not to mention acting as therapist to everybody in town even if it is while posing as Madame Maisy. You need to look in that crystal ball of yours and take your own good advice. You've done enough!"

"And you've got to quit worrying so," added Charlotte. "It's not like you. I'm afraid it's affecting your health."

Maisy's face twisted into a little grimace that made her look like a shriveled up five-year-old. A tear tracked its way down a deep wrinkle. She wiped it away with a trembling hand.

Well, at this, both of her nieces immediately teared up.

"Oh, Maisy, what is it?" cried Liza Jane.

She jumped out of her chair, knelt next to Maisy and held the old dear's hand. Charlotte blew her nose and cleared her throat in an attempt to get control of herself.

"Maisy, you have helped us out of so many jams we've lost count," she said. "It's time to let us repay the favor. Something's bothering you. We want to help."

Maisy let out a shaky sigh. She patted Liza Jane's hand. "Good Lord," she said. "Sorry to lose my grip." Then she smiled and added, "But sometimes it helps to let it out. My granny used to say, 'Tears or ulcers — take your pick.' She had a million sayings like that. Most of them turned out to be true as a plumb line — that's another one."

"So, are you going to tell us what's bothering you?" said Liza Jane.

"Okay, but get comfortable because the roots of this run deep and a long way back. You know your Uncle Dubby was in the oil business. He built rigs as a young man then got an engineering degree and started his own company. Before long, he knew as much about rigs and wells as anybody.

Made a fortune.

"A little over thirty years ago, he worked on an exploratory well in the Bay of Campeche."

"Ixtoc?" said Charlotte.

"That's the one," said Maisy. "As you probably know, the blow-out preventer failed, and it caught fire. Took ten months to cap it. Something like twenty thousand barrels of oil a day gushed into the gulf. You can imagine the damage."

"Sounds like what's happened with the Horizon well," said Liza Jane.

"The scenarios are almost identical," said Maisy. As if the stress of the disaster wasn't enough, there was Dubby's daughter, Alice —"

"The one who died?"

"Yes. From his first marriage. Y'all never knew her. She was a brilliant girl. But prickly as they come. When she was nineteen or twenty, she threw herself into environmental issues — more to spite Dubby than anything else was my guess. Egged on by her mother, too. The first Mrs. Downy was one spiteful woman.

"Alice hated the oil business, of course. Accused her daddy of polluting the environment, criminal negligence, you name it. Of course, she didn't mind that his dirty money was paying her tuition and providing her with the lifestyle she'd become used to. After the Ixtoc explosion, she sent Dubby pictures of Ridley sea turtle eggs smothered in oil — that kind of thing.

"He said things to her like, 'We'll see how much you care about a bunch of darn turtle eggs when you don't have gas for your car!' Like Alice his words were more for argument's sake than anything else. And then for his birthday, which came when the well had been gushing for six months, she sent him a copy of *One Hundred Years of Solitude*. I guess you saw how she signed it. Do you know another way to spell Ixtoc?"

"Toxic," said Liza Jane.

"That's right. The book was stuffed with Alice's notes drawing all sorts of parallels to the doomed paradise called Macondo. That was the straw that did it. It got him so upset his pressure went up and I swear I thought I would lose him. I sent that book back to her with my own note telling her not to contact us again." Maisy sighed. "I had no right to do it. To shorten a long, sad tale, that was our last communication with her. Alice died before she and her daddy ever made it up."

"Oh, Maisy. I'm sorry," said Charlotte.

"You did what you thought you had to do

at the time," said Liza Jane. "People weren't as aware thirty years ago. And oil production was Dubby's responsibility. He had to focus on that, try to fix the well."

"That's true. Of the four biggest industries in the Gulf of Mexico — tourism, fishing, shipping and oil, oil makes up more than half. That's nothing to sneeze at. Dubby and I were more interested in economic repercussions than environmental ones."

"But back then women didn't stand up to their husbands as much," said Charlotte. "And you said that for the most part Alice's views were just teenage rebellion."

"Yes, but because of people like Alice, we all have become more aware. And I stood up to Dubby all the time. He used to say the louder the argument the sweeter the make-up, so he expected it. I can't use that excuse.

"I grew up in a blue-collar family of fortune-tellers — carnival people, half of them. Hard-luck people. I don't need to tell you we didn't have much. I married your great uncle, Dubby because I loved him, but I admit I liked being rich a lot better than being poor. And to tell you the truth, I really didn't like Alice much."

"Wow," said Charlotte.

"Wow, indeed," agreed Maisy. "I learned a

257

tough lesson when Alice died. I've been trying to make amends ever since, in a way. I've given a lot of Dubby's money away to causes in Alice's name. I use my intuitive powers, which can be pretty darn powerful, if I say so myself, solely to help others.

"But when the Horizon exploded, it all came back. Same scenario. And then I realized it was in the Macondo oil field. It was a sign if there ever was one. And an admonition. If we'd done more back then maybe we wouldn't be dealing with this horrible mess now. And every day the oil creeps closer.

"When Harrison McMillan showed up here, and it was plain as the age spots on my face that you're still crazy about him and he's engaged . . . well, it was the past . . . my past errors in judgment catching up with me again. If I hadn't meddled in your business and engineered that trip to France, you wouldn't be . . . be so heartsick.

"So I'm wondering, Is somebody trying to tell me something? Could it be Alice or Dubby or maybe Marie and Simone? Liza Jane, I could have sworn it was your mother herself sending me a message. But who knows? Maybe I'm losing my gift along with everything else."

"Are you kidding?" said Charlotte. "You

haven't lost anything but your self-confidence."

"Charlie's right," said Liza Jane. "This oil spill has everyone upset. And for some reason, I think the destruction of Mama's birds goes back to it, too."

"What did you call me?" said Charlotte.

"You called her Charlie," said Maisy. "And you know what? It's a sign."

"Another sign?" said Charlotte.

This was a stretch, even for Maisy, but something had put the color into the old lady's face. She was smiling, sitting up straighter and the twinkle was back in her eye. Charlotte decided it best not to question her reasoning.

"Yep," said Maisy. "It's a sign, all right. I don't know what's going on yet, but I'm headed in the right direction. I'm getting a feeling. And it's a strong one."

"Great," said Liza Jane, who like Charlotte was dubious, but also was not about to do anything to dampen Maisy's renewed good spirits. She decided to ignore the abundance of signs and changed the subject. "Maisy, your daylilies sure look good this year."

Liza Jane didn't finish her sentence because she was interrupted by the roar of a boat rocketing out of the canal across the cove. Its dark blue hull flashed in the sun as the driver whipped it around and headed in the direction of the mouth of the bay.

Charlotte had told Maisy about her floundering escapade with Harry. She had assured Harry of her discretion in keeping his secret, but she needed the old lady's input. Though she doubted the signs Maisy read into things, the "gift" inherited from her paternal granny and the reliability of Crystal, Charlotte had to admit that Maisy had something extraordinary going on. Besides, if the destruction of the pelican statues was tied up in the Abbie and Harry charade, Maisy needed to know. Surely Harry would understand.

So she had confided in her aunt about the bogus engagement, about Harry's plea that she be patient, and how her instincts told her to trust Harry. But she hadn't told Maisy about the close encounter with the blue boat. And she hadn't told her about the incredible kiss on the beach because she would have had to explain that, now that she'd had time to think it over, it was probably a reflexive, emotional thing resulting from relief that they were alive.

And she might have been tempted to tell her that when Harry wrapped his arms around her, when she'd melted into him and his soft lips found hers, it was as if the whole world and its complications fell away. If Harry turned out to be a two-timing super rat, Maisy would shoulder the blame for Charlotte's broken (to smithereens) heart once again.

If she'd confided in Maisy about the boat, Maisy could have been keeping an eye out for it from her vantage point across the cove. But with the old lady fretting about everything from busted birds to broken hearts, Charlotte had decided not to burden her with it. When she had reported it to Foster, he'd agreed — it was best not to trouble Maisy.

"Besides," he'd said, "There's no way to prove it was anything more than inept operation of a water craft."

But he'd wanted a description of the boat and said he'd pass it on to his water patrol buddies "just for the heck of it."

As if reading Charlotte's mind, Maisy said, "I've been watching that boat. It's one of Butler Finley's VOO boats. That's his man driving it."

"The driver works for Butler?" asked Charlotte.

"Yep. Been with him about six months. Name's Matthew Clifford, but he goes by Cliff. He's a tough guy — unfriendly, intimidating — and a hot shot, always tearing around in that boat. I talked to Butler about him, but I can't see as it's done any good.

"Like I said, that blue boat is one of Butler's vessels of opportunity. Cliff drives it with a crew of three others. But I've seen him slipping out after the VOOs have checked in. He just unhooks the boom and goes where he wants. No running lights, either."

"Are there other VOO boats up in that canal?" asked Liza Jane.

"About six, as far as I can tell. But the canal twists way up in there, so it's hard to know for sure. The crew park their cars at the end of the road and walk to the boats every morning. They check in, gas up and get their daily assignments at the public marina in Sweet Key. One evening I was looking through my binoculars. You know I like to keep an eye on that nest of blue herons in the big pine over there. Anyway, I saw Cliff with a hose in the gas tank of that boat. I think he was siphoning the free gas he gets every day from the VOO program." She shook her head. "Like I said, that Cliff is bad news."

The subject of "tough guy" Cliff and his part in the VOO program had taken the bloom off Maisy's improved humor, so Charlotte looked at Liza Jane and said, "So what's new with the jazzman?"

"Jazzman, better known as Grant, has asked me to come to his ranch in Florida . . ."

"Really?" said Charlotte and Maisy at once.

"Strictly business." Liza Jane smiled. "Or mostly business, anyway. It turns out he's in desperate need of decorating help. He's been emailing me pictures of his place, and I've been emailing pictures and suggestions, and he likes my ideas."

"Oh, I can tell you really like him," said Charlotte. "This is so exciting!"

"I do like him, but don't go getting all moony about it, Charlie. Charlotte. Wow, I did it again."

"Definitely a sign," said Maisy. "I haven't had a good vibe in two weeks." She grinned at her nieces. "By God, I think I'm coming back!"

"Maisy," said Liza Jane, "Do you feel up to doing a reading for me . . . with Crystal?"

Maisy and Charlotte looked at one another. Liza Jane hadn't asked for a Crystal reading since she was a teenager.

Like Charlotte, she thought the old lady's gifts were keen insight, amazing intuition, near-infallible wisdom and an unparalleled appreciation of the outrageous, but as far as they were concerned, Crystal was a party trick. Charlotte, as well as Maisy, knew that requesting a reading was Liza Jane's way of perking up her old auntie.

"Like I said, I have this cold," said Maisy. "For some reason stopped up sinuses are an impediment to a clear reading. But call me in a few days. I should be rid of this cold by then. I'll get Crystal shined up, and we'll have one heck of a reading."

25.
MARSEILLES TO EAST OYSTER

It was a couple of weeks after Harry's and Charlie's big misadventure that the President of the United States made another visit to the Coast. Besides keeping national attention on the dire situation, another positive was that he had lunch at Casa Crab. Needless to say, this was the Crab's biggest happening ever.

As it turns out, politics not only makes strange bedfellows but strange luncheon companions as well. Life-long Libertarians, Crabman and his crabbie missus had their pictures made with the commander-in-chief. The photo made the front page of the East Oyster Register.

"And can you believe all three of 'em are smiling?" said Foster, easing himself onto the Gauguin stool by Charlotte's desk.

His face was red, and he was breathing hard. The front of his uniform shirt was sprinkled with powdered sugar. The buttons strained so when he sat down that Charlotte shifted over a little. If they started flying, she didn't want to be in the line of fire. It was obvious that East Oyster's chief of police had made a few too many stops by the Big O.

He smiled at Charlotte and said, "Got some good news for a change. The birds are back. Home to the roost. Safe and sound."

"I take it you're speaking of Lucy's statues?" said Charlotte.

"Yes, ma'am, I am. Now if I could just figure out who took 'em and when, I could concentrate on things like stolen boom, illegal VOO activity, drunk and disorderlies and what not."

"Do you have any idea how long the statues have been gone?"

"No. If I did, I'd have a better idea of when they were stolen."

"Did you find out who the collector is who bought the statues? Or who sold them to the collector?"

"No to both. I get the impression from the French police that they might just consider the East Oyster police department a bunch of bumpkins when it comes to art." He sighed. "But it's pretty much irrelevant because according to the Frenchies, no one involved has ever heard of Lucy Bradford."

"So the owner of the tapestries didn't buy the birds?"

"That's right. He has no connection whatsoever to the pelicans. The connection is the thief or thieves who stashed everything behind the café in Marseille."

"What about someone who worked at the café? I mean that's a strange place to leave a bunch of valuable art work."

"Again, no connection whatsoever." He sighed again. "Nope. Until they find out who stole the other artwork from the VIP collector — the stuff that was found with the pelicans — it's a dead end."

Foster sounded downright happy about this latest development.

"Not very helpful."

Charlotte was half referring to Foster's attitude, but he took it as a slight against the "gendarmes" and agreed.

"No, it's not." He sighed in a feigned attempt at dismay. "But the birds are back," he said, "And I don't think the perpetrators are dumb enough or desperate enough to try anything else around here."

"So you're giving up on finding these . . . perpetrators?"

Charlotte hadn't meant the question to sound accusatory (even though that's how she meant it), but Foster clinched his jaw and narrowed his eyes. He took in a big breath that puffed his chest out and made him sit a good two inches taller. It was an intimidating look that Charlotte figured was a handy tool in his line of work.

Staring straight ahead, he said, "I guess they've moved on by now. Anyway, I've got plenty to do with this oil spill business going on. Plenty of people with real problems. No offense, you being an artist and all, but rich people and their statues and pictures aren't that high on my priority list right now. Poor people are behind in their bills. They're gettin' conned. It's makin' 'em desperate. Desperate folks drink too much, beat each other up, do things they might not ordinarily do. I've had three domestic calls this week. The natives are getting restless, Charlie."

"What did you call me?"

"What?"

"You called me Charlie."

"I heard that McMillan fellow call you that. It kind of stuck in my head, I guess. It suits you."

"You think so, Fostie?"

"Fostie? Oh. Well, on second thought, Charlotte, maybe not."

Foster eased himself off the barstool. "That thing's a lot more comfortable than it looks," he said. "Oh, by the way. You're gonna love this. I've had a complaint about Maisy."

"The church again? Worried about her dabbling in the occult?"

"Nope. Ever since she raised all that money for Our Lady of Perpetual Succor and warned Father Fritz about his pancreas, she's off the hook with them. It would be your favorite newcomer, Abigail Pitt. She's accusing Maisy of child abuse."

"What?"

"Now do you see what I deal with? I'm deputizin' you to find out what's going' on over there. Has to do with the neighbor kids. Pitt says Maisy's payin' them money to tease her."

"What?"

"Just go over there and check on it, will you?" he whined. "I ain't got time for this kind of stuff."

Charlotte knew that since the case of the purloined pelicans had surfaced, Foster had been driving by the gallery at all hours. He'd personally checked her alarm system, and though the art scene was definitely not his scene, he'd come to the Arcadio show. She owed him this much.

"Sure," she said. "I can't wait to see what this is about."

Though she was relieved that Lucy Brad-ford's precious pelicans were back in town, she was disappointed in Foster's attitude. She was also worried about his physical and mental health. First Maisy now Foster! And it all went back to the oil spill. If Foster and Maisy weren't so all consumed with it, they would both be working on the case of the purloined pelicans. (Craig had everyone calling it that — even people who had no idea what purloined means.)

Nothing seemed to be nearing a resolu-tion — not the gushing oil, not the mystery of the art thefts and not the questions swirl-ing around Harry and Abbie. It was all so tiresome. Charlotte had adjusted to the empty space left in her heart by Harry McMillan, then adjusted to the idea that she might actually have him in her life again.

But his absence had the doubts growing again. Some deep-seated streak of self-preservation just wouldn't allow her to trust him completely until she had her proof, until she and everyone else knew the whole story. Until Harry had moved out from under Abbie's roof.

As the day went on, Charlotte continued to worry. By mid-afternoon her brain felt like mush. She'd made incorrect change twice, had forgotten to send in her registration for the upcoming art class, East Oyster Impressionists En Plein Air, and misplaced her favorite reading glasses. She was irritable and unsettled. With so many unanswered questions bouncing around in her head, it was impossible to concentrate.

She looked at the clock. *Ten till five, thank God!* She would lock up the gallery, have a glass of wine, sit on her balcony and not think about anything for an hour. Then she would tackle the weird events surrounding Lucy Bradford's pelican statues and try to put the hodgepodge of information into some sort of order.

As she walked toward the door, however, it opened. And in walked Harry. He stopped and smiled at Charlotte.

"I thought you might still be here. Hope you don't mind me showing up at closing time. I seem to be making a habit of it."

"No. Of course not."

"I forgot to pick up the plans. You know, to make the changes we talked about."

"I've been meaning to look at them again and just haven't had time. So much has been going on."

Harry seemed unsure how to respond. Finally he said, "Feel like doing it now? I mean if you can. But hey, you probably have plans or something."

Seeing Harry standing there so hopeful, her heart grew all fizzy, her worries evaporated and suddenly she felt downright energetic.

"No, that would be great. Let me just lock up."

Soon they had the plans rolled out on Charlotte's dining room table, pouring over every detail.

26.
A MINOR INFRACTION

The next afternoon found Charlotte back at Maisy's. She knocked on the kitchen door and called Maisy's name, but Taylor Swift was turned up so loud that she gave up and let herself in. She heard children's voices singing along with Taylor and followed them to the front porch.

Maisy was laid out on the wicker chaise. The neighbor's children, ten-year-old twin girls and a five-year-old boy — Charlotte thought his name was Beckett — were gathered around the old lady. One of the girls sat on the floor at the end of the chaise. A row of opened nail polish bottles was lined up before her. She was painting Maisy's toe nails — each one a different shade. The boy, whose tiny toenails were alternating crimson and white, was drinking coke through a straw in a can. He watched intently as his other sister worked on Maisy's chin with a pair of tweezers.

"How much a pet, Aunt Maisy?" asked the girl with the tweezers. (Children who made Maisy's acquaintance invariably ended up calling her Aunt Maisy.)

"A dime for every pet you pull out of my chin," she said.

"How many have I pulled today?"

"You have to keep track. I have way too many things to remember at my age. Kids don't have anything to remember."

"How about times tables?"

Maisy thought a moment, then said, "You got me there."

"Everybody hates the times tables," said Beckett.

'That's true," said Maisy. "They're like pimples."

Beckett made a face. "Why?" he asked.

"Everybody hates 'em, but you can't avoid 'em. Part of life."

"Did they have times tables when you were little?" asked Beckett.

"All the way to the twelves," said Maisy. "Which I never did learn. Made life harder than it needed to be, too."

One of the twins squeezed her face up in concentration as she worked on one of Maisy's pets. "I'll help you with your twelves," she said and plucked a whisker.

"Ow," said Maisy. "Okay. We'll work on it

tomorrow."

Well, Foster had it almost right, thought Charlotte. *Except that she's paying the children to tweeze her, not tease her.*

"Hi, everyone," said Charlotte. "What's going on?"

"Children, this is my niece, Charlie . . . sorry, now I'm doing it."

"Hi, Miss Charlie," the children said in unison.

Charlotte was about to correct them when she was interrupted by a voice behind her. She turned to see an attractive woman wearing a University of Alabama baseball cap. She balanced a drooling baby on her hip.

"Hi, Mom," said Beckett. "This is Miss Charlie."

"My niece," explained Maisy.

"Nice to meet you, Charlie. I'm Erin Lansky. We've just moved into the old Wilson place on the other side of Pitt Cottage. Maisy has been helping me with the kids." She jiggled the baby. "Robert here is teething and so fussy . . . well, you know how it is."

Charlotte laughed. "It's been awhile, but I remember those days. You have my sympathy."

"Okay, Olivia," said Erin. "Let's get everything picked up. Grace, help your

275

sister. So, how many pets did you get to-day?"

"Seven, I think," said Olivia.

"And seven times ten is . . ."

Grace started counting on her fingers.

"Seventy," said Olivia. "We're teaching Aunt Maisy her twelves tomorrow."

"Erin, stay and have a glass of tea with us," said Maisy.

While the children cleaned up and collected their pay from Maisy, Charlotte took the drooling Robert from his mother so Erin could drink her tea in peace. Soon the conversation turned to the renovation of Pitt Cottage and its owner. Charlotte asked Erin if she'd met Abbie.

"Oh, yes," she said. She made a little face and smiled at Maisy before adding, "But I'm afraid I didn't make a very good impression."

"You better start from the beginning," said Maisy.

"Okay. Olivia and Grace have it in their heads that they want to open a spa together when they grow up. They've been talking about it since they were seven. So sweet Maisy here came up with the idea."

"Might as well kill two birds with one stone," said Maisy.

"Actually, three birds," said Erin. "With

Robert teething and fussing, I needed a break. Olivia and Grace got to try out their spa skills, and Maisy is getting rid of her pets and getting a pedicure." She looked at Maisy's toes. "Although I doubt every toe a different color is what you had in mind."

"I kind of like it," said Maisy. "And I can't see my chin whiskers any more to pluck the suckers out. And we're working on times tables. Grace is less than enthusiastic about the tables."

"But Maisy, your toe nails," laughed Erin. "At least let me fix them for you."

Maisy waved a hand in the air. "They're fine. We can change them tomorrow if we get around to it. Besides, they're no worse than Harry's."

"Harry McMillan?" asked Charlotte.

"Yep," said Maisy. "Alternating black and gold. He's a big Vanderbilt fan, you know."

"But we've decided to overlook that," said Erin. She pointed to her crimson hat. "I mean he's so cute and everything."

"Harry really let the children paint his toenails?" asked Charlotte.

"After Abbie saw the children tweezing Maisy on the beach, she came to me all upset," said Erin. "When she found out I was not only okay with it but downright grateful to have the kids out of my hair for awhile, she said something like what kind of people are you? and stormed off. By the way, does she always walk that way?"

"Yes," said Maisy and Charlotte in unison.

"Well, that cute Mr. McMillan came over and apologized and let the children give him a pedicure. He paid them two dollars apiece." Erin shook her head. "I probably shouldn't say this, Charlie, but I just can't see him with that Pitt woman."

"I think Charlie might just agree with you," said Maisy. "More tea?"

Erin looked out to the garden where her children were swinging on a low magnolia branch.

"Thanks," she said. "I managed to throw a casserole together and do the laundry while they were over here. And the children are actually behaving themselves." She sighed. "Summer hasn't even officially started yet, and they're getting into trouble."

"I don't believe it," teased Maisy. "Children getting into trouble?"

"Do you know that yesterday the girls took the kayak across to Finley's Landing without telling me? They are not supposed to even swim without me watching them. And on top of that, they made up this wild story about going to a store over there."

"A store? The only thing over there is that

little shed," said Maisy.

"They tried to tell me that there were pictures for sale in there."

"Pictures? What kind of pictures?" asked Charlotte.

"Oh, who knows? It was just something they made up."

Charlotte noticed that Maisy was looking quite pale. Her hand shook as she placed her tea on the table.

"Maisy, what's wrong?" asked Charlotte.

But Maisy turned to Erin. "I don't want to frighten you, sweetie, but with all the VOO boats pulling in and out of the landing, it's not safe for the children to be over there. And you have spoken to them about strangers, haven't you?"

Charlotte figured she was thinking of the creepy Cliff.

"Of course," said Erin, "But I don't see . . ."

And so Charlotte told them both an abbreviated version of her floundering excursion with Harry.

"We're not trying to scare you, Erin, but there's just so much going on right now," said Charlotte. "We all have to be a little more careful."

"Charlotte, I can't believe you didn't tell me about that boat running you over," said

Maisy. "You could have been killed." She was interrupted by the children's voices calling from the front yard.

"Hi, Mr. Harry!" they all yelled.

Charlotte looked up to see Harry McMillan coming in from the beach. He was wearing a golf shirt, jeans and no shoes, and even from that distance she could see that his toenails were indeed black and gold.

"I thought I heard monkeys out here," she heard him say.

The girls giggled, but Beckett said, "No sir. It's just my sisters. Roll, Tide!"

"What did you say?" said Harry in mock anger. "Why, you —" He grabbed Beckett up and tickled him.

"Roll, Tide, Roll, Tide," gasped Beckett between giggles. Finally Harry set him down. As Harry made his way to the porch, smiling and waving and seemingly oblivious to his ridiculous toenails, the three women waved and smiled and sighed. Because every woman loves a man who is good with children and because Harry McMillan is nothing if not cute.

He accepted Maisy's offer of a glass of iced tea and sat down next to Charlotte who was still holding the drooling baby. Harry flashed a grin at her, rubbed a big hand over Robert's head and said, "How's it going,

Charlie?"

"Very well, thanks."

They sat there smiling at one another for a few seconds until Charlotte said, "So, we were just discussing your game day pedicure. Very nice."

He looked down at his toes. "And it only cost me six bucks. I definitely see a spa in Olivia and Grace's future."

Erin laughed. "I can't believe you're still wearing that polish."

"No remover. Abbie gets her nails done in town."

The mention of Abbie's name sobered the mood a bit, but the group rebounded nicely when Harry said, "Speaking of toes, looks like Maisy got the deluxe pedicure today."

Maisy laughed and wiggled her granny toes at Harry. "Scary, aren't they?"

About that time Robert started to make noises. His face turned purple then he relaxed and smiled at everyone. And they all became aware that adorable, drooling, stinky Robert was in need of a diaper change.

Erin smiled and stood up. "Sorry about that. Duty calls."

She started to gather the other three, but Maisy shooed her off, promising to keep an eye on the children and walk them home herself. As they left, Robert started to cry, and it was an ungodly howling.

"And for God's sake, give that baby some bourbon," yelled Maisy.

Erin and Harry laughed, but Charlotte was praying Abbie wasn't within earshot. With her anorexic sense of humor, she'd probably take Maisy seriously and call the nearest social services office.

Harry's cell started to ring. He looked at the screen, frowned and clicked it off.

"It seems that duty is also calling me," he said. "Maisy, could I borrow some of that polish remover? I promise to bring it back in time for your next spa treatment.

"Sure," said Maisy passing the bottle over to him. He leaned over and gave her a kiss on the cheek. Maisy smiled and even blushed a little.

Harry looked at Charlotte and said, "Goodbye, Charlie. Always a pleasure."

As soon as Harry was out of earshot, Maisy quizzed Charlotte about the details of her run-in with the blue boat.

"That was so odd — the children saying the shed over there is a store," said Charlotte. "Do they usually make up stuff like that?"

"No, they don't. And now, if you'll excuse me, I'm going to have a little chat with those rascals. And maybe go over a few rules."

"What rules?"

"Oh, water safety, minding parents, tres-passing, talking to strangers."

Charlotte watched as Maisy approached the children — the "monkeys" were back in the magnolia tree, laughing and swinging from its branches. Though the proximity to water held its own set of dangers, East Oyster and Palmetto Bay in particular were wonderful places for children to grow up. Charlotte hoped that one day her own grandchildren might be swinging from those branches and learning the ins and outs of boats and nets and caring for the delicate, threatened ecosystem she loved.

On her way out, she picked up the tea glasses and stowed them in Maisy's dish-washer. She wiped the counters off, grabbed her purse and headed for the car.

As she was backing out, she took one last look through Maisy's side yard to the water. A flash of yellow made her take a second look. It was Harry, in his kayak.

Whatever "duty" called him from Maisy's has certainly been taken care of promptly, thought Charlotte. She turned off the car's engine and watched. Harry pulled the kayak ashore at Finley's Landing and tied it to a pine root at the edge of the water. He waded around to a sandy spot and headed along the canal toward the shed the children had referred to as a store.

From her vantage point Charlotte could see through the trees where the front of the shed was just visible. Harry was now approaching it and looking over first one shoulder then the other — the VOOs would be returning soon, Charlotte remembered. He stretched his long frame until he could run a hand over the edge of the shed's roof.

"What the heck?" muttered Charlotte.

Harry had evidently found a key and was turning it in the lock. He disappeared inside, closing the door behind him. Seconds later he emerged, looked around, replaced the key and hurried back to the kayak. The last Charlotte saw of him, he was paddling up the cove like any innocent outdoorsman basking in the tranquilities of nature.

27.
HERMIT CRABS

Once Charlotte returned to the gallery, she called Foster and relayed the source of the child abuse allegations against Maisy. She and the police chief had a good laugh.

"It's good to hear you laugh," she told him.

"Feels good, too. This oil spill has just about ruined my sense of humor along with everything else. Thanks for dealing with Maisy. That's one less thing on my plate."

Charlotte clicked off and realized it was past closing time. She double-checked the locks and headed upstairs. As she walked into her apartment her cell began to ring again.

"Hi, Mom," said Mark.

Charlotte and her older son chatted about their lives for a few minutes until he said, "I almost forgot. I haven't even asked you about the big art show — with that Arcadio guy. How'd it go?"

"Really well."

Charlotte kicked off her shoes and settled onto the sofa. After a description of the evening of the Arcadio show, the discussion naturally turned to the oil spill. It wasn't a happy discussion.

Scientists had doubled their estimates of the oil gushing from the Macondo well. Apparently as of June third, a whopping twenty to forty thousand barrels — millions of gallons — had flowed into the blue-green waters of the Gulf of Mexico. Tarballs had washed ashore on Florida's pristine northwest shore (which was really just down the road). The few tourists who visited the beach were greeted with signs advising the public not to "swim in these waters due to the presence of oil-related chemicals."

The latest dour news report about shoreline cleanup was accompanied by pictures of crews' nets. They held piles of lovely seashells. Mixed in with the shells were black tar balls. The only good news was the president was looking for someone's "butt to kick." The bad news was he didn't know exactly whom that butt belonged to. Was it the oil company, the rig owner, the maker of the blow-out preventer, the service provider for the well owners or the inspectors who, it seemed, failed to inspect? Well, they were all spewing barrels of blame at one another, so . . .

Mark had seen pictures of little children in their bathing suits, shovels and buckets in hand, standing on the sugary beach he'd played on as a child. The children were staring at globs of oil that had washed ashore. Charlotte thought she and her son might both cry just talking about it.

It was Mark's dream to move back to East Oyster after graduation. Though he and his younger brother, David, were working on business degrees, they wanted to try their hands at guiding tourists and fishermen through the waters surrounding East Oyster. The unspoken worry that the spill had turned his plans into fantasy hovered like a shroud above the conversation.

On a brighter note, he mentioned a new girlfriend — Julia. Twice. This was a record. Charlotte had learned not to press for details, so merely said she thought she sounded lovely, and that she hoped to meet her. To her surprise, Mark said he'd been invited to spend the Fourth of July holiday at her family's lake house.

Wow. Meeting the parents?

"And she's never been to East Oyster . . . thought I might bring her down when summer classes are over."

He said this with an air of nonchalance, yet bringing a girl home to meet mom was special, and they both knew it. She could tell by his tone that she would get no more information concerning his relationship with Julia so she let the subject drop.

There was a pause, and Charlotte felt an urge overtaking her to mention Harry — to just say his name. Talking about him was a way of keeping him near, keeping him real. But Mark changed the subject, asking about Maisy and Liza Jane and finally, the pelican statues. Harry faded to the edges of her consciousness.

And so she filled him in, ending with her worries about East Oyster's overweight, over-worked and over-wrought Chief of Police.

"He has such an unhealthy lifestyle, and now his workload has increased with the oil spill. He hardly has time to keep up with a 'bunch of busted birds,' as he calls them."

"Yeah, seems kind of minor in comparison to . . . well, to the oil spill and real crimes."

Charlotte sighed. She figured that to most policemen art theft or vandalism is a victimless crime. Who cares if some wealthy person loses her etchings?

"I know I'm a little biased, Mark, but when we lose art, especially great art, we all suffer. I know Lucy Bradford was no Picasso, but her work is important, especially to folks here in East Oyster."

"Mom, has Mr. Finley gotten involved? I mean, doesn't he have a big art collection and all that?"

Charlotte laughed. "You're very good at changing the subject. But okay, I'll get off my soapbox for now. In answer to your question, I haven't seen Butler's collection in some time, but I understand from Liza Jane that he's added to it and that it's really impressive.

"It includes some very good local artists, including the Lucy Bradford pelican that was vandalized. He also has a Wyeth sketch, an Ansel Adams and a couple of watercolors by Walter Anderson. Of course owning art and really knowing art are two different things. Still, he's on the pelican board, and he has a personal interest, of course, since one of the birds belonged to him. So, yes, he is very involved. Why do you ask?"

"I just thought being the biggest of the East Oyster bigwigs, he could help out. I'm sure he has connections, can get things done and all that."

Charlotte thought about the growing friendship between Abbie and Butler. "Yes, he's all about connections. I hope something comes of it."

Promising to let Mark know of any developments in the bizarre things going on in East Oyster, Charlotte hung up. As she often did, she replayed the conversation with her son in her mind. Mark and his brother, David, were as upset as everyone else about the oil spilling onto their hometown beaches and wetlands, tainting their memories and possibly their futures.

Charlotte smiled thinking about the new girlfriend, but grew a bit apprehensive about her visit. She looked around the apartment, attempting to appraise it with detachment. At one time it had what Liza Jane referred to as "artistic panache." Now she'd probably describe the apartment as more shabby than chic. Whether Julia ended up coming for a visit or not, Charlotte knew she'd procrastinated long enough.

She went to the drawer of her desk and pulled out the plans Harry had drawn up. They looked even better than the last time she'd perused them. Yet she had to admit that half the thrill of the project was having Harry as her consultant. Without him, renovation seemed like nothing more than endless decisions on top of a pile of work.

The idea of tackling it alone made her feel sorry for herself. Which made her seem pathetic. Which made her feel even sorrier for herself. But it would have to be done — Harry or no Harry.

She'd always thought her sons would return home. She would have daughters-in-law, grandchildren and as always, her art. Before a blow-out preventer on an oil rig failed, before Harry McMillan re-entered her life, she was content. Not over-the-moon happy, but very content. Charlotte had learned to appreciate the three-quarters full glass that was her life and not waste time lamenting the one-quarter that was missing.

After all, she'd known head-over-heels romance and had enjoyed a good if short marriage with a wonderful man. She'd had every reason to look forward to a healthy, comfortable future. Now that future seemed as frightening as the plumes of oil making their way into their lives.

The oil well will be fixed, Charlotte told herself. *Things will be normal again. Mark and David will come home as they planned. Enough of this self-pity!* she berated herself. *Try to dwell on the positive!*

Taking her own good advice, Charlotte thought back to the Arcadio show. It had been good — no, great! It had been great.

Yet something was off. There was some

unease floating along the edges of her brain, a sensation that she'd missed something. As if there was a discrepancy somewhere. Something she'd forgotten? Some small but important detail she'd noticed, but been too busy to deal with? She went back over her mental checklist; putting away the receipts, locking up, turning on the alarms.

No, it was something I heard. Something that didn't gee-haw, as Liza Jane might have put it. The thing with Maisy? Telling Arcadio that Dubby, her dead husband, had suggested she contact him?

No, that was strange, but as her cousin pointed out, not all that strange for Aunt Maisy who had a healthy respect for "messages from beyond." Charlotte decided it wasn't that.

Then what was it? *Good grief, I've had so many conversations with so many different people, there's no way I'll remember.*

She hopped in the shower, still thinking about Arcadio, entertaining herself with the choices her friends and neighbors had made that evening. Surely, competition and price had an influence, but for the most part she could have predicted which paintings would have appealed to which people. This was very gratifying because she always worried when friends insisted she opine about what should be very personal selections.

There was only one person she had misjudged. She'd thought that Butler Finley would have chosen the biggest, priciest, and most surreal of the paintings. It was of celestial bodies reflecting off night water teeming with sea creatures. There was lots of interest in it, too. It hadn't sold, however, and Charlotte decided that in the end, it was a matter of price — not usually a concern to Butler. A shame, too. It would have been an interesting addition to Butler's collection.

And suddenly it came to her.

That's it. Butler's collection. The Walter Andersons.

According to Liza Jane, one of the two Walter Anderson watercolors was titled *The Hermits.* It was of two hermit crabs emerging from their shells.

"The picture reminded me of our crab races," she'd said. The subject of the races were the small crabs that moved into increasingly larger shells as they grew.

Liza Jane had always had a thing for the shy, ugly creatures in their pretty shells. As a child, she was obsessed with trying to get a good look at them before they darted back inside their shells, or catching one between shell houses.

Charlotte had indulged her younger cousin in hermit crab races while babysitting her at the beach. They would pick crabs out of the shallow water and put them side by side up on the wet sand. The crabs would slowly emerge from their shells and wobble back down into the water. Which ever crab made it to the water first won the race. Unfortunately for the crabs, Liza Jane could be entertained in this manner for quite some time.

That's why Liza Jane had mentioned it and why Charlotte had remembered it. But recently she had seen an article about an exhibition in the Museum of Fine Arts in Houston. It was titled *Water* and included some gulf coast artists. Along with Anderson's *Blue Crabs* and *Palmettos,* the catalog had listed *The Hermits,* on loan from the Walter Anderson museum in Ocean Springs, Mississippi.

Charlotte hadn't put it together at the time. But the conversation with Mark concerning Butler's art collection had jogged her memory. Like the impossibility of the broken pelican statues being in East Oyster, Alabama and Marseille, France at the same time, how could the Anderson watercolor be on exhibit in a Houston,

Texas museum while hanging on Butler
Finley's wall?

28.
SOMETHING (ELSE) FISHY

After her run Charlotte showered and had a breakfast of fresh Georgia peaches and yogurt while she worked on the painting of the Provencal farmhouse. She remembered its angles and sun-infused colors and painted in abstract, catching and exaggerating the planes and curves of stones and roof lines and the darting light in the splashing water. Every time Charlotte looked at the picture, it made her smile. Not only because of the memories blooming like the old aunts' roses, but because she'd painted the darkness out of it. The magical ambiance of the scene she remembered was once again reflected in the piece.

But now it was gallery time. She tidied up and headed out into a beautiful morning. When she reached the bottom stair, she noticed Pup sitting on a bench next to the courtyard's wall fountain. She was wearing jeans and a pink T-shirt. A pink and orange striped scarf was tied around her head. Coral earrings hung from her ears.

"Hi, Pup. What's going on?"

Pup stood up, walked over to Charlotte and wrapped her arms around her.

"What on earth?" laughed Charlotte.

"I just want to thank you for my picture!" There were tears in her eyes. "Those boys of mine throwed me a party. Had balloons, cake, ice cream. Used they own money, too. But Charlotte, when Derek give me that picture in that frame, well, I just couldn't believe it. I never thought I'd have nothing like that."

"I'm glad you like it. Where'd you hang it?"

"Front room. See it first thing when you step in the door."

"You know your grandsons all chipped in to pay for it, and Derek framed it himself."

"He told me you give him a discount and took time to show him how to frame it, though."

"I've been meaning to give him more responsibility. He's good with the framing. I think he likes it."

"He do. He really likes it."

Charlotte and Pup chatted about their boys as they entered the gallery.

"Mark called last night," said Charlotte.

"He's got a new girlfriend named Julia."

"What happened to Hannah?"

"Who knows? I never get details."

"So this one's Julia? I can't hardly keep 'em straight."

"I know. But he's bringing this one home. Oh, and that reminds me. We were talking about Butler Finley's paintings by Walter Anderson. I know you work over there on Tuesdays and was wondering if he still has one called *The Hermits*.

"It was hanging in his good front room last time I was in there. I dusted it myself, but . . ."

Pup clamped her lips shut.

"But what?"

"Listen. What happens in your house stays in your house as far as Pup Jones knows. I don't take gossip to town. But with everything going on around here, something's got me worrying. You got to promise me you won't tell nobody." She pressed her lips together again and looked at the ceiling. "What am I talking about? I know you got to tell somebody, so make it Maisy. But nobody else — not Liza Jane, not nobody but Maisy."

Charlotte shut the gallery's back door. "I promise," she said.

"All them paintings of Mr. Finley's ain't real."

"Aren't real?"

"They real, but they copies. Least, that crab picture is."

"Are you sure? I mean, how do you know?"

"Cause I heard Finley's new man talking about it."

"Okay. I'm confused. Who's the new man?"

"Sorry. This whole thing has got me like a cat on a hot roof. Anyway, the new man told me to call him Mr. Clifford. Hah! *Mr.* Clifford? He think my name is Hey, you. But I'll call him Prince Clifford, if he that's what he wants. Cause he is one scary dude."

"Who was he talking to? What exactly did he say? And scary, how?"

"Hold on, I'm getting to it."

"Sorry. But this is important, Pup."

"I was taking the trash out. Finley keep his trash behind a tall fence. Mr. Clifford was setting in his truck talking his trash mouth on his phone. But I'll leave out all the bad words." Pup closed her eyes in concentration and continued. "I heard him say, 'Yeah, yeah, I'm bringing it. In cash.' Then the other person talk, then Clifford say, 'Finley love it. Even better than the

Wyeth.' Then he say, 'I don't get it. Why anybody get excited over a picture of crabs hanging on his wall.' Then the other person talk, then Clifford say, 'Okay, I get it. Yeah, the signature is perfect this time.'"

Pup opened her eyes. "So I gets to thinking — you know putting two and two together and I'm still getting five. Something ain't right. And this movie comes on TV about art forgers, and it come to me. Maybe them pictures Finley so proud of is copies! And I'm thinking I don't want to be in the middle of this mess, so I ain't said a word til now."

"Lord, Pup. I don't blame you."

"Really? Cause it's been worrying me to death."

"In the first place, the man could have been talking about something else. I mean, maybe the frame was covering part of the signature or something. There are plenty of explanations other than Butler Finley is being sold fake art. You don't have any idea who Clifford was talking to? He didn't say a name or anything?"

"No, glad to say. I already know more than I want to."

"Have you seen anyone bringing art to Butler's or meeting with him about art purchases? Anything like that?"

"No. I only go to his place on Tuesdays, so . . ." She shrugged. "Well, except that new guy — little white guy with orange hair. He came by, said he was a admirer. Finley let him in, too. They was talking big art talk. The little guy knew his stuff. But that's all."

"Now that's interesting," said Charlotte. "But no one else?"

"Well, your old friend, Mr. McMillan and his fiancée stopped by for a drink one afternoon. They was awfully interested in Finley's art. But everybody comes by the house acts interested in the art. If they don't, Finley gets 'em interested. Loves to show off them pictures."

The women were quiet for a while, mulling over the situation. Finally, Pup said, "So why you interested in *The Hermits*? Kinda funny, you asking me about that same picture that's been on my mind."

"Because I think that same painting might be hanging in a museum. I'm pretty sure I remember seeing it in a brochure."

"What?" said Pup, shaking her head. "Just like that movie? What am I mixed up in now?"

"Maybe nothing. I'll check it out. If *The Hermits* is hanging in two places at once, I'll have to tell Foster. He'll want to talk to you.

But I'm sure he can keep your name out of it."

"I knew I shouldn't've said nothing! I'm quitting Mr. Finley today."

"I don't blame you for not wanting to get involved, but if there is something going on, you don't want to draw attention to yourself by quitting. That Cliff guy could be dangerous."

"Lord, I ain't thought about that!"

"I'll call the museum in Houston today. Like I said, there could be a simple explanation for this. I doubt it, but I'll call you as soon as I find out. Then we can decide what to do. And don't mention it to anyone, okay?"

"You kidding? These lips is sealed, baby. Now I got to get going." She took her cell out of the pocket of her jeans and held it up. "Call me."

Two hours later, Charlotte called Pup.

"Hi, Pup. It's Charlotte. Well, *The Hermits* is hanging in the Museum of Fine Arts, Houston as we speak. The curator even sent me a picture of it. It's the same."

"I knew it. Lord, Jesus, I knew it."

"I'm sorry, but we can't just ignore it. You know that," she added gently.

"Would you give me the weekend to think on it?"

"Pup, we really should tell Butler right away. He'll want to report it to Foster."

"Just wait a little while. I got to think on this. Got to pray on it. Please."

What the heck, thought Charlotte. *What's one more secret? What's a few more days?*

"Okay," she said. "Til Monday."

As Charlotte clicked off, she heard a tapping on the front door of the gallery. It was Craig, peering through the window. When he saw Charlotte coming toward him, he held up a cup of coffee and a bag from the Big O Bakery.

He sat on his coveted bar stool and placed two still-warm, napkin-wrapped almond croissants on Charlotte's counter.

"First of all, I'm still hearing what a fabulous evening the Arcadio show made," he said. "Leon is over the moon over his moon painting."

"No buyer's remorse?"

"Not a smidgen."

"Great. By the way, have you talked to Maisy today? She hasn't returned my call." Charlotte sighed. "She's so old, I always worry when I don't hear from her."

"Maybe she's on a brunch date. It's all the rage with the post Viagra crowd." He took a bite of his croissant and rolled his eyes. "I mean, they can hardly stay awake til lunch — much less dinner. They have to party early in the day."

"I hate to change the subject from the partying habits of the — what did you call them — the post Viagra crowd? But what's the latest on the oil spill?"

"I guess you know that they've expanded fishing restrictions to almost forty percent of U.S. federal waters in the gulf."

"I heard."

"And the oil slick has slipped in through the pass. It's officially in the bay. They're hoping it'll leave with the tide, but it's gotten into the marsh."

"Good grief, it won't get any better, will it?"

"This is scarier than a category five hurricane," said Craig. "Which could happen in a matter of weeks. Can you even imagine that scenario?"

"No, I can't. What if they can't plug it? Ever."

Craig looked so dejected at this notion that Charlotte quickly added, "But we just cannot allow ourselves to go there."

"Right," said Craig. "Gloom and doom thinking isn't going to help anybody."

"So what else is going on?"

Craig looked over one shoulder then the other, raised his eyebrows and said, "There's been a little development in the case."

"What case?" teased Charlotte, though she was dying to know. She pinched off a piece of her pastry and popped it into her mouth. A little groan of ecstasy escaped her. "Heavenly," she said.

"The case of the purloined pelicans, of course," said Craig.

"You love saying that, don't you?"

"Yes. It sounds better than the case of the busted birds which is Maisy's quaint euphemism for our local mystery. Besides, it reminds me of Perry Mason." Craig sighed. "I had a huge crush on Raymond Burr, you know."

"Well he was a huge guy."

Craig pressed his lips together and rolled his eyes in mock exasperation. "Do you want to hear the news? Because I can take it right on down the street if you don't."

"Sorry. Of course I do."

"Well, it seems that the pelican painting stolen from Pup's church has been located."

"Thank God. Where?"

"On Finley's Landing. Butler told me about it himself."

"Now that is interesting."

"You know he has bought up a bunch of boats and turned them into VOOs. One of his crew found it behind that old shed."

"Vessels of Opportunity?"

"Yep. He's the captain of a whole fleet of VOOs."

"I knew he was using his own boat which was bad enough. I mean, really! He doesn't need the money."

"Well, evidently, he qualifies for the program because folks renting his condos on the beach have all bailed on him. He's lost a bundle, Charlotte. I noticed that he didn't buy a painting last night. That was most odd."

"I guess. It's just that so many folks are worse off than Butler Finley."

"He has a right to try and recoup his losses, Char. Anyway, in addition to *Air Apparent,* he has eight other boats of various sizes working as vessels of opportunity. And he's paying the VOO crews very generous wages." Craig leaned in across the counter and added, "But between you and me, he's still making a killing."

"Okay, Perry Mason, so what does this have to do with the case of the purloined pelicans?"

"The latest art show success has turned our little Charlotte quite spunky, hasn't it?" Craig said. He took a bite of his croissant and smiled at Charlotte. "I think I like it."

"The case?"

"Right. Butler has been keeping some of his boats in that old canal thing across the cove from Maisy."

Charlotte remembered the blue-hulled boat blasting out of there almost killing Harry and her and gave a shudder.

"Well, it seems that Butler found the church's painting over at the landing. He is just livid over it. He thinks one of the VOO crew could be responsible which makes him feel responsible. Foster is looking into it."

"Wow," said Charlotte, wondering if the homicidal blue boat could be involved in the pelican vandalism and thefts.

They concentrated on their croissants, chewing and moaning in delight over the orgasmic pastries.

When they'd finished, Charlotte thanked Craig for the treat and the gossip.

"There's more," said Craig.

"More calories or more info?"

"Info. I don't want to be responsible for ruining that pretty figure of yours."

"Are you sure you're gay?"

"Absolutely, but if I weren't —"

Charlotte smiled at her old friend. She knew he was sincere in his compliments. And his sexuality. It wasn't easy being gay in a small, southern town — even one as diversity-loving as East Oyster.

"Leon and I were out at Lowe Point yesterday and who do you think we saw at Gilda's?

"I have no idea."

"Butler Finley and Ms. Abigail Pitt herself. They were having an intimate lunch in that little corner booth that looks out on the water — drinking wine and everything. They were practically canoodling."

"Really."

"Yes. So when Ms. Pitt went to the ladies' I slipped over to have a word, and that's when he told me about the VOOs and the painting being found and everything. I just can't help but think that there is somethin' abrewin' between Butler and Abbie."

Charlotte was tempted to tell Craig about Harry's and Abbie's baffling bogus betrothal if for no other reason than he'd get such a kick out of having another "case." But as much as she loved her friend, he had some of the loosest lips Charlotte had ever encountered. She just wasn't sure he'd be able to keep such a development to himself.

To assuage her guilt, she said, "Craig, I've decided to lower the price on those bar stools before you wear the paint off of them."

"How much?"

"Oh, ten percent."

Craig stood, leaned across the desk and kissed her cheek.

"I'll think about it. But no discount. They're worth every penny you're asking. Have a good day."

"You, too. And, Craig?"

"Hmm?"

"I kind of had a crush on Perry Mason myself."

Craig was still chuckling as he pulled the door shut behind him.

29.
FEEDING THE MONSTER

It was Saturday afternoon. Nevin was working a rare weekend shift. Charlotte had just gotten comfortable on her chaise. She'd left a message for Maisy to call so they could discuss the latest turn of events in East Oyster's art world. As usual, there were more questions than answers.

For example, was Butler's fake painting somehow tied in with the faux pelican statues? Was it an incredible coincidence? Had the oil spill and the economy driven the honest folks of East Oyster, Alabama, into lives of crime? Had this kind of thing been going on under their very noses and they were just now getting wind of it?

Charlotte decided to give her brain a rest until she heard from Maisy. As a distraction, she picked up Harry's plans. She was giving them a final look when the clarinet ring tone from her cell told her Liza Jane was calling.

"Hi, L.J. What's up?"

"Put your party pants on because I'm taking you out to celebrate."

"What are we celebrating?"

"There's a decent band playing at the Crab."

"Sounds great, but it's been a tiring week."

"It's Saturday night!"

"I'm ten years older than you, remember? There's no way I'm going out tonight."

At seven o'clock, Charlotte found herself wearing her party pants and climbing into Liza Jane's SUV. At seven-thirty, they eased over the patchwork of oyster shells, asphalt and red clay that makes up the parking lot of Casa Crab. The place was packed.

"Is this free beer night or something?" asked Charlotte.

"Good band, remember?"

"Anybody I've ever heard of?"

"Who Else."

"Who else but who?"

"Who Else — that's the band. Obviously, you have not heard of them. But I think you'll like them. They have a great female singer. Sometimes she does old stuff. No offense."

"None taken," said Charlotte in a wounded voice.

Liza Jane laughed and continued searching for a parking place. She finally found one close to the road. They hopped out and made their way around pot holes and puddles to the Crab's front door.

The establishment's disgruntled, dyspeptic owner sat at his usual perch on a stool behind the love of his life — the cash drawer.

"Hi, Crabman," said Liza Jane.

"Ten dollar cover, unless you're a commercial fisherman. They get in free," he said, and held out a meaty hand. "Credit, debit or cash."

"My treat," said Liza Jane when Charlotte opened her purse.

"In that case, it'll be my pleasure to relieve you of twenty dollars, Ms. Bradford."

Liza Jane handed him a twenty, smiled sweetly at the old goat and ushered Charlotte to a table where they ordered fried shrimp with sides of hush puppies and slaw along with two beers.

"Asian shrimp, due to the spill," said Janine Jett as she set their plates down. "Never thought I'd see the day. They taste pretty good, but cost twice as much."

"How's Bobby?"

"He's alive."

Charlotte and Liza Jane waited for her to elaborate, but she simply said, "I'll check back with y'all in a few minutes."

By nine o'clock there wasn't a seat left in the place. Even the outside porch was standing room only. Guitars, keyboard and a very large female singer had somehow managed to fit into a corner of the Crab. The air-conditioning had gone into overdrive, but with all the hot bods, the Crab was still pretty steamy.

If anything, Liza Jane had understated the entertainment. Charlotte loved the mix of old and new tunes, the traditional as well as funky sounds the three members of *Who Else* put together. The female singer and lead guitarist had great voices with unbelievable range.

It wasn't long before a couple of Liza Jane's young cowboy buddies walked over.

"Would you ladies consider sharing your table?" the tallest one said.

"Well, it's kind of girls' night out," Liza Jane said.

"It's fine with me," said Charlotte who had totally gotten into the swing of things. The great music, general convivial atmosphere of the Crab crowd and Liza Jane's infectious party vibe had conspired to put Charlotte in a very un-Charlotte mood.

The cowboys were cute, charming and insisted on buying the cousins a couple of Pink Meanies to show their appreciation for the shared table.

"Woo," said Charlotte. "Is it just me, or is the bartender being a bit heavy-handed tonight?"

The cowboy who'd gotten the drinks caught the bartender's eye and gave him a thumb's up. The bartender grinned and responded likewise.

Charlotte laughed and said, "Remind me to sip this."

But of course, she didn't.

Besides being pretty and quite tasty, like its namesake killer jellyfish (so mean it eats other jellyfish), the Pink Meanie cocktail has quite the sting. There is even a sign posted in the women's restroom (aka Gull's) warning female customers. It is an actual jellyfish warning sign like you'd see at the beach — the signature umbrella-shaped body with trailing tentacles encased in a circle and crossed with a line. Only the Crab's version is pink.

Charlotte couldn't figure out why the very cute, very young guy named Brady wanted to sit and talk and dance with the likes of a woman of Charlotte's advanced maturity. So she decided not to try and just have a good time for a change. Besides, she was wearing her party pants — that pair of butt-enhancing white jeans that Liza Jane had complimented her on. She'd also gotten a cut-n-color from Honey the hairdresser and was wearing a chest-and-waist enhancing (yet tasteful and appropriate-for-her-age, she would report) striped top. And though a bit on the rusty side, Charlotte was a really good dancer. In other words, the outfit, hair and dancing ability bolstered by a Meanie-induced shot of confidence, had her feeling almost as cute as Brady.

When she and Brady had returned from yet another spin around the tiny, packed dance floor, she looked into her glass and exclaimed, "Oh, no! My Meanie's all gone!"

Of course, Brady said (in a manly voice) that he could fix that.

"No, what I mean is, I had intended it to last me the whole night!" Thankfully she didn't add, I'll be up all night with acid reflux! Because that's what she was thinking.

But she and everyone else at the table were laughing, and before she knew it a brand new Pink Meanie was sitting before her. And gee, it tasted even better than the first one. She looked at her watch. Ten forty-five. She would not allow herself another sip until eleven.

It was at this point that she happened to glance out onto the porch and see two familiar faces. Charlotte could tell by the glowering — yes, glowering, she decided — expressions on their faces that they were not having nearly as much fun as she. And this made her so happy that she took an unauthorized sip of her Meanie. You see, the two unhappy faces belonged to none other than Abbie and Harry.

How long have they been here? she wondered.

Liza Jane leaned across the table and said, "They've been here for an hour."

Charlotte smiled at her devious cousin. "Really?" she said.

Liza Jane smiled back and nodded and headed over to the band as they ended the set. Charlotte quickly lost interest in Liza Jane's activities because Brady was complimenting her on her shirt. And her smile. And her personality.

She just said, "Oh, that is so sweet," which sounded like something she would have said in junior high. But thanks to the Meanies, she didn't care. However, in order to mask her small social lapse, she took another unauthorized sip of her drink.

This seemed to satisfy Brady who smiled at her like she was queen of the rodeo or something.

He really is nice, she thought as he excused himself to the men's restroom (aka Buoys).

She was beginning to understand L.J.'s attraction to guys like Brady.

Charlotte occupied herself by trying to remember how long it had been since her last sip of Pink Meanie. Finally, she lifted the glass, studied the amount left in it and decided that she'd hardly had any at all. She allowed herself another swallow.

As she set the glass down Brady slid into the chair beside her. Except when she looked, it wasn't Brady at all. It was Harry.

"Hello, Harry."

"Charlotte."

Charlotte felt her face twisting up with emotion. Tears sprang like missiles from her eyes.

Darn these Meanies! she thought.

She grabbed a cocktail napkin and dabbed at her eyes, aware she was probably smudging her mascara, but again, thanks to the Meanies, she didn't care.

"How dare you call me Charlotte!" she hissed.

Harry had had a couple of Meanies himself. As a matter of fact, he'd had three. This was enough alcohol to make him completely oblivious to Abbie's growing discomfort as he scowled at the tall, young, good-looking cowboy who had spent the better part of the evening pressed up against Charlie on

317

the dance floor. *When not plying her with alcohol,* he reminded himself.

Abbie, who'd been nursing a lite beer and a growing resentment over Harry's total infatuation with Charlotte, decided she couldn't take it any more. Thankfully, she had taken her meds which enabled her to ask calmly, "Harrison, may I have the car keys, please?"

Harry absent-mindedly handed them over and didn't notice his fiancée's absence until she was halfway back to Pitt Cottage. To his credit, he did try her cell, leaving an apologetic message and asking her to call once she was home safely. But when he saw the young stud in the cowboy boots — the one who'd been buying Charlie drinks all night with only one thing on his mind — head for the head, he'd decided it was time to take action. All thoughts of Abbie evaporated into the heavy atmosphere of Casa Crab.

He didn't have a plan exactly when he took the cowboy's place next to Charlotte, but he did plan to take charge of the situation. The circumstances called for a level of formality, hence his decision to address her as Charlotte. It seemed to have had a sobering effect on her at the art show, so it seemed the best way to begin. When she started to cry, he realized that he'd probably gotten off on the wrong foot.

This was just about the time Brady, the quintessential southern gentleman, exited the Bouys'. It only took one good, hard look for him to ascertain the situation at his table. In the time it had taken for him to relieve himself, some old dude had not only moved in on Charlotte, for whom he'd been buying drinks all night, but now the guy was making her cry. Brady squinted up his eyes, set his square jaw and adopting what he thought of as a menacing swagger, he started across the room.

Liza Jane had pretty much orchestrated the whole evening. (She'd heard from Craig that Harry was a fan of Who Else and would be in attendance at the Crab for their performance.) She now watched the proceedings unfolding at Charlotte's table like a mother hawk and wasn't about to let young Brady, pumped up on testosterone and tequila, gum up the works.

She neatly intercepted Brady, flashed him a mega-smile, looked up into his flinty, squinty eyes and said, "What's the problem, cowboy?"

"Something unpleasant is going on with your cousin, and I plan on fixin' it," he said in a deep, slow drawl.

Liza Jane was reminded why she loved

319

these young bucks and almost lost sight of her mission. But she got hold of herself and said, "They're old friends. What do you say we have a beer and let them talk it out?"

Brady looked over at the table where things seemed to have simmered down. Besides, he didn't really want to get into it with an old guy. He grinned at Liza Jane, took her by the arm and led her to the bar.

Oblivious to Brady and Liza Jane, Harry was now trying to solve the unsolvable dilemma of how to win Charlotte's complete trust without providing her with a complete explanation as to exactly what he and Abbie were doing in East Oyster. He realized he'd pushed Charlotte's patience far beyond most women's endurance level, but he had to have more time before the whole story came out. He owed Abbie that much.

"Charlie, I'm sorry." He shook his head. "I know you've heard enough apologies from me to last a lifetime. It's time for some explanations." The band was starting up again, and the tables were too close for serious conversation, so he said, "Do you think we could step outside for a few minutes? I have something I need to tell you."

Charlotte's curiosity was so overwhelming, her judgment so impaired by Pink Meanies and her desire to clear Harry so great that she agreed.

Out in the parking lot, a sea breeze rustled palms. From where they stood, near the quiet side of Casa Crab they could see the moon floating like an enormous pearl over the gulf. It reflected a ribbon of light across the water and bathed Charlotte and Harry in its glow.

"First of all," said Harry, "I'm sorry I called you Charlotte."

The sea air had Charlotte's Pink Meanie fog lifting somewhat. But it was just enough for her to realize that she was in no shape to discuss the ins and outs of Harry's and Abbie's plan to find the person responsible for her brother's death.

"That's okay," she said. "I guess I over-reacted a bit. But Harry, if you brought me out here to discuss the strange tale of the faux fiancée this is neither the time nor the place. I intend to have my wits about me when we talk about it." She inhaled a deep breath of fresh air and let it out. "I swear these Meanies have got me so I can't think straight."

"That's not why I asked you to come out here. I was watching you tonight, and I re-alized that I couldn't let another day, another minute go by without telling you one thing. And I wanted to say it in the

321

moonlight . . ."

Charlotte looked into his misty eyes, the moonlight setting off his lovely features, the absolute magnetism of him so close and thought if she didn't hear those three wonderful words from Harry she would explode. She threw her arms out in exasperation and almost lost her balance in the sand.

"What, Harry? What?"

Harry grinned at her as he had that first day at the café in Cassis.

"I love you, Charlie. I have always loved you."

Charlotte was so overcome with joy and relief she thought she might faint. She noticed Harry looking at her expectantly.

"Oh, Harry! I love you, too." She threw her arms around his neck and kissed Harry McMillan like he hadn't been kissed in over twenty years.

A half-hour later a wind-blown but happy Charlotte entered Casa Crab with Harry. Crabman gave them a suspicious look, but waved them through without asking for another ten bucks each. Liza Jane and Brady, who seemed to have lost all interest in Charlotte, were on the dance floor. When Liza Jane saw Charlotte and Harry, she could tell by their faces that something very good had taken place. She smiled to herself and gave the female singer a little wave.

The singer nodded and said into the mike, "Okay, for all you Abba fans out there . . . y'all do remember Abba, don't you?"

Approximately a fourth of the room cheered in the affirmative.

"Well, we're gonna make sure that after tonight, everybody will remember Abba. We'll start with my favorite — a little song called *Dancing Queen*."

Charlotte and Harry looked at each other.

"I think they're playing our song," said Harry, holding out a hand."

"And I think I know who's behind this," said Charlotte, looking over at her cousin. Liza Jane gave an innocent little shrug and turned back to Brady.

The keyboard player ran a finger over the keys in the song's familiar opening and the singer began, "You can dance, you can jive, having the time of your life." And anyone in Casa Crab who hadn't known Abba became an immediate fan.

Charlotte and Harry launched into their old disco routine as if they had been doing it every Saturday night, and it was so impressive (and strange) that the dancers on the floor stepped back to watch them. Charlotte became the Dancing Queen of her youth and once again Harry was king. As the keyboard finished up, Harry dipped Charlotte without dropping her and with only a moment's hesitation planted the Hollywood kiss of all Hollywood kisses on her.

When he had her upright again, she was flushed, dizzy, a bit embarrassed but extremely happy. The tipsy crowd thought the whole thing was a hoot and cheered. Charlotte grinned at Harry, who took several well-deserved bows.

Liza Jane turned back to Brady and said, "Now aren't you glad you didn't beat him up?"

30.
PAYING THE PIPER

The following morning Charlotte woke up with a colossal headache, a tongue that felt like it was wearing a sweater and a case of bed head so severe that she startled herself when she looked in the mirror. Unfortunately, these were the typical symptoms of a Pink Meanie attack. The sting of the Meanie, though severe is rarely fatal, and responds fairly well to a double dose of the usual hangover remedies.

Charlotte started with strong coffee and dry toast followed by antacid tablets followed by a couple of Advil followed by a drive to Downydew for a swim in the bay. (All East Oysterites know that having one's head completely submerged in cool to cold water does amazing things for the critically hung over.)

As she was turning into Maisy's drive, Butler Finley's BMW exited the Pitt driveway. In it were Butler and Abbie. Butler wore a coat and tie, and Abbie had a feathery fascinator attached to her gleaming brunette head. Charlotte remembered that it was Sunday. Naturally, Butler was always in the front pew of Our Lady of Perpetual Succor (referred to as Our Lady's, for brevity's sake.)

So Butler and Abbie were going to church together?

Charlotte's headache intensified and her stomach took a little lurch. She had momentarily forgotten that any thought more complicated than where are the aspirin can exacerbate a hangover. She massaged her temple and foolishly continued thinking.

Maybe Liza Jane is right. Maybe there is something going on between Abbie and Butler. And maybe she has lost interest in Harry.

This final thought made her smile. But the small rearrangement of facial muscles intensified her headache, so as she parked behind Maisy's house Charlotte decided to put all thoughts out of her Meanie-soaked brain

The old lady's car was gone. Like everyone else, she was probably at church. As Maisy says, East Oyster is one church-going town. There are more churches than there are gas stations — a different denomination on

326

every corner. The thought made Charlotte feel just the tiniest bit guilty, but she was grateful to have the place to herself. Besides, in her present state conversation of any kind was impossible. And she didn't trust herself too far from a bathroom.

The oil had retreated back through the pass when the tide went out, leaving the bay in its pre-violated state, but Charlotte noticed a black "tide line" along the sea grass to the left of Maisy's beach as she swam lazily back and forth. She wondered about the baby shrimp and crabs that started their lives in the grass. Had the oil gotten to them?

As predicted, the cool water had the desired effect, and Charlotte's head stopped throbbing and subsided to a small, dull ache. Her stomach quieted down, and her achy muscles responded gratefully to the weightless stretching of her limbs as she paddled around.

When Maisy got back from St. John's eleven o'clock service and found her niece floating like a cork at the end of her pier, she ascertained the problem and fixed them both bowls of bland soup with saltines and cokes over ice. Charlotte pulled on a cover-up and slumped into a chair on Maisy's porch.

After the second coke, Charlotte realized that her headache had finally disappeared, and though she was still a bit shaky, she felt well enough for both thought and conversation. She told Maisy about the forgery hanging in Butler Finley's house.

"Pup already filled me in," said Maisy. "She came by yesterday. Very upset. She should tell Foster right away. But only Foster. Not Butler. Only Foster."

"I think you're right," said Charlotte.

"We were out here fishing when you called. By the time she left, I guess you were already out on the town." She smirked at her niece.

"So, how did you know I have a hangover?"

"I ran into your buddy, Harry this morning. Said y'all closed down the Crab." She shook her head. "He looked almost as bad as you. He'll be here in a few minutes."

"What? Harry's coming here?"

Charlotte put thoughts of art forgeries out of her mind as she remembered the shock she'd received when she'd looked in her bathroom mirror. She hadn't had the nerve to recheck her appearance, but she figured it couldn't have improved by much.

"Yep. Should be here in about ten minutes. I hope you've got a comb and some make-up in your purse because you're look-ing a little peaked, if you don't mind me saying so."

As Charlotte hurried to Maisy's powder room, the old lady called, "There's a hair dryer in the drawer."

When Charlotte emerged from the bath-room fifteen minutes later, she was almost her old self. This was a good thing because Harry McMillan sat at Maisy's table enjoy-ing the same lunch that the old lady had served Charlotte. He was wearing a yellow golf shirt he'd probably slept in and a pair of faded khaki shorts. He was barefoot.

When Harry saw Charlotte, a grin spread across his unshaven face and his bloodshot eyes lit up with happiness. He slowly (pain-fully?) stood up as she approached the table.

"Hi, Charlie," he said, still smiling. He started to sit back down but winced, then let himself into the chair slowly. "I think I did something to my back last night."

Maisy's eyebrows went up and she pressed her wrinkly little lips together to suppress a smile.

"We were dancing, Maisy," said Charlotte.

"Oh." The old lady seemed disappointed.

"I think it was that last move," Harry said. "Guess I'm a little rusty."

Charlotte laughed and sat down at the

table. "You should have seen him, Maisy. He was very impressive. Cleared the dance floor at the Crab."

"And don't forget the applause," said Harry.

"Right. And he received a very enthusiastic round of applause."

"Actually, we got a round of applause," said Harry. "We all know Fred is nothing without Ginger."

"That is so true," agreed Charlotte.

When Harry had finished off a second bowl of soup and his second Coke, he turned to Maisy.

"You've saved my life, Maisy. I feel almost human again. You know, I seem to remember that in St. Yves, a dip in the sea was the ultimate cure for the over-served."

"Charlie here has already taken a swim," said Maisy.

"Proof that it works," said Harry, smiling at Charlotte who hadn't even noticed Maisy's mispronunciation of her name. "Would you ladies care to accompany me out to the pier?"

And so the threesome strolled back out to the pier where Harry stood on the edge of the lower section (which East Oysterites refer to as the crab wharf), pulled his shirt over his head, dropped it onto the sun-silvered boards, held out his muscular arms and fell backward into the bay. Charlotte remembered him doing the same thing in St. Yves all those summers ago. It was good to know that a lot of the boy remained in Harry McMillan.

"God, this feels good," he called.

So Charlotte peeled off her cover-up and jumped in.

"What are you waiting for, Maisy?" called Harry.

Maisy kicked off her shoes and took off her watch. And in her church clothes, from the highest level of the pier, the old character executed a first-rate cannonball.

It took another forty minutes or so, but finally Harry announced himself hangover-free. They climbed out of the bay and lay in the sun. They closed their eyes and watched the hot rays turn the inside of their eyelids red as they had all done when they were kids.

But soon Charlotte's fair skin started turning pink so they moved into the shade. Maisy handed out ice cream sandwiches. (She kept these in her freezer for the neighbor children who had come to expect it whenever they visited.) No one had mentioned oil, art or Abbie the Pitt for hours. It was simply glorious!

However, their minds eventually returned to the serious matters that plagued their equanimity. It was Maisy who first broached the subject of the recent troubles.

"Harry, why don't we tell Charlie what we were discussing yesterday?"

"Maisy and I have decided to throw a party."

"Really. What's the occasion?"

"The return of the pelican statues to East Oyster," said Harry."

"I'm totally there," said Maisy when Charlotte looked doubtful.

"Abbie has agreed to let us have it at Pitt Cottage," continued Harry.

"Sooo, I take it that this . . . this pelican party falls into Abbie's plan to find the mystery man she holds responsible for her brother's death?" Charlotte said, thinking it out as she spoke.

"Yes," said Maisy and Harry at once.

Charlotte was starting to feel out of step with these two. When she thought about it, they were all a bit out of step with one another.

I have ideas I'm not sharing. Pup and I — and now Maisy — know about the fake art and Cliff; Harry and Abbie know who it is they followed to East Oyster that they blame for Tim's death. Harry has confided in some "authorities" who may or may not be in contact with Foster. Harry has told me he is in love with me, but I doubt that he's shared that with Abbie. How did he know where the key to the shed on Finley's Landing is located? And then there's Aunt Maisy. Between her instincts, people's propensity for confiding in her and Crystal's revelations, there's no telling what else she knows. If we all shared info — not to mention trust in one another — maybe some things would be cleared up!

Charlotte became aware that Harry was speaking to her.

"Hey Charlie . . . you still with us?"

"Sorry, I was just thinking." And she relayed her views on the benefits of sharing information. "I mean we can trust one another, right?"

But Maisy and Harry were silent. Finally Maisy said, "It's . . ."

"Complicated?" Charlotte interrupted.

"Yes." She reached over and rubbed Charlotte's knee, which had an oddly soothing effect. "I understand your frustration. It's just that we have to be extremely careful in whom we lay our trust. And in whom we confide." She smiled sweetly at Charlotte. "As Foster is fond of saying, loose lips can indeed sink ships."

Charlotte knew that when Maisy spoke in

333

this formal manner it meant that she was deadly serious.

But surely she's not suggesting that I can't be trusted not to blab to the wrong person!

"I can keep a secret," said Charlotte with a little sniff.

Harry and Maisy looked at one another. Maisy's eyebrows rose as if to say, *I don't know.* Harry shrugged.

But as much as they wanted to confide in their beloved blabbermouth, they just couldn't take the chance that her very loose lips might botch their well-laid plans — or worse — sink her own ship. After all, there was real danger in dealing with these people, at least one of whom was a criminal.

And so for the next hour and a half Harry, Maisy and Charlotte shared *most* of what they knew and *almost* everything they thought they knew. And when Charlotte pressed for the identity of the mysterious person Abbie had tracked to East Oyster, Harry said it was turning into a dead end and so he'd better not say.

This was obviously a fib. When Charlotte started to object, Maisy reached over and rubbed her knee and said, "Harry is right not to confuse the issue with erroneous information."

The "authorities" Harry was working with

were known as ORCA or the Organization for Research into Crimes against Art. Yes, art. The trouble that Abbie's brother had gotten himself involved in was all about art — and the looting, trafficking, fraud and forgery thereof.

ORCA was academic in nature, but worked closely with the FBI and police departments large enough to have an art detail — such as the LAPD — as well as museum security firms. They even had a blog where missing artwork and known criminals were listed. This was where Harry had come across them. They had indeed been in touch with Foster, but had gotten a cool reception from the overworked, over-stressed police chief. So they were counting on Harry, following his and Abbie's progress and offering assistance in the way of advice as well as piles of art info stored in their many files and databases. Discretion was paramount, the ORCA official assured him, to a successful conclusion in the quest of the — to use Craig's description — pelican perps.

"So there is a connection between Tim's suicide and the pelican art," said Charlotte.

"Well, we don't know that for sure," said Maisy, but the look in the old lady's eye had Charlotte thinking that Maisy had a pretty good idea as to what was going on.

Thankfully, Charlotte didn't have to raise the question of Harry and the key to the shed. The issue of Finley's Landing and the children's notion that the shed was a "store" was broached by Maisy. Harry explained he'd overheard the children and wondered if some other stolen loot might be stored there.

"I'm pretty sure it was Cliff who almost ran us over when we were floundering that night," he said. His eyes narrowed and he clenched his strong jaw, sending a delightful, little shiver through Charlotte. "I went to check the whole area out the next morning," he continued, "Just after the VOO boats left. The shed was locked, but I found the key on the edge of the roof."

"How'd you think to look there?" asked Maisy.

Charlotte was wondering the same thing.

"Because at my height, that's probably where I'd have put it. Cliff is even taller than I am, and so that's the first place I looked. Anyway, the shed was empty. I went back after the kids called it a store, thinking maybe Cliff was behind all of this and was using the shed to stash . . ."

"Hot art?" suggested Charlotte.

"Maybe. Although that seemed unlikely

with all the VOO activity going on there. Just like before, the place was empty. But you know what? It smelled like the gallery . . . like oil paint." He shrugged. "I don't know. Maybe I imagined it."

This left the subject of Charlotte and Harry. Had Harry revealed his true feelings for her to Abbie? Charlotte didn't want to raise the touchy subject in front of Maisy. And she really didn't want to hear the answer. No, it would upset the Abbie's fragile constitution. *We've come this far. Just trust me a little longer.*

There was also the amazing coincidence of the Marseille/East Oyster connection and Harry's connection to that part of France and this part of Alabama. The fact that Maisy didn't seem concerned about this — well, it eased Charlotte's apprehensions. She decided not to think about it.

Once they'd thoroughly discussed the strange occurrences and correlation of events in little, old East Oyster, they voiced theories — each in various stages of completion — as to what exactly was going on and how it was all connected. Next they formulated a plan to go about proving once and for all, which theory was correct. This naturally led to rudimentary plans for the party where, as Maisy put it, "all would be revealed."

First of all, Pink Meanies would not be served. Though it might be helpful if the suspects were bombed, and Harry and Charlotte needn't worry — they'd sworn off the wicked concoctions for life — the infamous Meanie was still a danger to the other innocent party-goers. Lemonade and beer and bottled water would be the beverages of choice.

Since the moratorium on local seafood was in effect, hotdogs, potato salad and coleslaw provided by the Backyard Grill would have to suffice. Maisy insisted on picking up the tab. She also agreed to set up her tent on the front lawn of Pitt Cottage since Abbie did not allow spooky crystal balls — or Maisy, for that matter — in her house.

The festivities would begin at seven-thirty and be well under way after sundown when it was cooler. And darker. Because subterfuge works better in the dark. Maisy and Harry would see to it that all of the unusual suspects would be gathered. That was paramount.

"And we need to run this by Foster," said Maisy. "He probably won't like it, but he'll go along. Now if you two will excuse me, I'm in need of a nap. Make yourselves at home. Just pull the back door to when you leave."

Having talked the particulars of "the case" to death, Harry's and Charlotte's conversation turned to the renovation of her apartment. When she told him she'd hoped to get it far enough along to host her son's new girlfriend in mid-August, he let out a low whistle. But then he smiled at her and said, "Can we start this week?"

"You can do that?"

"I think so. Unfortunately, there are a lot of desperate people looking for work. They would probably start this afternoon if they could. I bet we can get most of the inside work done in a couple of weeks. Even the kitchen, if we don't make changes to the plans. We can finish up the outside after the kids have left."

"You're sure we're not cutting it too close?"

Harry kissed her cheek and reminded her of her own words concerning trust.

"Trust me, Charlie. It's all going to work out."

Charlotte believed him. She felt optimistic about the outcome of not only her apartment renovations, but everything — even the horrible, dreadful oil spill.

As she parked next to her courtyard gate,

she had already begun mental lists of what she would need to do to ready her apartment for the invasion of workers that would happen in a few days: Move and cover furniture, empty closets and cabinets, go over paint colors and kitchen appliance choices with Liza Jane . . .

Her cell began to chime. It was Craig. As usual, he had news. Foster was in the hospital. He'd had a heart attack.

31.
LIFE GOES ON

The second in command at the East Oyster police department was a guy named Douglas Feiffer. Rarely rivaled in incompetence, Deputy Feiffer made Mayberry's Barney Fife look like Sherlock Holmes. To darken the cloud of his persona, Douglas's ineptitude was surpassed only by his lack of people skills. So it wasn't surprising that behind his back and occasionally to his face, the usually kind-hearted citizenry referred to him as Duggie, Deputy Phife or even Barney. You have to earn disrespect in East Oyster.

Most of the townsfolk figured their own bumbling deputy was at least partly responsible for his boss's hospitalization. And now, at least for the time being, the short arm of the law was in charge. The folks sighed and shook their heads and asked each other, could things get any worse?

Well, of course they could.

Every U.S. gulf state — Texas, Louisiana, Mississippi, Alabama and Florida — had now been soiled by the spill. In some cases, visitors were forced to pack their bags (and their wallets) and leave the shores.

When the beaches weren't closed, workers close to heat stroke in protective suits vied with bikini-clad sunbathers for a spot. It was a bizarre sight. Mostly, the clean-up was effective. Most areas were quickly put back into pristine condition.

On other days, as Craig reported, "The sun and the water are the same. The restaurants and shops and bars are the same. But no one is there. On Friday, there was just one blue heron looking out across the gulf. Like he was wondering, you know? It's eerie is what it is."

Craig wasn't alone. The sight of tar-removal workers and equipment — or worse, empty beaches during the height of tourist season — sent a ripple of angst along the entire gulf coast from the Texas Coast to the Florida Keys.

There were smidgens of good news. Giant sheets of oil were being burned or skimmed off. Hurricane Alex was downgraded to a tropical storm, though it still threatened to push even more oily water farther into delicate ecosystems.

Coastal inhabitants were exhausted from worrying about Hurricane Alex. Downgraded to a tropical storm, he didn't do much damage after all. But the episode was a cruel reminder that hurricane season was indeed upon them. Storm tracking is a headache for weather-weary coast dwellers, but throw in a busted behemoth of a well and millions of gallons of oil, and you've got yourself a major migraine.

Not surprisingly, the Fourth of July came and went with a sputter instead of the usual bang.

Meanwhile, the little group of amateur sleuths were on a conference call deciding that they had no option but to go ahead with their plans to party themselves into some answers. It was the Cocktail Cove solution to most things, and there was no sense in upsetting poor Foster who was facing not only rehab but a mountain of depressing dietary restrictions. And they certainly couldn't let Deputy Feiffer in on things as he would surely screw everything up. Pup was especially glad to hear all this because it meant that she wouldn't be required to "get herself in the middle of it." At least not yet.

To ease their consciences about not consulting Foster or the now acting-chief-of-police Feiffer, Harry, Maisy, Charlotte and Liza Jane (who had been deputized by Maisy and sworn to secrecy by the rest of the group) were overly kind to Feiffer even though power had gone straight to his empty head and made him more inept and insufferable than ever. They also brought cards and flowers to Foster and stowed healthy casseroles in their freezers for him to feast on upon his release from the rehab center.

All of this took place as the plans for the Pitt party shaped up and framers and plumbers and painters demolished Charlotte's apartment. Enormous plastic sheets separated the spaces to be renovated from the spaces to be merely painted. Her bedroom and dining room furniture was crammed into the non-reno space.

Every evening she crawled across her dining table to get into her bed, praying that she wouldn't have to make a trip to the bathroom during the night. She ate take-out for dinner and breakfasted at the Big O. One had only to look at Foster to know where that road led.

There was no time for painting (excepting walls). The picture she was working on had been moved down into the gallery's store room, but she was too tired to deal with it anyway. She was getting to bed later, getting up earlier and was lucky to eke out a twenty minute run in the mornings.

The bright spots in this sea of chaos were that she could see progress daily if not hourly, she loved all the changes, and Harry was there every day. Together they solved the many small and not so small problems inherent in redoing an old space. For the most part, they managed to laugh their way through the stress.

Many days they had lunch in the courtyard, careful not to discuss "the case" or their relationship lest the workers overhear. And this turned out to be a good thing because they talked about the renovations, about their children, about books and art and fishing, about the weather — anything and everything but "the big stuff." They got to know each other all over again.

Was it the same as it had been when they'd discovered each other in Saint-Yves-Sur-Mer? They each turned this over in their minds. And if anyone had quizzed them about it, their thoughts would be surprisingly similar, their answers an unequivocal yes. If there was a difference, it lay in their maturity.

Seeing each other through time-worn eyes made them grateful. They understood what they'd had and that it was rare and special. They understood the enormity of their loss. As Maisy would have put it, "second chances are fate's treasures." All these years later, the hollow spaces in their hearts were beginning to fill. Though they had not spoken these thoughts aloud, it was in their eyes and weary smiles as they hurried past one another during the hectic days of renovation.

Harry reluctantly retired to the guest quarters of Pitt Cottage each evening since Abbie insisted that the faux engagement continue. It was critical to their plan, she said. And they had both witnessed the other side of Abbie when things didn't go her way.

Still, it made little sense to Charlotte since Abbie was spending more and more time with Butler Finley. The oil spill was a prime topic of conversation. But according to Craig, the tongues of East Oyster were beginning to wag about Butler and Abbie.

And Abbie has to be aware of this, thought Charlotte. *So why is she insisting on the engagement charade? Because she still has a thing for Harry?*

Charlotte filed these questions away in her mental to-be-answered-later folder.

When she broached the subject with Harry, he sighed a tired sigh and said, "I don't really know." And with a touch of irritation he added, "Look, Charlie, I'm just trying to keep her from completely losing it. We're so close to the end of all this."

She vowed not to ask him again, but desperately needed to talk it over with someone. She was practically in withdrawal from not being able to hash things out with Liza Jane.

Liza Jane, who had apparently shed her cougar skin, was spending more and more time in Florida. Short emails concerning appliance choices, etc. were all Charlotte was getting from her cousin these days. But she had promised to help Charlotte "fluff" her apartment as soon as the paint dried. That was great, but even more than decorating expertise, Charlotte needed a girlfriend fix!

According to Maisy when they finally got around to the reading Maisy had promised Liza Jane, the subject of her love life had Crystal humming. That's all Maisy would say on the matter, but since the reading, Charlotte's cousin, best friend and main confidante was spending every spare moment with Grant.

And why not? thought Charlotte.

Like most businesses along the coast, Pelican's Nest Interiors was suffering the destructive ripple effects of an oil spill on top of a flailing economy. No money and fears of oil-covered beaches and tainted seafood meant no tourists which meant no wear and tear on condos and beach houses.

Who needs or wants to spruce up lease-less rental properties? Who's going to spend money on the luxury of redoing a beach house that the owners might not be able to enjoy (or continue owning) for the foreseeable future?

Liza Jane sent regular updates on the ranch restoration in the form of pictures emailed to Charlotte. Since she was involved in her own redo, Charlotte was fascinated watching the process as Liza Jane worked her magic on what she referred to as "a sprawling man-cave." Day by day she transformed the tired furnishings and paint colors into a modern, masculine, comfortable home that any rancher would be proud to own. It was still full of leather and cowhide and antlers, but the fresh paint, light slipcovers, new lighting and a few abstracts from Turner Gallery had it looking fresh and modern.

The most impressive transformation, however, was in L.J. herself. To the dismay of East Oyster's frisky male population, she'd apparently traded in the whole herd of young bucks for her one authentic cow-boy.

Charlotte agreed with Maisy that "love looks good on Liza Jane." In the opinion of Pup and her church friends, Lucy Bradford might just calm down now that her wild offspring "had herself a man." Craig, who had a soft spot from here to Cuba, was enthralled that someone had managed to "lasso Liza J's heart" and wanted all the details. Charlotte had no idea what Abbie thought about her match-making gone awry, but it was a safe bet that she wasn't happy about it.

Liza Jane and Grant rode the ranch by horseback and pickup. They joined committees to raise money for victims of the spill. Weekends found them heading to New Orleans to soak up jazz and look for fixtures, furniture and art for Grant's house. They signed up for cooking classes under the city's hottest new chef proving that wonders indeed never cease. Because as far as Charlotte knew, Liza Jane had never boiled an egg.

Derek worked more hours now that school was out for the summer. His framing skills improved, and he was finally getting the hang (so to speak) of working in a gallery around so many precious things. But Charlotte noticed that he was becoming more interested in the goings on upstairs and jumped at any chance to be helpful to Harry or his subs. Swinging a hammer or playing assistant to electricians and plumbers was obviously more intriguing to Derek than unpacking lovely pieces of art and helping customers decide on just the right matting for their purchases.

Pup had returned to Butler's house on consecutive Tuesdays since they had discovered the forgery. The fact that no one had clued Butler in on the fake art adorning his wall had them all nervous, but Maisy had declared continued secrecy paramount to success. Exactly to the success of what, Charlotte and Pup couldn't say, but they'd learned long ago the futility of arguing with Maisy Downy.

According to Pup, Cliff was around Butler Finley's house more than ever. As far as Cliff was concerned, Pup was of no more interest than one of Butler's yellow labs. Insulting as this was, ultimately it was a good thing. She'd easily eavesdropped on him chatting away in his truck as she let the dogs in and out, watered the potted ferns or took the garbage out. "Besides," Charlotte had said, "Who wants the attentions of the Cliffs of the world anyway?"

Pup had to agree.

Pup heard Cliff mention "the Pitt woman" and "pelicans." And once, she'd heard him mention the name of the person he was talking to. Someone named Ed.

"I ain't heard no last name. Could be anybody. But with all the laughing and cussing going on, the guy was a big buddy of his," said Pup.

"Was he talking about pelican statues?"

"I don't know. I was just catching bits, you know. But I think it was statues 'cause he said something 'bout pieces of pelicans."

"The only pieces from the East Oyster pelicans are in the police department." Charlotte sighed. "When you threw out the pieces of Butler's pelican . . ."

Before Charlotte could finish her sentence, Pup interrupted. "Now hold up a minute. I ain't throwed out nothing!"

"I thought Butler said you threw out the pieces of his bird — not knowing a crime had been committed, of course."

"See? I'm gonna end up in trouble over this 'fore it's all over. I did not want to be in the middle . . ."

"Calm down, Pup. We are absolutely not in trouble! I bet Butler will give you a reward for finding out about the forgery. And as far as exposing his disloyal em-

351

ployee, Cliff, is concerned, you're doing him a huge favor."

"Now why am I doubting that? Kill the messenger! Ever hear of that?"

This time it was Charlotte who had to agree.

32.
HALLELUJAH, BABY!

By the middle of July there was news of yet another "cap" on the well. Understandably, folks were skeptical. After all, the Macondo well had worn more bizarre, ineffective hats than Eunice Toowell. Why should this one be any different?

But subsequent testing indicated that the flow of oil into the gulf had indeed been stopped for the first time since April twentieth. Though a relief well would have to be drilled to complete the fix, glimmers of hope began to make their way into jaded coastal souls. And before long, hope turned to belief. It looked like the nightmare of spewing crude was finally over. There were high-fives and exclamations of joy from Texas to Florida, but no one put it better than Pup.

When Derek told her the news, she grinned at her grandson and said, "Hallelujah, Baby!"

The government announced that three

quarters of the oil that had leaked into the Gulf of Mexico had been cleaned up or broken down by natural forces.

"It's good news, alright," said Maisy. "Depending on whose estimate you go with, that well leaked from two to four and a half million gallons of oil. By my calculations that leaves about a million gallons of oil in the water and marshes and beaches. I know it's a big gulf, but that's one heck of a lot of oil. We'll be dealing with this for years to come."

Still, capping the well was great news. It was so great that everybody came down to the beaches that were once again like miles of hot powdered sugar gleaming in the sun. Gulls and pelicans wheeled above salty water clear and green where waves broke over the sand bars then turned cobalt in the distance where sharks and billfish and blue-fin tuna and the big red snapper hang out. Dolphins raced and played everywhere. Children waded and splashed and built castles out of pristine sand.

And in the distance, just out of sight, sat the wells pumping the oil the nation depended on.

Charlotte and Liza Jane joined the crowd for lunch at Casa Crab. They smiled and laughed with their neighbors and toasted to the future. And though they didn't voice their thoughts aloud, they thought about the wells coexisting with the fragile environment and they wondered, *Can we curb our greed, meet our needs and preserve nature's incredible bounty? Can we have it all?*

33.
MAKING HEADWAY

Three days before the pelican party, Charlotte couldn't remember being as happy or as exhausted. The oil spill was really behind them! Smiles of optimism lit up the faces of her neighbors. Folks were out on the water, fishing and skiing and visiting. Tourists trickled back to the condos and restaurants and shops.

In addition, the swarms of workers at Charlotte's apartment had dwindled to a few men and women doing touch-up work. She and Harry and Liza Jane had worked like dogs arranging furniture, hanging drapes and filling cabinets and bookshelves. When it was done, Charlotte couldn't believe the transformation.

A wall with a wide opening and pocket doors now separated the living and dining area from the enlarged kitchen. The space for Charlotte's painting was revamped and enlarged. One of the windows was now a door leading out onto the far end of the balcony, admitting more light than ever. The living room was elegant but comfy. Best of all, it maintained its views.

There were actual walls on which to display paintings and photographs. Charlotte's extensive collection of art — including bowls and china and Craig's coveted bar stools — transformed the apartment into that elusive ideal of a homey showplace.

Liza Jane directed the placement of the many paintings, drawings and photographs. But Charlotte insisted on hanging some paintings herself — *The Gathering,* the *Midnight Charade* poster and *Pescar,* the Arcadio masterpiece given to her by Harry. *Pescar* found a spot in her bedroom where it is the first thing she sees each morning. The movie poster hung above bookshelves holding her art books, and more than once Charlotte found herself winking back at the actress captured in the kitschy scene.

The Gathering hung on a prominent wall in the living area and could be seen from almost anywhere in the apartment. As Harry helped her place the large canvas on the wall, the spirits positively shimmered. Charlotte figured her ghosts were as happy as she that they were back where they belonged.

The walls were painted something called almond. Woodwork and windows were clean white. Most of the original furniture was slip-covered and reupholstered in soothing tones of the sea and garden. The new guest bedroom and bath were stunningly appointed by Liza Jane. A new pewter chandelier hung over Charlotte's mother's dining room table.

Freshly painted kitchen cabinets were fitted with glass-fronted doors and cool pewter hardware. Stainless appliances winked amid marble counter tops.

The looming specter of the pelican party with all manner of East Oysterites roaming her pristine premises had Abbie flying off to her therapist's for a final session. This freed up Harry, who had been diligent about returning to Pitt cottage every evening after work so as not to ruffle Abbie's fragile feathers.

He now sat on Charlotte's balcony enjoying the view and a cold beer. Charlotte poured herself a glass of wine and sat on the other chaise. A breeze from the bay flitted between them. Harry and Charlotte breathed simultaneous sighs of relief and chuckled.

"Feels pretty good, doesn't it?" said Harry.

"Does it ever," agreed Charlotte. "I can't

believe the last worker is gone. To think, I'll have my beautiful new apartment all to myself!" She smiled at Harry. "Thank you, Harry."

"I'm the one who should be grateful. I love doing this kind of work. It's what I've always wanted — to do work I love . . ." He smiled at her and added, ". . . and finish off the day with you."

Charlotte looked at Harry. She still couldn't believe he was here with her. It was almost as if they had never been apart.

"Promise me we'll have lots of evenings like this," she said.

"Still doubtful?"

"Oh, I don't doubt you. Really, I don't. It just doesn't seem like the obstacles will ever go away."

"You've been more patient than any man could ask. It's going to be over soon. Keep the faith."

"I'm trying," said Charlotte.

"By the way, I have some news about the pelican thefts. Promise not to tell Craig?"

"I do not tell Craig everything!"

"Okay, okay." He sipped his beer and continued.

"I've been in contact with a cousin of mine who lives in Marseille. I'd already heard about the statues being found there.

You know, before you and Maisy and I had our meeting."

"How on earth did you find that out?"

"Charlie, everyone knows everything in this town. It's the only place I've seen that can hold a candle to St. Yves in the gossip department." He took a sip of his beer. "Anyway, this cousin of mine works for La Provence, the newspaper in Marseille. And she owes me a favor. You'd like her." He grinned at Charlotte. "She loves to snoop."

Charlotte was so interested in Harry's info that she didn't object. Instead she acted as if she hadn't heard the tease and said, "Go on, please."

"Claire . . . that's my cousin . . . called in a few favors of her own. It turns out that the Marseille police have been suspicious of a certain art collector for a while. The tapestries that were found with the pelicans were probably en route to him."

"But I thought there was no connection between the collector and the East Oyster statues."

"That's what I'd heard, too. They haven't found whoever left the loot behind the restaurant, but listen to this." Harry leaned forward and lowered his voice. "The collector happens to be an American. His name is Joe Finley."

"Finley?"

"Pretty coincidental, huh? Claire also found out that our pal Joe Finley has left Marseille — and probably France — for parts unknown. His high-end apartment in Marseille was cleaned out. He left owing the landlord two months premium rent."

"Harry, I'm pretty sure Butler Finley's nephew is named Joseph Finley."

"Why am I not surprised?" he murmured.

"If it's who I'm thinking about, he left here years ago after he got into trouble. I can't remember exactly what it was." She shook her head. "But it was a terrible embarrassment to the Finley family." She took a sip of her wine, thinking back to what she knew about East Oyster's first family. "You know what? I'm pretty sure Joseph Finley . . . Joe inherited Finley's Landing. He still owns it as far as I know. Although from what I've heard, Butler's dying to get his hands on it."

"Lot of coincidences, Charlie."

"So if Joe was the ultimate recipient of the pelicans, then who was his connection here? Who swapped birds? Who vandalized the birds?" She thought for a few seconds, chewing her lip in that way that Harry found adorable. She sat up straight. "It has to be Cliff!" she said, answering her own question. "He is in on this with Butler's nephew, Joe, who owns Finley's Landing where Cliff hangs out in that blue boat he almost killed us with."

"You think this Joe would steal from his own uncle?"

"Yes. I bet he had Cliff switch Butler's hermit crabs with a forgery because he resents his Uncle Butler's money and prestige."

"Whoa, Nancy Drew. This isn't a storybook."

"Well, I think that's as good a solution as any." She frowned and sipped her wine. "But who made the fake pelicans? And why?"

"If the fakes hadn't been discovered then the thefts could have gone undetected for . . . well, maybe forever," said Harry.

"Then who broke them?"

Harry shook his head. "No idea."

"That reminds me of another question," said Charlotte. "Did you ever find out anything about the clay?"

"What clay?"

"The Indians' clay . . . you know, when you talked to Eddie Hillman."

"I never talked to Eddie Hillman."

"You weren't out by the clay bed?"

"No."

"Because Eddie said you were." She realized her voice had an edge to it, but she couldn't help it. Why would Eddie make up such a tale? "He said you were asking all sorts of questions about the clay."

"And you believe Eddie." It was a statement, not a question. Harry's voice was low and flat, almost menacing. He frowned and his jaw muscles grew taut. It was as if Harry — the Harry she thought she knew — was being sucked right off of the balcony.

And who is this mean Harry taking his place?

They sat staring at each other for an eternity of seconds, she wide-eyed with surprise and indecision and he all flinty-eyed with anger. Finally he stood.

"I thought you were all about trust," he said.

When Charlotte didn't respond — to this day she couldn't tell you why — he walked around the balcony and stepped through the French doors with their fresh coat of paint. He crossed the polished pine floors to the dining room, sneered at the large basket of white orchids on the table and walked into the kitchen, pulled out Charlotte's new trash receptacle and tossed in his empty beer bottle.

And what was Charlotte thinking as she hurried after him into her lovely, sparkling kitchen?

He doesn't even recycle!

The absurdity of the thought snapped her back to her senses, however and she said, "Harry, wait. I trust you. I do. I'm just confused. And tired. We're both tired."

He was at the door now, but he turned, rubbing his forehead with his thumb. Finally he gave her a weary smile.

"You're right," he said. "You're absolutely right. So I tell you what I'm going to do. I'm going back to Abbie's, get cleaned up and take a nap. And if it's okay with you, I'll be back at eight. With dinner." He looked around at the beautiful, new kitchen. "We should be celebrating, not arguing. Okay?"

"Oh, that is definitely okay," said Charlotte, sniffing back tears of relief.

"All you have to do is let me in the door. I'll have everything for dinner. You will let me in the door, won't you?"

"Yes. Absolutely."

He walked over to her, took her face in his hands and said, "Don't give up on me, Charlie."

And he kissed her mouth. And then that spot just under her jaw. He kissed her mouth again. Slowly. And when he had them both breathless, he stopped.

"See you at eight, right?" he whispered.

"Right," croaked Charlotte, leaning into her new marble counter top for support.

She could hardly stand up. And the thought occurred to her, *Harry McMillan is the only man I have ever known who can literally make me weak in the knees.*

As Charlotte soaked the day's dirt and stress away she sipped the rest of her glass of wine, shaved her legs and thought about the details she'd learned that afternoon. For some reason, the little caution lights began to flicker in her brain. But who or what were they cautioning her about? Not Harry, surely.

I will not doubt Harry. I can't, she thought, reminding herself that emotionally speaking, she'd pretty much bet the farm on Harry.

Therefore, Eddie Hillman has to be lying. And why would he implicate sweet, innocent Harry? Because Harry, the stranger in town affianced to Abbie the Pitt, is the perfect person to implicate. Everybody is already suspicious of him. Not to mention Abbie.

Charlotte was very relieved to have reached this conclusion. She finished off her wine, added a bit more hot water to her bath and hopped back aboard this re-assuring train of thought. So why did Eddie lie? *Because he has something to hide, of course.* She sat up so quickly that water sloshed on the floor. *Pup said Cliff was talking to someone named Ed!* Who was obviously his buddy.

It has to be Cliff who stole the birds and replaced them with fakes — I mean how many art thieves/forgers can there be running around East Oyster, Alabama? If he is involved in swindling Butler, then it has to be he — and Eddie — who have done all of this crime.

So Cliff and Eddie are in this together. But they hardly seem like they would know enough about art to pull this off. They're more like . . . like minions. So who is their boss? Joe Finley? Who owns Finley's Landing? It all seems to revolve around the landing.

And what about Erin's children and the "store" they discovered. Just kids' imagination?

The more she thought about it the more she thought not. The first chance she got she was going to investigate the "store."

Yes, that has to be it. Joe Finley, creepy Cliff and Eddie Hillman are behind it all. And the center of their operation might just be Finley's Landing! I can't wait to tell Harry.

34.
THE LOOK OF LOVE

But at a quarter of eight, Charlotte was feeling more like Grace Kelly than Nancy Drew. She'd dressed in her new black slacks, very high black, strappy heels and a creamy, silky, slinky top that she'd been told looked great on her.

The table was set with lovely linen mats and napkins, pearl-handled silverware she'd bought that long ago summer in Provence and her mother's pale china. She lit the citronella candles on the balcony, dimmed the interior recessed lights, poured herself a glass of wine and popped a Windham Hill CD into the player.

Then deciding the scene had seduction written all over it, she turned the lights up, turned off the CD and buttoned her blouse all the way up. She tucked her flirty bangs behind her ear. It was too quiet. The blouse and her hair looked funny. So she got the music going again, fluffed her hair out and unbuttoned her top button. She left the lights at their brightest.

Harry showed up promptly at eight wearing a crisp yellow shirt and the smile that never failed to melt Charlotte's heart. He put a large shopping bag on the counter. He bent to kiss her lightly on the cheek, then stood back and looked at her.

"You're beautiful," he said.

"Thank you," said Charlotte, with a becoming blush. "And you are looking especially handsome tonight," she said.

"New shirt," he explained.

"Now what on earth do you have in that bag? It looks like a week's worth of groceries!" she teased.

With a flourish, he took an aluminum square out of the bag. "Shrimp, crab and artichoke casserole." He gestured to Charlotte's new oven and said, "Do you have any idea how to work that thing?"

Charlotte laughed. "Not really. But I bet we can figure it out. The instruction book has got to be around here somewhere. What else do you have in there?"

More containers came out — enough wild rice and mushrooms for four, plastic bags of exotic salad fixings and a bottle of vinaigrette dressing. Next came half a dozen still-warm yeast rolls and tiramisu from the Big

O bakery.

"Hope you're hungry," said Harry.

"Starving," said Charlotte. She realized she was looking ravenously at Harry and quickly added, "It's perfect. All my favorite dishes." She handed him a glass of wine and after a couple of tries had the oven preheating. While Harry was sorting out the salad fixings she slipped into the bathroom for a Prilosec.

When they walked into the dining room, Harry looked at the beautiful settings and gave a low whistle.

"Who's coming to dinner?"

"Oh, nobody special. I eat like this every night."

The day was fading into dusky breezes from the bay as the lights of Semmes Street began flickering on. The citronella candles were turning to delicate feathers of light. They danced and winked along the balcony railing. Harry raised his glass.

"To us," he said.

"To us," said Charlotte.

The evening quickly progressed from good to really, really good to down right dreamdate status. The conversation was light, sparkling with flirting and laughter, and it had the closeness between them growing second by candlelit second. The air was heavy with the scent of magnolia and jasmine and bay. It was also heavy with tension — the good kind. No, make that the great kind.

The former lovers brought out the best in one another. They filled in each other's spaces. Together Harry and Charlie were complete, happy — beautiful even — in a way they weren't when they were simply Harrison and Charlotte. And they had the good sense to know it.

When the meal was ready, Harry dimmed the lights in the dining room and reset the music. Charlotte loosened her blouse a bit and kicked off her shoes. They drank wine, feasted on Harry's gourmet take-out and when Charlotte claimed she was too full for tiramisu, Harry dropped a spoonful into her mouth, kissed a smudge of chocolate from her top lip and promptly forgot about his own dessert. Charlotte thought she might spontaneously combust right there at her dining room table.

About this time the CD player came forth with an instrumental version of *The Look of Love.* It was just like a scene from one of Charlotte's old movies. In fact, the setting could have tumbled right out of her favorite film, *Midnight Charade.*

Harry, not one to squander a romantic

moment, God bless him, took Charlotte in his arms and they danced as if in a dream. Slowly, sensuously. In the pale light, she watched his handsome, peaceful features. She loved this man. And he loved her.

The next morning Charlotte and Harry enjoyed one of those dreamy breakfasts that can only be had by new lovers — or in this case, re-newed lovers. Along with the previous night's dinner, Harry had smuggled in fresh strawberries and peaches, as well as almond croissants and a container of whipped yogurt and cream. They consumed this with juice and coffee and head-over-heels happiness at being together.

They sat in the shade and privacy of the narrow balcony facing Palmetto Street and watched the world come alive on the bay. The early hour was still cool and glistening with dew and bursting with the promise of a stellar day.

Charlotte took a bite of her croissant, sipped her coffee and said, "It was very thoughtful of you to bring breakfast."

Harry smiled. "I'm a thoughtful kind of a guy."

Charlotte dipped a strawberry into her pot of yogurt and grinned back.

When they'd had their fill of food and flirting, Harry and Charlotte finally climbed down off their cloud and faced the realities of the day.

Abbie was due in that afternoon, and Harry was expected to pick her up at the airport. The pelican party ostensibly held to celebrate the return of Lucy Bradford's famous pelicans was scheduled for the following day. Though Maisy (with Liza Jane as her assistant) had made all of the arrangements for the rentals and refreshments and entertainment, Harry thought it best that she and Abbie not come face to face until the actual event.

Of course, there was also the chance that Charlotte's presence might upset Abbie's delicate balance. Even though Harry had not confessed his intentions toward Charlotte to his faux fiancée, Abbie was observant enough to realize that whatever Harry and "Charlie" had had in France, at least some of it lingered. So, of course, she was jealous.

As everyone knew, any emotion in Abbie was apt to go viral with the slightest provocation. And jealousy, that most mercurial of emotions, is known to instantly morph from the smallest seed into a fire-breathing dragon in people of normal temperaments. Lord only knew to what monstrous proportions it could grow in Abigail Pitt!

Thus it was decided that Charlotte, too, would keep her distance until the party began. Liza Jane as well as Grant, who was coming in town expressly for the big bird soiree, would be allowed to pitch in before the festivities. This decision put the burden of pulling it all together on Harry, whose entertaining experience included having the guys over to watch the game or cooking a few steaks on the grill. But our Harry was no fool. He'd enlisted Maisy as a behind-the-scenes organizer.

So he assured Charlotte that with Maisy as a sort of ghost host, he was up to the challenge. Besides, the main reason for the bash was the execution of the elaborate scheme they'd hatched (the details of which Charlotte was still not totally clear on). It was not to win party-of-the-year award. And, unless she made Abbie nervous, Liza Jane would also be there for back up. Charlotte reluctantly agreed. His arguments were rational. But the whole thrown-together operation had her very uneasy.

35.
An Embarrassment of Pelicans

The next evening found Maisy, Charlotte and Liza Jane on Maisy's pier enjoying preprandial frozen margaritas. Maisy was attired in her best gypsy duds. These included a faded black bodice that had once belonged to her paternal granny, a pink peasant blouse and a gauzy, floor-length crimson skirt. She was bare-footed as this allegedly helped in receiving transmissions from Crystal. But really, she just needed the feel of the grass on her gnarly little toes.

Liza Jane was gorgeous as usual in a simple but form-fitting skirt and top. Her pile of luxurious hair was pulled into a ponytail. Gold earrings and sandals finished the outfit.

Unsure of the proper attire for a pelican celebration/ sting, Charlotte was dressed more or less like a cat burglar. She wore black slacks and a sleeveless black, high-necked top. But with her new hair cut and her body toned from daily runs, it was very becoming — even for a mid-summer lawn party.

Maisy generally liked to keep a clear head until she'd gotten Crystal cranked up to her ultimate capacity. It wasn't until the messages began emanating from the ball, and she and Crystal were "operating on the same wavelength" that she would accept a cocktail. But tonight, Maisy decided that "a little nip" was in order.

"Frazzled nerves interfere with readings worse than anything," she'd explained and proceeded to fire up the blender.

Liza Jane threw a look at Charlotte.

"It's not like you to be nervous, Maisy," she said.

"Nerves get old just like everything else. Mine aren't quite what they used to be, that's all."

Maisy noticed the frowns on her nieces' faces and added, "Don't worry, girls. It's all going to work out. Crystal told me so."

Well, gee, now I can relax! thought Charlotte. *I have the assurances of my secretive, faux-engaged lover as well as my octogenarian auntie who acts on suggestions from her deceased husband and her crystal ball — which is on the blink half the time.*

Liza Jane simply shrugged and took a big

375

sip of her margarita.

Charlotte shook her head and wondered for the millionth time, *what have I gotten myself into?*

At a little past seven, Maisy downed the rest of her drink, and when Charlotte and Liza Jane declined her offer of a second toddy, she stowed the remains of the margaritas in the fridge.

"Waste not, want not," she said. She rubbed her tiny hands together, adjusted her flowing skirt and said, "Y'all ready? 'Cause I believe it's show time."

Charlotte suppressed a groan as she and L.J. followed Maisy to the porch where the old lady had left her gypsy wig and the bowling bag that housed Crystal. She nodded at Lucy Bradford's famous statue and said, "Would one of you mind grabbing *Miscegenation?* I've got my hands full with Crystal."

Charlotte carefully picked up the statue and thought about her own cross-eyed Lucy Bradford original which was already at Pitt Cottage. Liza Jane had transported it along with a whole flock of its clay brethren and sisters to Abbie's that afternoon. Now that Charlotte's bird, *Dee Dee,* was in jeopardy, she realized how attached she had become to the goofy thing with its crossed eyes.

It wasn't worth nearly as much as Maisy's famous piece, but Charlotte would be devastated should anything happen to it. She knew the loss of *Miscegenation* would be an even bigger blow to Maisy. Not only was *Miscegenation* extremely valuable, it was the only thing the old dear had of her crazy yet much-loved niece, Lucy. As far as Liza Jane was concerned, the loss of each bird was like losing a piece of her mother.

"Maisy, are you sure you want to take a chance with this? Aren't you worried?"

"We agreed to use the birds as bait. Right, Liza Jane?"

Liza Jane nodded. "It's too late for second guesses now," she said.

They're right, thought Charlotte. *And what's the use in adding to Maisy's stress by questioning the plan?*

In an attempt to lighten the mood, Charlotte lifted *Miscegenation* and said, "Ready when y'all are. The early bird gets the worm."

Maisy smiled thoughtfully and said, "Yes. But remember, Charlie, it's the second mouse that gets the cheese."

Liza Jane and Charlotte looked questioningly at one another as their aunt adjusted her wig in the hall mirror. As usual, Maisy didn't concern herself with the back where her own wiry, platinum hair poked through the wig's black curls. She leaned over Dubby's old bowling bag and unzipped it for a last check on Crystal. Her face was immediately bathed in an iridescent glimmer of green.

"Hah," she said. "Crystal's raring to go!"

She zipped up the bag and headed out across Downydew's front yard, crossed over the beach and started up Pitt Cottage's lawn. Her nieces dutifully followed, Charlotte cradling the fabulous pelican statue in her arms and praying she wouldn't trip. Maisy slipped into her gold and yellow tent which had been set up in front of the hydrangea hedge close to Pitt Cottage's front porch. Liza Jane headed to the house to check on her mother's endangered birds.

Charlotte paused to admire the pre-festivity progress. There were lanterns hanging amid the streams of Spanish moss that floated from the oak branches. Beneath these were serving stations covered with red and white checked cloths. Charlotte recognized employees of the Backyard Grill busily setting out hot and cold covered dishes, stacks of paper napkins and plastic utensils in readiness for the crowd, which would soon be swarming over the grounds.

Miniature skiffs placed near the food

overflowed with ice and drinks. Round tables covered in the same checked cloths were clustered into groupings along the perimeter of the lawn. Each was centered with a lantern glowing from a nest of palm fronds.

The decorations were a bit dated and hokey, close to an exact replication of those in a party sequence from the movie that had put Pitt Cottage on the tourist maps. The famous scene had even taken place at day's end when the moss-draped oaks were beginning to stand out in black relief against the backdrop of East Oyster's renowned sunset.

About this time, the sound track from *Midnight Charade* started up from speakers concealed in the palmettos. Charlotte, feeling as if she'd been transported right into her favorite movie, was rooted to the spot. She gazed around her, almost forgetting that she was holding twenty pounds of miscegenation in her arms.

The sun was at its flamboyant best this evening. The gaudy orb glowed so large and orange that it had the sky blushing with color and oak-and-moss shadows creeping melodramatically across the lawn. Charlotte, her senses in artistic overload, breathed in the scene and began to sway to the opening strains of the title song from

Midnight Charade.

She closed her eyes, soaking up the cinematic ambience and imprinting the picture on her brain. She had to paint it! Just the thought of capturing it on canvas made her feel lighter, optimistic even. She decided that Maisy was right. Everything would work itself out.

That was when someone turned off the music, slamming Charlotte back to reality. The entwined pelicans had grown heavy in her arms. Her black, cat burglar ensemble sucked up the lingering sun rays. She began to perspire and felt her hair erupting into frizzies in the heavy air. She opened her eyes and beheld a most disheartening sight.

Harry and Abbie — looking a bit like the movie star couple from *Midnight Charade* — were walking toward her. Abbie's thick, dark hair was caught up in an elegant do, her dark eyes dramatically and perfectly made up. A white linen dress had her looking like some kind of snow queen in spite of the humidity. One of her perfectly manicured claws was attached to Harry's arm. Her engagement ring caught the light and winked at Charlotte, throwing its sparkle into her eyes and making her squint.

Harry didn't seem to notice any of this. As a matter of fact, he looked annoyingly complacent about having the woman whom he'd described as unstable clutching his arm. Charlotte's lovely bubble of tranquility began to deflate, and as Abbie turned to smile up at Harry, it crumpled to nothingness in the grass.

As usual, Abbie's smile morphed into a frozen grimace when she turned her attention to Charlotte. Harry, on the other hand, was smiling at Charlotte if she were Venus herself standing there in the grass. The woman he saw was beautifully backlit in the afterglow, her hair curling softly around her pretty face and framing those lovely, light eyes that seemed perpetually on the verge of a smile.

"Oh, good, Charlotte," said Abbie in her bored monotone. "You remembered the fortune teller's birds. If you'll take it into the house, Liza Jane will show you where it goes." She spoke slowly and deliberately, and Charlotte surmised correctly that Abbie was well medicated for what promised to be a stressful evening.

"Here, let me have that," said Harry, taking *Miscegenation* from Charlotte's arms. "Abbie, I think some of the guests are arriving. Maybe you should greet them."

"Of course, Harrison. Charlotte, do we need to go over your part in this . . .

charade?"

"No. I think I've got it," Charlotte said with a touch of annoyance in her voice.

But then she looked into Abbie's slightly unfocused eyes and felt something akin to compassion for the woman.

After all, Charlotte thought. *I have Harry and our future together. Abbie has . . . demons. And a very iffy future.*

So Charlotte added kindly, "But thanks. Let me know if there's anything —"

But Abbie had turned toward the house.

One of Charlotte's duties was to make sure that all of the "players" in the evening's drama had in fact made an appearance and that they hung around until the final act. Per Maisy's instructions, Pup's grandson, Derek, was stationed at the rear entrance of the property. Craig and Leon manned either side of the lawn where it met the beach. One of Derek's brothers was to keep an eye on a path leading from the Pitt yard to the Lanskys next door.

Unless someone took off into the thick underbrush in the dark, these were the only ways out of party central. If anyone in the least bit suspicious started to leave, the party guards were to detain the suspect with any one of a dozen phony excuses (concocted by Leon, who'd had a lot of experience in this area) and contact one another by cell phone.

Charlotte was doubtful. Actually, she thought the entire plan was the most ridiculous thing she'd ever heard. But when pressed for a better idea, she'd agreed to go along with the charade, as Abbie called it, charade being an obvious allusion to *Midnight Charade,* the movie she hated and Charlotte loved with equal passion.

Craig referred to their scheme as a sting; Maisy, as a come to Jesus meeting; Pup, as this mess; and Liza Jane, as an adventure mama would have loved. Matthew Clifford (aka Cliff), Eddie Hillman, Mayor Toowell, Butler Finley, Police Chief Foster and acting Chief Feiffer referred to the soiree as simply The Pelican Party since, as far as she knew, none of them had been apprised of the real focus of the festivities. Charlotte wondered. Was this multiplicity of designation by the participants symptomatic of the group's lack of cohesion as to what they were about and whom they hoped to expose?

The principals in what Charlotte was starting to think of as a farce, had been lured to the party by the promise of any combination of free food and beer, civic duty, sincere love of the pelicans and their significance to the town, curiosity, and/ or the chance to see *Miscegenation.*

The word was out that this was East Oyster's last chance to view the most valuable and notorious of the Bradford birds. Maisy had announced that in light of previous events, she felt compelled to take stringent measures to ensure her statue's safety. Hereafter, *Miscegenation* would be housed in a museum in of all places, Denver, Colorado — which might as well be Mars as far as most of the area bird lovers were concerned. Because like Liza Jane's cowboys, they saw little reason to ever leave the county.

Charlotte took a pen and the neatly typed list of the "players" out of her purse. It took her about twenty minutes to locate and check off the names. All except Cliff. She called Derek. He too had checked everyone off his list except Cliff.

She made the rounds of Pitt Cottage once again, stopping only to provide the party guards with fresh lemonades. It was getting quite dark by this time. Folks were lining up for food or taking their places at the tables. Many had walked out onto the pier where Pup and Grant were keeping vigil. Someone turned up the music. People began to dance. Children with flashlights

384

dashed around the beach chasing sand crabs. Every light inside the house seemed to be on. People moved around inside like fish in a bowl, balancing beers and plates of food.

Charlotte headed to the house in search of Cliff. She passed Maisy's tent glowing a bilious yellow green in the shadowy corner of the yard.

Well, at least Crystal is functioning. Even if this nutty plan isn't, thought Charlotte.

She went into the house and back to the dining room where the pelicans were displayed. Ribbons stretched across the wide doorways so that the birds could be admired only at a safe distance. Folks were in the doorways pointing to the different birds and discussing them, telling stories about each one, why it was their favorite, or the tale of why Lucy sought to bequeath a certain bird to a certain person.

There were at least twenty pelicans of varying sizes on Abbie's new pine table. In the center sat *Miscegenation.* The glories of each were easily appreciated since the table was large enough to accommodate twelve people. Charlotte wondered if Abbie even had eleven friends, and realized that she hadn't seen the woman — the supposed hostess — since she'd first arrived.

But her first concern was locating Cliff — if he was there. As frustrating as this was, when she caught sight of her pelican nestled there with the flock of delightfully wacky birds in various pelican postures, she had to smile. Some of the pelicans were in flight, one was a tiny, funny fledgling, one even stood on its head, but all had the great pouched beaks, proud heads and round, iridescent eyes that left no doubt as to what kind of bird they were.

"Amazing, aren't they?"

It was Harry. She'd been so engrossed in the pelicans she hadn't even noticed him come up behind her.

"They are. *Dee Dee* looks so happy with all of them, doesn't she?"

Harry smiled. "That she does. But I'll be happy when she's safely back on the balcony."

"Oh, that reminds me." Charlotte looked around her and lowered her voice. "I haven't located Cliff yet."

"Look over there," said Harry.

He nodded toward the hall doorway on the other side of the room. Sure enough, there stood Cliff and Eddie Hillman. And next to them was the red-headed guy who managed to be wherever there was art. Each of the men had a beer. Eddie and Red were eating hot dogs. Cliff munched a burger. They looked as innocuous as the statues they admired.

Charlotte frowned. Could she have been wrong about Eddie? Was Red just an art-loving tourist taking an extended vacation? Could they all have been wrong about Cliff?

It was at that moment that the lights in Pitt Cottage went out.

36.
THE GOOD, THE BAD AND THE REALLY, REALLY UGLY

Charlotte heard mild shrieks of surprise, lots of laughter and the voice of acting Chief of Police Feiffer telling everyone to remain calm.

"Sure thing, Barney," a man answered.

More laughter ensued. But Charlotte was not laughing. Because someone was pushing by her, through the ribbon and into the dining room where the pelicans were now a bunch of sitting ducks.

"Harry?" she called.

If Harry was there, he wasn't answering.

People plagued by tropical storms and hurricanes are used to power outages and feeling their way in sudden darkness. So this crowd waited patiently for their eyes to adjust to the dark then made their way calmly and politely out of the crowded house to the porch and the lawn. They figured the lights would return in a few minutes, and if they didn't? Well, there was a sky full of stars. There was plenty of cold beer and lots of friends and neighbors to share it with.

When Charlotte's eyes had adjusted to the sudden darkness, she could see that there were people in the dining room with the pelicans. Thank goodness one of them was Douglas Feiffer. He was handing *Miscegenation* to someone behind him. Charlotte guessed they were getting the valuable pieces out of harm's way. But when he reached for *Dee Dee,* something sparked in Charlotte's brain.

"Wait just a minute, Feiffer!" she called. "That's my pelican. I'll take her, thank you."

The other man who Charlotte now recognized as Eddie Hillman snatched *Dee Dee* and disappeared through the butler's pantry and into the kitchen. Charlotte only hesitated a second before running through the big dining room and into the pantry where it was very dark. Someone rushed in behind her and grabbed her arm. Someone who felt and smelled just like Harry.

"Charlie, what do you think you're doing?"

"He's got *Dee Dee.* And *Miscegenation.*"

"I don't care about those stupid birds. You could get yourself kill—"

Harry was interrupted by the sound of

tires spinning on Abbie's oyster shell drive-way. Then there was the unmistakable sound of one car hitting another before taking off down the drive.

"They've kidnapped *Dee Dee,*" gasped Charlotte.

"It's a bird, Charlie," said Harry. "Not a child. Just a clay bird."

"Right," said Charlotte, getting a grip on her nerves.

"Wait here," said Harry, and he ran through the kitchen and out the back door. Of course, Charlotte was right behind him.

As Harry and Charlotte exited the house, they ran into Grant who had abandoned his post on the pier when Derek appeared. Derek had been told by "that Clifford dude" that his grandmother needed him out on the pier. "Some kind of accident." Grant figured something was up. Because other than berating herself for "getting in the middle of it," Pup was fine.

As Grant hurried around the side of the house, he heard the crunching sound of metal meeting plastic. About that time Harry and Charlotte came tearing out of the kitchen door.

"What's going on?" Grant called.

"Somebody made off with some of the statues," Harry called. "You check out here.

I'll get the lights on."

Due to his work on Pitt Cottage, Harry knew that the breaker box was located behind a panel on the back porch, so he had no trouble locating it in the dark. He opened the panel and flipped the switches. Lights, music and hot food were immediately restored. Like an awakened merry-go-round, the party came back to life.

Foster had been out by the beach when the lights went out. Instinctively, he knew this was no random power failure, and he hurried into the house. As he entered, Feiffer was announcing that there had been a pelican theft. Foster shook his head, shooed the flock of gawkers back outside, found Charlotte and asked exactly what had transpired.

When she'd finished her brief and breathless recitation, Foster said, "So, Feiffer, who did you give the birds to? And for God's sake, why?"

"I gave them to Butler Finley's man, Clifford. He said I'd better hand them over or they'd be stolen, and I'd have to answer to Mr. Finley."

When Foster went outside to the driveway, the getaway car, if that was what it was, had vacated the premises. It was also discovered that it was Pup's eight-year-old red minivan that had been hit by the alleged getaway car. Charlotte only hoped *Dee Dee* wasn't in the same shape as Pup's tail light, the sad remains of which lay in the shells of the drive.

"Don't no good deed go unpunished, and that's the truth!" said Pup when she saw the damage.

"We'll get it fixed for you, Pup," said Harry before Foster could ask what good deed she was talking about.

Of course, Foster would have to be told about their inept meddling. But as sorry as Charlotte felt for Maisy and her loss of *Miscegenation,* her auntie was the one for that job. Which reminded her. Where was the old thing? And for that matter, where was Abbie?

Charlotte went to the side of the house where she could see over the hydrangeas to Maisy's tent in the front yard. She was hoping to see Crystal glowing like a haint through the canvas. But the tent was dark.

The remaining birds were loaded into Liza Jane's van to be transported to the police station for safe keeping — at least over night. Foster held up Liza Jane's car keys and quickly assured the owners of the remaining Bradford statues that Feiffer would be assigned to duties other than art protection. It was only then that they breathed a sigh of relief and agreed to let their precious pelicans be incarcerated.

The van, which was parked in a well-lit space by the house, was locked by Foster himself. He gave the keys to Liza Jane and had a brief but intense tete-a-tete with Feiffer. No one heard the exchange, but when it was over, Feiffer looked like he might burst into tears.

Several of the bird owners formed a sentry around the car that held their art. At this point a patrol car with two officers pulled up.

Charlotte heard Craig mutter, "If that's the fashion police, the mayor's out on the porch."

But the police car was responding to a call from their chief. Foster hopped in and they left in a cloud of oyster shell dust, barely missing Pup's car.

By now everyone at the party knew that two more of their beloved beacons of the hope and spirit of East Oyster had been stolen. The event that was to have been the bright spot in a very dark time suddenly had all the cheer and optimism of a wake. Folks shook their heads and drifted off down the beach or to their cars. And as the little group of amateur sleuths gathered on the porch and watched their friends and neighbors leave, they were rightly filled with guilt.

"Well, that was ugly," said Maisy.

"Where have you been?" cried Charlotte. "And where's Abbie?"

Maisy pulled off her wig, tossed it onto the coffee table and collapsed into the snowy white cushions of Abbie's sofa.

"Abbie's fine," said Maisy. "She kinda fell into my tent when the lights went out. I gave her a little something for her nerves."

Everybody's eyebrows shot up at this. Abbie was already well medicated. What on earth had Maisy given her?

Their reaction wasn't lost on Maisy.

"Don't worry," she said. "It was just some of my special tea." A mischievous grin crept across her face as she added, "She's sleeping it off over at Downydew."

The next thing they knew, Butler Finley walked up. "Who's in charge here?" he asked. "Not that twit, Feiffer, I hope."

"Foster's back on the job," said Maisy.

"So where in the heck is he?" asked Butler. "I understand there's been another major art theft, and that there's a van load of Lucy Bradford pelicans sitting out in the driveway. Good God, does anybody have any sense in this town?"

"Please have a seat, Butler," said Maisy, looking sternly in his eyes and using that mesmerizing tone she generally employed only for séances. "And try to calm yourself. Foster's around here somewhere, probably scooping up clues by the boatload. In the meantime, would you like me to fill you in on the details?"

Butler perched himself on the nearest ottoman. "Okay, he said, "So what happened?"

Maisy and Harry glanced at one another, and Charlotte thought she saw a signal transpire between them. It was just a narrowing of the eyes, an almost imperceptible nod of the head, but it was there. She was sure of it.

Then Maisy began a recitation of the evening's events in excruciating detail. Once she had the others' attention, Harry placed his hand on the small of Charlotte's back. He nodded toward the butler's pantry and they slipped out of the room.

"Where are we going?" asked Charlotte, following him into the yard.

"You up for a boat ride?"

Charlotte was up for just about anything involving Harry McMillan. "Sure," she said.

Harry stopped long enough to plant an appreciative kiss on her mouth. "Did I mention that I'm crazy about you?" he said, then turned in the direction of the pier. Charlotte, lost in a little love cloud, didn't immediately follow until Harry called, "C'mon, Charlie!" She remembered *Dee Dee,* her darling pelican, and hurried after him. Minutes later they were climbing into Maisy's boat.

In the meantime, Foster — with the help of the Alabama Marine Police, an especially zealous member of ORCA (Organization for Research in Crimes against Art) and twins Olivia and Grace — was not only scooping up clues, but criminals as well.

37.
PIRATES IN THE COVE

Due to an even-fussier-than-usual baby Robert, the Lansky family had left the pelican party early. They took the narrow path that snaked from Pitt Cottage's front yard to their own large back garden. Olivia and Grace grumbled about having to leave the party and begged to stay out and play a while longer. The girls' parents, too tired to argue, made them promise to stay in the back yard and went in to deal with brothers Beckett and Robert.

It was the twins' nature to test the limits of everything, especially parental regulations. So when the lights went out next door, the girls did not rush inside to Mommy and Daddy. Instead, they made their way through the underbrush, stopping at the very edge of the property line separating the Lansky yard from the Pitt yard.

When the girls emerged from a bunch of sticky palmettos, they found themselves staring at Pup's van. Seconds later a black car swerved backward into the red car, crunching Pup's taillight. They heard the two men in the back seat of the black car cursing as it took off across the parking area and down the drive.

The remains of Pup's taillight were scattered in the oyster shells. But there was something else. Nested in the center of the plastic shards was a small silver bird. Grace stretched her arm out, careful to keep the rest of her body in her own yard, and snatched it up.

She held it up for her sister's inspection. "Look! It's a silver baby pelican."

Just then, their mother called, "Grace, Olivia! Time to come in!"

Meanwhile Foster had alerted the marine police of possible nefarious goings on at Finley's Landing. Cliff and Eddie Hillman were just blasting out of the canal in the infamous blue-hulled boat when the police cruiser took chase. The whole thing was over in a matter of seconds however, because Harry had reattached the boom across the mouth to Cocktail Cove. It became tangled in the blue boats' propeller, and twenty yards later the getaway vessel was dead in the water.

The police car carrying Foster had just

arrived on the Finley's Landing side of the cove. Radio contact confirmed that the boats and lights not too far out in the bay were indeed the marine police and the disabled Cliff and Eddie. Butler Finley's pirated boat with its hopelessly entangled prop was being towed back to the canal.

While Foster and the two East Oyster cops waited to take Cliff and Eddie into their custody, Harry and Charlotte came ashore not far from the shed. After alerting Foster to their presence, lest they get mistakenly shot or tazed or something, Harry aimed his flashlight in the direction of the shed. His beam caught a slight figure there in the shadows, illuminating the fiery red of his hair. It was the curious fellow who'd been skulking abound East Oyster!

"Good Lord," muttered Charlotte. "What the heck is he doing here?"

When questioned (rather menacingly by Harry), Red admitted to being involved in the pelican business. But merely as an overzealous ORCA affiliate craving a little adventure outside the museum.

"Do you have any identification?" asked Harry, who had been working closely with the ORCA authorities and had never been apprised of the torch-headed fellow.

But Red produced a laminated ORCA

I.D. with his grinning picture right there on it.

"I'm kind of working on my own," he said.

He'd come to town after getting wind of the pelican caper through the ORCA newsletter. He'd quickly deduced that Cliff and Eddie were up to no good and had been following them.

"Art is my *raison d'être*," he explained rather dramatically.

Inside the shed were *Miscegenation, Dee Dee,* and *Amber,* a small, ocher-colored bird with breasts (not one of Lucy Bradford's best efforts) that belonged to the mayor. As Harry aimed the flashlight around the interior of the shed, a lavender pelican sitting on a nest of coral seemed to come alive in the brief light. It was the famous back door to Pitt Cottage.

In between baths, brushing teeth and reciting bedtime prayers, Erin Lansky had discovered the silver pelican and pried the truth out of the twins. Like everyone, she knew exactly whose car it belonged to. Like the rest of the interested parties, she quickly put two and two together. And like the rest of them, she did not come up with four.

Erin had Foster's number in her cell phone (from the conversations regarding

Maisy, the children and their "spa"). So after getting most of the story out of her twins, Erin immediately called Foster to tell him that the stolen getaway car was indeed Butler Finley's. It seemed that Cliff, Eddie Hillman (and possibly Butler's own black-sheep relative, Joe) had made him the ultimate patsy, stealing his art and using his own boat and car to carry out their despicable plots.

"And it doesn't take Hercule Poirot to figure out that those two ungrateful bums are behind all this art theft and vandalism!" added Erin.

Foster wisely made no comment. After promising to bring the twins with her to Pitt Cottage the next morning, Erin clicked off.

Cliff and Eddie were put into a second police car that arrived, lights flashing and siren wailing, just as the culprits were being brought ashore. They would be transported to a paddy wagon that made the circuit through the small towns of Creek County to what is known as big jail in the county seat. The pelican art found in the shed would be taken to the East Oyster police station to join the rest of the flock in protective custody.

After verifying the authenticity of Red's

ORCA card, he was instructed "not to leave town," which made him feel like a bona fide player in an art theft sting. And when he was further instructed to meet the next morning at Pitt Cottage along with Charlotte and Harry it was all he could do not to throw his arms around Foster and kiss him.

As Harry and Charlotte puttered back across Cocktail Cove, Charlotte said, "It looks like we're close to wrapping up the case of the purloined pelicans."

"It does look that way," said Harry.

"But . . . ?"

"Well, for one thing, I'm wondering, where this leaves Abbie."

It always comes back to Abbie! Abbie and her problems and her strangeness. And her hold on Harry.

Between feeling sorry for Abbie, feeling guilty because she couldn't stand the woman and feeling jealous — or at least confused — over her relationship with Harry, Abbie had put Charlotte through the wringer emotionally. If an end to Abbie's quest to find the person responsible for her brother's death didn't come soon, Charlotte felt like she might just lose it, too.

When they returned to Pitt Cottage, the caterers were gone, everything cleaned up and the parking lot empty except for three cars — Charlotte's, Harry's and Abbie's. Harry walked Charlotte to hers. As she clicked the keypad, Harry gently turned her toward him.

"Hang in there, Charlie," he said. "Okay?"

It would have been nice if he'd taken her in his arms, but then Abbie might be watching.

38.
WHODUNIT?

The next morning found them all gathered a la Agatha Christie on the porch of Pitt Cottage. Since Abbie was still groggy from the "special tea" administered to her by Maisy, Harry was the de facto host. He had whipped up a batch of lemonade and procured pastries from the Big O. Charlotte was very impressed.

Foster looked longingly at the almond croissants but resisted temptation and grabbed a couple of bland cookies instead. After washing these down with a glass of diet lemonade, he cleared his throat and took out his phone.

Everyone was silent as he scrolled through his notes and checked off the attendees: Mayor Eunice Toowell, who had coerced Foster into this unorthodox proceeding, Maisy Downy, Abbie Pitt, Harry McMillan, Charlotte Turner, Butler Finley, Liza Jane Bradford, Grant James, Erin Lansky and twins Grace and Olivia Lansky. Miss May Doody, who'd lost and regained a pelican, was there. Craig and Leon were there, too, though Foster hadn't invited them. But what the heck, Craig might know something. Also, a very nervous Pup and Derek were there. The little ORCA guy, who really did go by the nickname Red, was there swigging lemonade and munching his third chocolate éclair. The now-back-to-second-in-command, Douglas Feiffer, was occupied with paperwork at the station and not present.

"Okay, I know everybody'll be glad to get this wrapped up," said Foster, hitching up his pants which Charlotte noticed were noticeably looser.

Affirmative murmurs floated from the crowd.

"The mayor and I thought we needed a meeting of the minds, so to speak, of the concerned citizens involved in this."

Eunice adjusted the skirt of her plaid jumper and smiled encouragingly at Foster. She gave a nod of her elaborately coiffed head, and he continued.

"As you all know, Eddie Hillman and Matthew Clifford were arrested last night. Unfortunately, when the paddy wagon stopped to pick up a couple of DUI's in

Powder Key, they escaped."

This time murmurs of outrage and disbelief rang out from the group.

"I know, I know," said Foster. "But take it easy. I just got word they were recaptured." He chuckled. "A couple of pit bulls treed 'em when they tried to steal a pickup. And your birds are safe."

Butler Finley stood up. They all expected him to tear into Foster concerning the rampant incompetence of area law enforcement, but he smiled an ingratiating smile and said, "Uh, sorry Foster. I'll have to cut this short. Just got a text from my insurance agent."

He headed for the door. When he got there, Foster said, "I'm sorry, Butler, but I'm gonna need you to stick around. We all have things we'd rather be doing."

Butler raised his chin defiantly, but before he could speak, Foster added, "I'm going to have to insist. The mayor wanted to keep this informal, but if we have to, we can take it back to the station."

Butler opened his mouth to speak, thought better of it and fell silent.

Foster smiled genially. "It'll just take a few minutes," he said.

Butler was not happy, but returned to his seat. "If it's only a few minutes," he said, at least getting the last word.

Olivia and Grace hung on every syllable, obviously enjoying being included in this adult drama. Grace whispered into her sister's ear three or four times before being shushed by her mother. She scrunched her face into a pout but did as instructed.

Abbie sat as close to Harry as possible without climbing into his lap. She was paler than usual, her thin lips pressed into a line. She twisted her engagement ring round and round her finger, and seemed on the verge of jumping out of her chair. It seemed whatever nerve potion Maisy slipped into her tea had worn off.

Foster quickly went over the sequence of events, starting with the broken pelican in the park. He filled everyone in on the French connection at which point Craig said, "Hate to bring this up, Butler, but I heard that your cousin, Joe Finley was behind the whole scheme to steal art and substitute it with fakes."

Butler clasped his hands together across his knees and stared at his Gucci loafers for a few seconds while shaking his head. When he looked up, his face was a mask of disappointment and resignation. He smiled sadly at his neighbors.

"Well, all families have them. Black sheep.

And the Finleys are no exception."

"Except for one thing," said Foster. "Joe Finley is in the Philippines as we speak. Has been for the last two weeks." He reached into his shirt pocket and pulled out the silver pelican. "This belongs to you, Butler, if I'm not mistaken."

"Everybody knows by now that Cliff took my car. That ungrateful . . ."

Olivia raised her hand. Erin gave her a stern look. She put it down.

"Just a minute, sweetie," Foster said to the child.

"There's one other thing I'd like to clear up. Pup, did you throw out the pieces to Butler's busted bird?"

"No, I did not."

Butler smiled sadly at Pup. "I am so sorry, Pup. I just assumed — Obviously, it was Cliff who disposed of the pieces."

"Glad that's cleared up," said Foster.

He then continued a recitation of the events of the case, touching on Cliff's extensive rap sheet and the fact that Eddie had been stealing from his fellow tribe members for years. Of course, he'd lied about having seen Harry around the clay bed, diverting suspicion from himself to the mysterious newcomer, Harrison McMillan. Foster punctuated his story with the apprehension of Cliff and Eddie the previous evening. Butler stood, obviously intent on getting back to his insurance agent, but Foster continued.

"There are a couple of things that just don't add up. First of all, Cliff and Eddie don't know squat about art. And Charlotte, when they jumped into Butler's car, did they get into the front or back seat?"

Charlotte thought back to the previous night, replaying the scene in her mind. Finally she said, "The back seat, I think."

"Then who was driving?"

"Gosh, I don't know," said Charlotte.

Grace raised her hand, wiggling it wildly, as she often did in Miss Homer's English class. Erin whispered a firm remonstration into her daughter's ear. That's when Olivia raised her hand.

"For heaven's sake, Foster," said Maisy. "Let the children speak."

"Okay, Olivia," said Foster. "You go first." He looked from one to the other. He knew their names but couldn't tell them apart.

"I saw who was driving the car that ran into Pup's car."

All eyes were on Olivia.

"It was . . ."

She was interrupted by the slamming of the screen door. Butler Finley was sprinting like a gazelle around the house to his dented car which was parked once again behind Pitt Cottage.

Foster, in spite of doctor's orders to the contrary, started make chase.

"Whoa, Foster," said Maisy. She held up a car key with the unmistakable BMW logo attached to a sterling silver F. "Harry and Grant, would you please detain Mr. Finley for us?"

But they were already out the door.

Maisy moved to the spot vacated by Harry and took Abbie's trembling hand. In spite of the tears dripping down her face, Abbie didn't look vulnerable, as you might expect. The expression on that mascara-smudged visage was one of triumph. The tears were tears of relief. She'd known all along.

The person she'd tracked to East Oyster was Matthew Clifford, but the man responsible for the missing pelicans and the art forgeries and her brother's sad demise was none other than East Oyster's most prominent citizen. That's right. The Butler did it.

39.
BACK TO THE FUTURE

A few days later Harry took Abbie and Red to the airport. Abbie was flying back to her shrink and friends up east (yes, she actually had friends). Having accepted a generous offer from Harry to purchase Pitt Cottage, she hoped never to return to the land of humidity and ghosts and alligators. Avenging her brother's death had so filled her with belief in herself that Maisy and Crystal predicted a somewhat normal, if not blindingly bright, future for Abbie.

"Yep, it's the best we can hope for," said Maisy.

Charlotte, Liza Jane, Leon and Craig were on Maisy's porch, sipping margaritas while Maisy cleared up the hazier details of the case of the purloined pelicans.

It turned out that cousin Joe, the Finley black sheep, had indeed been involved with Butler whose stocks and real estate investments had dwindled to less than nothing.

411

The scheme started out relatively innocently. Being "in the know" when it came to all things political, Butler was aware of the soon-to-be-implemented Vessels of Opportunity program before anyone else in town. Joe offered the use of his land — for a cut in the profits, of course. With the help of Cliff and Eddie, the Finley cousins bought boats and hired crews and were first in line for oil company money.

But then Cliff began stealing gas from the program. Time sheets were doctored. A little skimming soon turned into out-and-out theft. "Easy money," said Cliff. "Nobody gets hurt," said Eddie. The desperate Butler, who was born with a talent for whitewashing his own short-comings, had been bitten hard by Cliff's easy money bug. Based on Butler's still-impeccable credentials, Joe's knowledge of art forgers and fences and the like and the prior success of their VOO venture, they hatched yet another plot. And another. Butler had sold his art just in time to avert financial disaster. Joe's forger came up with replacements in time to avert the social disaster of the loss of Butler's precious collection.

Joe also knew a "genius in ceramic forgery" who could reproduce the Bradford pelicans. The yahoos in Alabama wouldn't be able to tell the difference, he said. Forgetting that there is no honor among thieves, Butler jumped at the chance to cash in on his fellow yahoos' naiveté in what he considered a victimless crime.

These lucrative enterprises were clicking along quite smoothly until the day Butler gave Abbie a lift to the airport. He'd spotted Charlotte hiding in Maisy Downy's palmettos, and a small shiver of apprehension danced up his spine. Since he had plenty to hide, it never dawned on him that Charlotte was spying on Abbie. That was the day he began looking over his shoulder.

Then there were the excessive attentions of the lovely, young, wealthy, engaged Abigail Pitt. Even through the myopia of vanity and self-denial, Butler could see that this was a bit unusual. And when the pelican caper started falling apart, as it were, Butler started to sweat like a Michigan tourist in August.

It was his strategy to make a hasty retreat to cousin Joe's sugarcane plantation in the Philippines. He'd already checked the extradition treaty or lack thereof, packed up his fake paintings and purchased a planter's hat from the J. Peterman catalog. He planned to live out his retirement from crime beneath that hat, hosting soirees on

Joe's veranda and elevating the sub par social life of the area. Strangely enough, he still saw himself as a man of class and lofty ideals.

Like most thieves, however, his conceit and greed quickly exceeded his common sense. He'd lusted after *Miscegenation* since he'd first laid eyes on the two entwined pelicans. Egged on by Cliff and Eddie, he decided to make it his own through one final heist the night of the pelican party. He would then gather the stash from the shed, ship them to Joe, and follow Cliff and Eddie out of the country.

As to the mystery of how and why the birds exploded in the first place, Butler reluctantly explained. He'd gotten a frantic call from Joe. The faux birds were afflicted with a glazing problem. It was only a matter of time before the birds would discolor and their lack of authenticity become apparent to the most casual observer.

"The only answer was to get rid of them," said Butler.

Upon hearing this, the ever-resourceful Cliff simply picked up a discarded slingshot in the park, found the largest piece of ice in his R. C. Cola and shot the bird to pieces. The same method was employed in the destruction of May Doody's bird. May tearfully gathered up the pieces which she left on her back porch. While she was at Hawkins Hardware buying a case of super glue, Eddie Hillman simply sauntered down May's driveway and slipped the pieces into his backpack.

When berating Foster on his lack of professionalism, Butler noticed the webbed foot with the inauthentic thumbprint and dropped it into the pocket of his sports coat. He then went home and took the silver-plated corkscrew presented to him by the East Oyster Connoisseurs Club and destroyed his own forgery right there on the baby grand piano.

Cliff buried the pieces and blamed Pup for discarding them. When and if Pup got wind of it, well, who would take her word over Butler Finley's? All the while he was throwing Pup under the bus, Butler was playing his fondest role (that of selfless benefactor) by offering a reward for her church's missing painting. After Eddie carelessly left it behind the shed on Finley's Landing, and it was found by one of the many honest VOOs, Butler magnanimously returned it to the church.

While keeping a hawk's eye on the nefarious Cliff, Abbie had observed Butler coming and going to the landing at odd hours.

Though Abbie could hardly swim and was terrified of the dark water, she'd taken Harry's kayak across the cove after dark.

"That's how determined she was to get to the bottom of her brother's death," said Maisy. "That's when she overheard a conversation between Butler and Cliff. It was clear that Cliff took his orders from Butler. It was Butler who'd framed her brother, Tim. And it was Butler whom she blamed for Tim's death."

Like Abbie, Maisy and Harry were keeping tabs on the activity at Finley's Landing. After learning that Maisy had "sensibilities in common" with his aunts, Harry and the octogenarian fortune teller began to share information. This was in spite of strict instructions to the contrary from the "authorities" at ORCA. But Harry knew that if Maisy's sensibilities were anything like his aunts', they were nothing to sneeze at.

The next morning Harry went straight to Turner Gallery. Charlotte looked up when he entered, and when she saw it was him she smiled. Harry's face said it all. Abbie was gone. He had fulfilled his promise to her and to her brother, Tim. She pressed her lips together, but her eyes filled with tears. As she was wiping the first one from her cheek, Harry came to her and put his arms around her.

"I can't believe it," he whispered. "It's finally our time, Charlie. For the rest of our lives. It's our time."

"Our time," she repeated. "Promise?"

"I promise."

He reached into the pocket of his sport coat and took out a small, moth-eaten, velvet bag. He opened it and fished out a ring. It was a square-cut diamond nestled in an antique setting of platinum.

"It was Simone's," said Harry. "She and I always wanted you to have it."

"Oh, Harry, it's beautiful. And so special that it was Simone's."

"It's yours no matter what, but I was hoping it could be an engagement ring. For a real engagement. What do you think?"

"Oh, Harry!"

She threw her arms around his neck and kissed him.

"Does that mean yes?"

"That definitely means yes."

The bell on the gallery door jangled as Eunice Toowell and Craig Bloom entered.

Craig looked at the mayor and said, "Do you think we should come back later?

"Yes!" said Harry and Charlotte together.

After Harry had slipped Simone's ring on

Charlotte's finger, she put the closed sign on the door, took Harry by the hand and led him through the back entrance.

"Where are you taking me?" he asked.

"I have a surprise for you, too."

Sunlight surrounded the arched shape of the cottage's front door where a blush of roses climbed into cerulean sky. The statue of the children, Marie and Simone, was represented in pewter tones, the angles of their arms and legs bringing them to life as silvery water droplets rose to fill the entire scene.

When Harry looked at the painting, it was like coming home. He heard the splashing water of the fountain and felt what it represented — the discovery that had saved his grandfather and the town of St. Yves. He smelled the roses climbing to the roof and beyond. He felt the sunlight, warm on the old stones and a breeze rippling olive leaves in the distance. It was his cottage in Saint-Yves-Sur-Mer.

"Amazing," was all he could say.

"It's for you, Harry," said Charlotte. "Do you recognize it?"

"Yes. It's St. Yves. It's our house in St. Yves."

EPILOGUE

Just in case the fates decided to turn on Harry and Charlotte again, they married the next week. Charlotte's sons, David and Mark were there. Mark brought his girlfriend, Julia who fell in love with East Oyster. Harry's daughter was there. He had been emailing her about Charlotte since he'd come to East Oyster. When she saw Charlotte's painting of the house in St. Yves, she knew Charlotte was the woman for her dad.

A reception was held at Downydew. In the tradition of Cocktail Cove, it was a great party. Charlotte's and Harry's honeymoon was spent where else? In St. Yves.

Leon, who gets along famously with Nevin Schamm, runs the gallery when they're away. The rest of the time the McMillans reside in Charlotte's lovely apartment above Turner Gallery.

Harry bought Pitt Cottage, which will

soon reopen as the Midnight Charade Bed and Breakfast Inn. He is still in the process of re-restoring it to its former vintage glory, recapturing the setting and ambience of the famous movie while keeping the modern amenities. Liza Jane plans to decorate it. He hired Derek for the summer. Pup is head of housekeeping.

In addition to his other crimes, Butler faces prison time for filing fraudulent claims to the tune of four hundred thousand dollars to the Gulf Coast Claims Facility by making up a bogus janitorial and cleaning business. Pup had plenty to say about this, but none of it is printable.

Red was promoted from ORCA volunteer to an actual paid position in the organization. But most gratifying was having lived the adventure. His name has already become legend among thrill-seeking ORCA volunteers everywhere.

Liza Jane and Grant are still together, traveling, ranching and enjoying jazz. Craig has predicted an engagement by Mardi Gras. Leon agrees.

The relief well was a success, though the number of sick and dying dolphins is much higher than normal. And scientists blame the out-of-control Macondo well for the devastation of a once brightly-colored deep sea coral community about seven miles southwest of the well. Mats of tar still lurk beneath the sand.

But for now sun sequins dance on crystal green and blue water. The most beautiful beaches on the planet once again beckon all of their stewards — locals and tourists alike — to enjoy them forever. People fish, shrimp, and partake of the gulf's amazing bounty of seafood. No one can predict the long-range results of the worst environmental disaster in U.S. history, but the environment and custodians of that environment are making a remarkable comeback.

Maisy is her old self again, using her considerable influence and insight to lobby for an overhaul of the design of blow-out preventers on off-shore wells; a revamping of the safety regulatory system for off-shore drilling; definite, effective plans for clean-up in case of, God forbid, another spill; and checks and balances in the power of those in charge of regulations and safety.

Charlotte and Liza Jane worry about their octogenarian auntie wearing herself out, but Maisy claims her work on behalf of the environment has her "feeling like a girl of sixty again."

Soon after she returned from her honeymoon, Charlotte called Maisy.

"I need your professional opinion on something," she said.

Twenty minutes later Maisy stood in front of *The Gathering.* "It's a sign all right," she said.

The spirits still rose heavenward out of the mist. The scene maintained its peaceful, magnetic aura. But something had changed. There were three more spirits. Like the others, they were barely discernible in their translucent state. But they were there.

"I didn't paint them, but it's my work, my technique, my paint," said Charlotte. "What does it mean? Who are they?"

"Why Simone, Marie, and Lucy of course," said Maisy.

"And you know this . . . . how?"

"Think about it. Those spirits have been in a snit ever since the Macondo well blew. Just about drove me crazy and shorted Crystal out more times than I can count."

In response to the perplexed look on her niece's face, Maisy said, "Simone, Marie and Lucy were romantics. But the loves of their lives were always family and the beautiful places they called home. Now Harry has finally found what he's been searching for since that summer in St. Yves." She reached up and patted Charlotte's face.

"He's found you, Charlie. He's home."

Charlotte smiled at her wise, old auntie.

"And you know what?" she said. "I've found Charlie, too. I've found the young woman I was in St. Yves. To think, I could have gone the rest of my life never really knowing she was lost."

"I'm happy for you, sweetie," said Maisy. "And for Liza Jane. She's content for the first time in her life. Contentment is the most underrated state of being, you know." She clapped her hands together. "The well has been capped, and Lucy's pelicans, both real and clay, are safe."

She rolled her eyes heavenward and threw up her hands. "And thank you, Jesus, the spirits are at peace!"

They hadn't heard Harry enter. He walked over and stood with the women watching *The Gathering*.

He rested his arm lightly around Charlotte's waist.

"We've all been given a second chance," he said.

"Yep," said Maisy. "And we better not screw it up." She winked at Harry. "It doesn't take a crystal ball to see that."

ABOUT THE AUTHOR

Margaret P. Cunningham's short stories have won several national contests and appeared in magazines and anthologies including eight *Chicken Soup for the Soul* books. She grew up on her father's nursery in Mobile, Alabama, where she lives with her husband, Tom. She enjoys writing, reading, gardening and "beaching it" with her friends and family.

The employees of Thorndike Press hope you have enjoyed this Large Print book. All our Thorndike, Wheeler, and Kennebec Large Print titles are designed for easy reading, and all our books are made to last. Other Thorndike Press Large Print books are available at your library, through selected bookstores, or directly from us.

For information about titles, please call:
  (800) 223-1244

or visit our Web site at:
  http://gale.cengage.com/thorndike

To share your comments, please write:
  Publisher
  Thorndike Press
  10 Water St., Suite 310
  Waterville, ME 04901